Further details of these titles can be found at www.apbateman.com

For Clair, Summer and Lewis

Chapter One

Alaska was as good a place to hide as any. Better, in fact. It seemed that people from the lower forty-eight states migrated to Alaska for a variety of reasons. Some wanted a simple life. They ran from the complexities and pressures of modern society, sought solace in the state's emptiness, its honesty.

Other people were just on the run.

Stone recognized the defensive expression some people wore when he had attempted to interact with them. It was a beacon to warn people not to pry. If the eyes were the window to your soul, then the shutters were up on most of the people in the diner. As were most of the people in the small towns he had passed through to make it even this far north.

He watched the woman sitting at the table across from him. He had been watching a while. She was in her early to mid-thirties, wore her brunette hair long and she was effortlessly attractive. But that was not why he watched. Not the only reason, at least. She was drinking a hot chocolate. The frothy foam had stuck to her nose and she neither seemed to notice nor care. If it had been a date, he would have fallen in love with her a little right there and then. A little more, at least, because she was having a strange effect on him. More than an emotion, a feeling inside that he hadn't felt for a long time, and a lot of women ago. She was looking over a stack of papers, frowning at the wording, making notes in a pocketbook. She seemed troubled. And Stone recognized trouble.

"Katy McBride," the waitress said, pouring a refill into Stone's cup. It was his third. He still hadn't ordered any food. He figured this would be the last time the waitress would swing by for a free top-up unless he ordered a plate of something, but he wanted to organize a bed for the night before he filled his stomach.

"Thanks, Katy," Stone said.

"Not me."

"What?"

"The woman over there," she smiled and nodded to the woman on the other side of the narrow diner. "Go and talk to her, she's real nice."

"I…"

"Goodness, you could not have made it more obvious!" she chided. She looked around, Stone figured for the owner, who he guessed was the man who was busying himself on the grill, and then she sat down opposite him. Relaxed, unguarded. "You can't take your eyes off her. It's really sweet." She paused. "Unless you're figuring on being a stalker, then... I guess, not so much."

More composed now, Stone shook his head as he replied, "Of course not! I was just looking, that's all. Is there a crime against that around here?"

"Nothing's a crime around here," she said flatly. "Nothing is anything in particular around here."

"You don't like the wilderness?"

"I'm done with it, is all," she replied, shaking her head. "I want something to happen that doesn't involve a bear rooting around the garbage cans or a new road sign being replaced, just to be shot to pieces within a week like the one before it." She paused. "What's with that, anyway? Why do guys have to shoot up signs all over the state?"

"Guys do it all over," Stone replied.

"I guess."

"Been here long?" Stone figured her for just nineteen or twenty.

"My whole life," she said, looking towards the counter. The guy at the grill was dishing up fries to go with a burger the size of a softball. "I'm going down to Seattle to get some work in the coffee shops soon. While I'm working, I want to finish my nursing training. After that, then I guess it would be good to keep heading south, at least until the Golden Gate Bridge."

"Keep going," said Stone. "All the way to Santa Monica Pier."

"You've been?"

"I have," he said.

"Is LA really that great?"

"No, it sucks. The freeway is hell. But the drive down the coast is epic. And you can get a great bowl of clam chowder on Santa Monica Pier."

"I bet," she replied, dreamily. "And I've always wanted to visit Monterey Bay, The Big Sur. That's where they filmed *Big Little Lies*. It looks so... sophisticated. Have you seen that show?"

"No. Must have missed that one," Stone replied breezily. He hadn't exactly watched much TV in the past eight months. Except for the news. And only to see if he appeared on it.

"It looks so beautiful, Monterey Bay. And warm! So much warmer than here. God, I want more warm weather in my life!"

"You started training to be a nurse up here?"

"I did, then had trouble keeping up with the work. It's the distance between classroom segments in Anchorage and the work placements in places like Juneau and Fairbanks. I've worked things out now, Seattle has great medical training, and it will be far better money once I have trained. Better money working in the coffee shop than here in this dump." She paused. "Sorry, this place isn't so bad. You should try the short ribs."

"Great," Stone said somewhat distractedly.

She laughed. "Stop looking over my shoulder!"

"Sorry."

"I'm Sam, by the way," she said.

"Hi Sam, I'm… John," he said stiffly. He could not get used to not using his real name and had to think about which card he would pay with. The names had not matched in Albuquerque, and he had taken to the road quickly, changing his car as a result and heading back east five-hundred miles or so, before heading north, having already indicated to the chatty waitress where he had been heading.

"Nice to meet you, John. So, are you going to ask her out?"

"Hell no!" he said, a little too quickly. A couple of the other diners looked over at him. He ducked his head a little. "No. I don't know her. Besides, I'm just passing through."

"It's how it's done out here."

"What do you mean?"

She smiled. "Well, people live off grid. They come into town for supplies, a drink, get a fix of burger and fries or a pizza and then they go back for weeks or even months. Usually for the whole winter. They shoot caribou, fish for salmon. Live out of tins of beans. Town is town and the inhibitions are down."

"So, time is short. Make hay. Or at least make love…"

"Exactly!" She checked the counter once more, then picked up the coffee jug and started to get up. "You see what you like, and you go for it. None of that long-winded dating game stuff out here. You hook up as soon as you can. Shit, the nights are cold enough on your own, anyway."

Stone smiled. He sipped some coffee and looked at her as she stood up. "Thanks, I'll bear that in mind."

She bent down, whispered in his ear. "She could do with a friend," she said and walked back to the counter. Her order was waiting and the man behind the counter was glaring at her and shaking his head. He did not know he was losing his waitress soon, so Stone guessed she would have the last laugh.

Stone frowned at the comment, then looked back at Katy McBride. She still had not wiped the foam from the hot chocolate off her nose. She was frowning at the paperwork spread out on the table in front of her and did not seem to be making any headway. He finished his coffee and dropped a few extra dollars down for Sam and her nurse training fund. Then he got up and nodded to her as he left. She looked surprised that he had not gone over and talked to Katy McBride, but she was laden with plates of ribs and steaks and was already behind on clearing the empty dishes from the other tables. Her matchmaking services would not be required.

Outside, the air was cool. The sun was high in the clear blue sky and there was still a little thin ice on shady ground. He hefted the backpack over his shoulders and fastened it, before slinging the shotgun onto his right shoulder. Bears were waking up all over and he had been forced to fire a warning shot at a hungry-looking grizzly the day before. It had been rangy and thin and scraggly, but when it stood on its hind legs, it had been over ten-foot tall. It had been Stone's first encounter with a bear, and he hoped it to be his last.

He was heading into town. The diner on the edge of town had been his first stop. Tired, cold and in need of a rest, he had taken half-an-hour or so to regroup, reassess before turning up someplace new. He needed a place to stay, had camped rough last night, but tonight he was heading someplace warm and with a shower. And a big steak with something full of carbs and fried on the side. Washed down with a beer or two.

The verge was too rutted and hard to walk on, the frozen ground threatening to turn an ankle, so he walked down the patchy and poorly maintained asphalt road and as it stretched out in front of him, he could see the town looming ahead.

Lame Horse.

It was, even by Alaskan standards, a hell of a name for a town.

He heard the pickup behind him. Too close to town to hitch a ride, he stepped into the side of the road and continued to walk. The truck slowed and drew up alongside, the passenger window open.

"You ran out on me back there." Stone looked at Katy McBride. "Figured you'd come over at some point. You spent enough time looking."

"You've wiped the cream off your nose."

"That's what you were looking at?" she asked, seemingly embarrassed.

Stone smiled. "Well, that as well."

"I'm Katy," she said. "But you already know that. Sam isn't exactly subtle. Or quiet."

"You must have me down as a stalker."

She smiled, put the selector into park and switched off the engine. "Not exactly. And I wouldn't be here talking to you if I thought you were. Where are you heading?"

"North."

"Where have you been?"

"South," Stone smiled. "Not really got a plan."

"That goes for half of Alaska's population," she said. "The other half found the plan didn't work out so much."

"I figured as much."

"So, you're on foot?"

"Clearly."

"Alaska isn't the place for that," she said. "Hundreds of miles between towns and the threat of bears this time of year." She paused. "Cougars, too." She smiled when she saw Stone's expression, clearly leaning towards the double entendre. "That's mountain lions…"

"I know," he grinned. "I'll bear that in mind."

"I'm guessing you didn't set out that way? Without transport, I mean."

"No. I had a truck." Stone rested his hand against the doorframe and leaned closer. He could see she was slim under all the clothes. But she looked strong. Her hands were calloused, and her fingernails were trimmed. Or bitten down. He could not tell. "Some guys relieved me of it."

"Seriously? Did you call the police?"

Stone hesitated. Everybody in Alaska was running from something. He could not afford too many questions. "Not yet," he said.

"I'll take you to the Sheriff's office in Emerson," she said. "It's about four hours' drive."

Stone shrugged. Questions led to answers. Which led to problems. "It's OK. It was just a pile of junk anyway. I'll get some more wheels when I hit civilization."

"Good luck with that," she said. "Well, OK. I can offer you a lift to Lame Horse," she said. "But it's only there." She pointed and laughed. "Anyway, it was nice to meet you…"

"Rob."

"Really?" she smiled. "I thought it was John. Or at least that's what I heard you say to Sam back in the diner…" Stone shrugged, annoyed with himself for making the slip. "Well, it was nice to meet you, *Rob*…"

Stone smiled, looking at her behind the wheel. She was half the width of the wheel and it made her appear vulnerable. There were a few tiny crow's feet at her eyes, but he suspected they were what his grandmother had called laughter lines, and her face was pretty and kind looking. He had liked the look of her in the diner, and he liked the look of her more now that he was so close to her. He shrugged and said, "Oh, hell, I'll take that lift." He opened the door and Katy started the engine. It was a rough-sounding diesel and had seen better days. She pulled out from the side of the road and the box got up to third gear and fifty miles-per-hour was showing on the clock when she started to slow. She pulled across the road and stopped outside the motel.

"That was worth it, if only for the awkward silence," she smiled. "This is the only place to stay in town. It's also a bar and diner. Surprisingly good, considering where we are." She thumbed behind her at a wooden shack. "That's another bar, but it's a bit of a dive. A drinking den where all the world's problems are put to rights. And usually where trouble can be found."

"Sounds like any other bar." She laughed and he asked, "So why did you go to the diner outside of town?"

"Privacy," she said. "Small towns, big gossip. The motel owners are nice, but they *do* like to talk."

"Not much of that in a small town, I guess. Privacy, that is."

"It will get really busy in a week or so. May is the month for that."

"Yeah, how so?"

"Gold fever will hit, again. The ground is thawing, and the casual labor will come drifting in," she paused. "Is that why you're here?"

Stone shook his head. "No, I'm just heading north."

"What's up north?"

Questions. Problems. He should have kept walking.

Stone opened the door. The cold air swept inside the heated cabin. "I just want to keep moving," he said. "See how far I can get before the end of the summer."

"OK," she said, a little puzzled. She seemed to sense that she had pushed too much and backed off. "Well, nice to meet you, Rob. Or John... Enjoy your time in Lame Horse before heading north."

Stone nodded a thanks and closed the door behind him. He watched the pickup pull away and head down the strip. He kept watching until it was out of sight. Another time, another place and talking to Katy McBride would have been high on his agenda. That had been right up until they had pulled into the town of Lame Horse, and he had seen his truck parked outside the dive of a bar opposite.

Now he had something else on his mind.

A drinking den where all the world's problems are put to rights. And usually where trouble can be found...

Chapter Two

The bar was a shack made almost entirely from eight by four plywood sheets. Or chipboard. Stone was not sure which, DIY was not his skillset. And nor was it that of the person who had built the bar, either. One interior wall consisted solely of doors, all nailed at various angles. Stone had seen a similar concept before in Manhattan. Strangely, it had worked there, but that place would have employed an interior designer at five-hundred bucks an hour and spent money on an artist distressing the doors with a hammer and brushes and paint, and some of the doors had previously been on the dressing rooms of small theatres on 42nd Street and Broadway. Many had been signed by musicians and actors. And the guy putting them up had a spirit level and a set square and had used hidden fixings. Here, they had been screwed in and it simply worked to keep out the draught.

There were four men in all. One behind the bar staring at an early baseball game on a fuzzy television set that had been new once. Right about when Stone was in his second year of elementary school. The man did not look up, but Stone had entered quietly. Two men sat at the bar, one watching the game, the other watching his life ebb away in his reflection at the bottom of the glass. Both were bearded, sixty, grey and had lived their best years two-decades ago.

The other man was in mid-thirties, tattooed and wore a single grade of hair over his head and face. The same length, like he was wrapped in Velcro. He had been chewing on a big sandwich and was now frozen, the sandwich halfway from plate to lips when he caught Stone's eye.

This was Alaska. Practically everybody owned a gun, and most still carried one like it was eighteen-sixty. The state had seen the gold rush, the lawlessness it had brought with it, and in many ways times had not changed. The gold was still here, the miners used more high-tech surveying and excavation techniques, even updated their *Facebook* status, and *Twitter* accounts between shifts, but there was still an old feel about the place. Nowadays, the guns were more about freedom of expression and democratic rights, but out in the bush bears, wolves and cougars were a real threat. Most hikers and tourists from the lower forty-eight carried bear spray and that was usually enough. Some carried a shotgun with non-lethal rubber bear rounds, and that too was usually enough. But Alaskans carried guns, packed a spare and had two in reserve. Stone could see a big stainless steel .44 revolver in a leather holster on one of the bar-fly's hips. He was in no doubt there were more guns in the room.

Stone could not see any other play, so he dropped his rucksack on one of the chairs opposite the young man, placed the shotgun down on the table. He sat down, moved the weapon, and pressed the muzzle against the man's stomach. He didn't look at the other three men, but he sensed they had watched and two of them had turned back to the game, the other to the mystery in the bottom of his glass. The guy managed to swallow his mouthful, put down the rest of the sandwich.

"Keys," Stone said.

"Look, man…"

"Keys."

"Hey, dude, I'm sorry," the man hesitated. "Anyone would have done the same thing."

"I wouldn't have," Stone paused. "Where's your buddy?"

The man smiled, his demeanor changing. "Right behind you."

"I bet," Stone shrugged, then said, "You going to take a seat?"

"No, figure I'll stay standing," the voice was deep, but it went with the guy. Stone knew him to be around six-three and two-twenty. He was tattooed and his head was shaved too. "Move the gun away from my brother."

"Or?"

"Or I'll bust open your damned head!"

"You think you can do it without me pulling the trigger?" Stone shrugged. "Twelve-gauge, three-and-a-half-inch magnum, double-oh buckshot. Good for bears. And no good brothers, too." Stone felt the man near him, his breath - stale and foul-smelling. Cigarettes, coffee, beer, and a distinct lack of brushing. He could smell the man's body-odor as well. He looked at the three men at the bar. The game and the bottom of the glass were no longer so interesting now that the other brother had changed the dynamic of the confrontation.

The man stepped nearer. He wore an open denim waistcoat over a leather jacket. Biker style. The open flaps of material brushed Stone's right ear. "I might just break your neck before you can fire."

Stone shrugged. "You won't."

"Oh, he will," the man opposite him said with a smile. "He'll kick *your* ass, that's for sure."

Stone pushed his chair backwards into the man and flicked the shotgun up like a whip, the ventilated rib running along the top of the barrel cracked into the man's face and forehead with a sickening crunch. Stone kicked the table in front of him, driving it away with his heavy hiking boot, pushing the table into the other man's waist as he made to stand. The man was knocked off balance, became entangled in his own chair and stumbled. Stone stood up and took a big step aside from the table and chairs, the flailing legs of the guy whose face was bleeding but looked to have been improved by the broken nose and split lip.

The man regained balance and turned, but Stone wasn't where he thought he would be. He looked at his brother, sprawled and groaning, then at Stone, who had the pump-action shotgun leveled at him. "You're making a mistake…" he growled.

"Wouldn't be the first time," Stone paused. "And it sure as hell won't be the last."

"Oh, it *will* be."

Stone reached into his pocket with his left hand, withdrew a ten-dollar bill and dropped it onto the table. "For the mess," Stone called out to the barman. "We'll be going now," he added. He nodded towards the man on the floor. "Pick your brother up. We'll take this outside."

The young man was attempting a staring contest, but Stone hadn't even entered. He lifted the shotgun and leveled it, one-handed, at the man's chest. He got the message and stepped around the table to help his brother to his feet. The bigger man still clutched his nose as he limped towards the exit.

Stone looked back at the bar and the baseball game was still on, the mystery solved at the bottom of the glass, the man starting on another drink. The three men did not seem bothered. They had all seen a hell of a lot worse.

Stone hooked the strap of his rucksack and slung it over his left shoulder, keeping the Remington shotgun in his right hand. Both men seemed to hesitate at the door. Stone stopped. Three paces was generally considered to be a safe distance if you had a gun. Any less and he could be drawn into hand-to-hand combat. "Move on," he said. They did, but as they stood on the deck, at the top of the four wooden steps, they stopped again.

"Help you?"

Stone could not see the owner of the voice. He stepped forwards a pace and jabbed the shotgun into the younger man's back, right on the man's left kidney, then he stepped back again. The taller guy had his own problems, his face was still bleeding. The younger man dropped down the steps, his back arched and contorted at the stab of pain, but he didn't drop to his knees. He was tough enough. He straightened up and side-glanced Stone defiantly. Stone looked at the new arrival. He was in his mid-sixties and looked like he'd had a hard life. He was as broad as a barn door and tough looking. He was tall too. Six-four. Four inches taller than Stone, and perhaps thirty-pounds heavier.

"I said, can I help you?"

"I heard," replied Stone. He kept the shotgun steady. It was just as well because the man had one of his own. "I don't see that it's any business of yours, but these two men stole my pickup when I stopped to help them out a couple of days ago. Their car was out of fuel."

"Where was this?"

"About three-hundred miles back."

"And you walked here, when?"

"Like I said, not that it's any business of yours, but this was two days ago, and I got into town just now. Hitched some rides, walked a few miles."

"These men have been here a while." The man paused. "Longer than a couple of days."

"No longer than yesterday."

"Maybe you have them confused with some other guys?"

"Not a chance." Stone paused. "So why are you lying for them?"

"I'm not lying for them. And like I said, they've been here a while."

"And that definitely makes you a liar."

"Careful, boy…"

Stone glared at him and said, "There's no mistake. Besides, I doubt there are two other guys this ugly, or who smell so bad, in the vicinity." He paused. "Not the whole west of Alaska, for that matter. Present company excluded, obviously."

"Smart guy," the man said.

"It's better than the alternative, that's for sure. How's that working out for you?"

The man looked at the two men in turn, then nodded towards the pickup. "Give him the keys, and we'll end this here."

The younger brother looked defiant. "But…"

"But nothing!" the man snapped. He lowered his shotgun. "Give him the God-damned keys!"

The bigger, older brother dug into his pocket and retrieved the key bunch. He walked down the steps and tossed them at Stone's feet. Stone made no attempt to catch them, holding the shotgun as steady as a rock.

"We've got our stuff in the truck," the younger man protested.

"I'll be keeping it," Stone said. "Call it compensation."

"Bullshit!" the older brother snapped, his nose still bleeding. "It ain't worth that."

Stone fired the shotgun at the ground between all three men. The mud splattered them, and gravel flew up into their faces. Stone racked the slide and chambered another round before the big man with the gun had time to move. He had moved two paces to his right as he had pumped the slide and now had one of the eight-by-eight support posts lining the porch deck in front of him. It wasn't much, but it was more cover than the other men had.

"I'll take what's there," Stone repeated calmly. "Call it a lesson. You learn that when you cross some people you come off worse. You learn from this and move on. You come my way again looking for trouble, and I will end it. Permanently."

The younger man looked like he was about to do something stupid, and the older guy stepped between them. "Get in my truck," he said. "Now!" Both men walked over to a new silver-colored Chevy truck with an engine so large that it could kick-start a power station. They opened the doors and got inside in the same subdued manner two chastised schoolboys might have. The man turned back to Stone and stared at him. "So, are you heading out?"

"No."

"Why not? Nothing here but wilderness."

"Same all over this state."

"Dangerous place, the wilderness. Predators everywhere."

"You'd better take good care then," Stone replied. He still had the shotgun steady in his hand, the buttstock squeezed under his armpit, his elbow resting on his hip. It was a well-practiced method of firing with one hand. In Stone's former line of work, he always needed his other hand free.

"I think you know what I mean."

"You're a liar, so forgive me if I ignore what you have to say."

"It might pay for you to keep moving."

"Are you running me out of town?" Stone smirked, glancing at the shotgun in his hand and the man's shotgun which still pointed to the ground. "Because I seem to have the advantage here."

"For now. But advantages change."

"I don't run. So, I'm feeling inclined to stay and leave when I'm good and ready."

"Look, it's a big state, half the size of the rest of America," the man sighed. "I need these two guys, and it might save a lot of trouble if they didn't come back to have another go at you."

"It won't be any trouble. They come back, cause me trouble and I'll cripple them."

"That's a felony, to threaten like that."

"It's not a threat, it's a promise."

"There's a difference?"

Stone smiled. "The difference is that a threat infers the chance of consequence. I made a promise. There *will* be consequence. And it will be what I say it is."

"Hard ass, eh?"

Stone shrugged. He kept the shotgun aimed at the man, but he noted that the man did not appear overly concerned. Stone curled up the toes of his right foot, lowered the weapon and rested the tip of the muzzle on the last half an inch of his boot's toe cap, all gap, and no toes. No chance of getting debris in the barrel, and it acted like a launchpad should he need to get the weapon back on target. Push-pull. Push with his foot, pull with his right hand. Both weapons were no longer threatening, but Stone was confident he could win a quick draw. "What do you need those guys for? Are you related or something?"

"Nope. But I need them to work for me."

"Mining?"

"Why are you interested all of a sudden?"

"Just getting the lay of the land."

"Not a good idea to stick around."

"And I suppose that is a threat?"

"No. Just being practical," the man said. "Those boys are staying. I need them. They will inevitably come into town. If you're here… well, you just laid down the gauntlet. There'll be trouble. You don't need to be here. You've got your truck back, got their belongings as compensation. Just hit the road and nobody has to get hurt." He paused, held up a hand. "Practical, is all."

Stone considered this for a moment, shrugged. "I'm getting a steak, staying the night, and having some breakfast. I think I will have seen enough of this place by then."

The man nodded. "Good idea." He turned around, then hesitated, turned back, and looked at Stone. "I didn't catch the name."

"I didn't throw it."

The man smiled, turned his back on him and walked to his truck.

Stone watched him leave. Watched as the truck drove down the strip and disappeared. He was hungry and the next town was over a hundred miles to the north. He was too tired to start the drive, needed to rest. He had walked thirty-five miles today, between the truck rides. He gathered up his rucksack and walked over to the pickup truck.

Despite what he had told Katy McBride, the truck wasn't a banger and was only four years old and in good condition. It had only covered a hundred-thousand miles. Nothing by Alaskan standards. Barely run in. He had part-exchanged it for a vehicle he had purchased in Seattle. He thought the Alaskan plates would help him to blend in, but short of a flashing beacon he could not have drawn more attention on the drive up. The Alaskan people knew their own and everyone he met had asked him where he was from and where he was heading. The Seattle plates hadn't helped.

He opened the rear door and looked around inside. The men had bags and loose clothing scattered on the rear seats. There were grocery bags, and a good deal of garbage, the men having eaten their way through a couple of gas station picnics on the three-hundred-mile drive. A few drive-thru meals as well.

He found the cellphone. A burner. A drugstore pay-as-you-go. He had seen the two men, both texting and scrolling away on their smartphones. He had seen the basic phone, been curious why they should have needed a third. Their old Pontiac Firebird, beaten and worn-out, had died on them. With no working fuel gauge, they had underestimated pit stops. When Stone had happened upon them, they had been broken down on a quiet stretch of road, ill-prepared for the Alaskan bush and about to face the prospect of a freezing night, and no apparent protection from bears. They had exhausted their mechanical expertise; the car was dead. It looked as if the fuel pump had objected to no fuel supply going through it and cracked like a brittle plastic bottle. The two men were in trouble. Stone, who had kept a classic Mustang on the road for many years to the detriment of his bank balance, had popped the hood and investigated, but he estimated about four major problems that needed a ramp, a welder, and a seriously competent mechanic before they even addressed filling it with gas. He offered to take them to the nearest large town, but there were not many to choose from. Hope Falls was going to be the best bet. Either that, or the four-hundred miles south to Anchorage. The two men had not wanted that at all. They were adamant they needed to head north. They were due to start a well-paying job, and work had been short, and money even shorter. Stone had enquired about their line of work, assuming mining or fishing, but was swiftly shut down. Alaska. Everyone was running from something.

After a dozen miles the bigger of the two men had needed to take a call of nature. Stone had stopped the truck and the man had taken himself off into the undergrowth. Stone had not talked with the younger guy. The man was not the talkative type. He had gotten out, circled the truck and smoked a cigarette. Stone waited at the wheel. When the man returned, he had pointed at one of the rear tires. He said it was down on air and they should check it before moving off. It looked a little spongy, but there was no sound of air escaping and as Stone was not carrying a pump, they decided it would be better to change to the spare.

Stone felt foolish now, as he reflected on the events. More annoyed with himself than anything. He had spent almost ten years as a soldier. A life of regimentation and professionalism, but later, as he served in special forces, he had learned to out-think his enemy, to counter them. He had been taught to follow his instincts and be suspicious of most things, and of all people. After the military, his world had changed, but his instincts had only been honed further. The Secret Service had almost given him a sixth sense and he had lived this far, to his mid-thirties, by trusting his instincts and staying ahead of the game. He had not seen the younger brother let out the air. He had not noticed the exchange of looks between them, although he recalled them now.

Stone had taken out his rucksack and dropped it on the dry, frozen earth. He had then hefted out the jack and the wheel brace and the two brothers had changed the wheel quickly. One received a text, but not on his smartphone. The other had looked at it, but he could not recall whose phone it had been. Stone was putting the tire into the spare wheel rack underneath the pickup bed, when the younger brother bent down to help. The phone had dropped out of his pocket and skidded in front of Stone as he crouched under the tailgate of the vehicle. The message was still open on the screen. It had been enough. The brothers had moved, as had Stone, but they had been quicker. The older man had Stone's shotgun in his hand, jacking a round into the chamber, but Stone was fast and had thrown the tire iron at the man's shin. The shot had gone wide, and Stone had taken off through the undergrowth, zig-zagged his way through alder bushes, which were stunted and wispy from the cold. The brothers had not followed, but they had taken off quickly. Stone returned from a devious route through the alders and saplings and headed a hundred yards back up the road to find his rucksack, the jack and the wheel brace discarded in the dirt. The truck had left deep wheel ruts where the big V8 had spun the wheels. Night had come all too soon, and Stone had camped out. He was no stranger to surviving and had excellent bushcraft skills, and he had a fire going soon enough, cut the alder to make a bed to insulate him from the frozen ground, and he had struck out along the road in the morning. After a couple of hours, an eighteen-wheeler had stopped and given him a lift to the next town and the driver had shared a flask of coffee with him. Stone had enough money for a few more stops yet. He bought an old and well-used Remington pump-action at the general stores and enough shells to load it and carry a few in reserve and he had followed the roads north and west. He had known which direction to walk in, having recalled the body of the text. He had known where to find the two men, but he had also needed to know more. It was in his nature.

Stone watched the road that led out of town. The truck had long gone. But he figured it would be back soon enough. And he figured he had not seen the last of the two brothers, either. He had seen the text, and that was enough. Whatever they had traveled here to do, the text had potentially incriminated them. It had simply read: *Lame Horse. I need it done. No witnesses.*

Chapter Three

Stone drove the pickup across the road and the dirt parking lot and parked at the rear of the motel. He switched off the engine and got out, then reached in under the driver's seat. He felt for the package he had taped up a week earlier. It was still in place. He leaned across the foot-well and did the same with the other seat. The two men had not searched the vehicle, and he felt a huge sense of relief to know he still had funds and protection in place. Money and a gun. He didn't need much more than that. He took out the .45 model 1911 and checked the chamber. The brass cartridge glinted in the late afternoon sun. The pistol was a tried and tested design and originally made by Colt. Many manufacturers now made the weapon after its patent had run out. This one was a Remington and as standard as the original GI model as it was possible to get. Checkered walnut grips and fixed low-profile sights. Stone tucked it under his jacket into his belt and fished out a spare magazine from underneath the seat.

He bundled up the men's clothes and shook them through. There was nothing in the pockets, so he balled them up and pitched them into a beaten and rusted metal dumpster nearby. As he shouldered his rucksack, he looked out east, catching the setting sun behind him glinting its ebbing reflection on the snow-capped mountain ridge. He shivered. Partly because of the cold, and partly because of the message on the guy's phone. Why would the man need a burner? And what did someone mean by no witnesses? *I need it done…* What could they have been referring to? All Stone knew was that it could not possibly have referred to him. Nobody knew that Stone was here, because if they did then the Secret Service, the FBI and most likely the Alaska State Police and National Guard would be turning up with weapons loaded and locked, and with enough blues and twos for the arrest to be seen from space. So, did the person who had sent the text want Stone out of the picture, or somebody else? And it struck Stone that Lame Horse was not a big enough town for many witnesses to be present in any case, no matter what somebody didn't want to risk being witnessed. And the big guy in the new truck. Where did he fit in? He certainly had some authority over them, so he would have to be the one paying them, and the nature of their employment had meant that the man had attempted to deflect from them. Given them a jelly weak alibi that had evidently melted away by the fact they had Stone's truck with all their things in it.

The burner phone had locked itself and long since run out of battery. Stone would have to find a charger and even so, getting into a four-digit screen lock and working the variables to unlock it would take more time than he had. Not to mention ten thousand possible variables. But he knew that the answer would be in that phone, either in its address book, or in a thread of messages.

The motel foyer was made from the same chipboard as the bar, but the guy who had installed it clearly had better carpentry skills than the guy who did the bar across the road. Stone figured it would be well-insulated because as his boots hit the floor and he walked to the desk, there was no echo. Or it could have been that the thirty or more deer, elk, moose, and bear heads mounted upon the walls did something to cushion the sound. There were a good many photographs, too. The sort where overweight, balding dentists and accountants pose with a hunting rifle over a slain animal. Stone figured the motel to be a lodge for tourism hunting, often called trophy hunts.

"You're not a hunter…" a man said as he stepped out from the back office. "I can see the look on your face."

"And what look is that?"

"Well, most people who hunt tend to look at our little collection of trophies and appear envious," the man paused. "You looked just a little incredulous…"

"Incredulous!" a woman chided. "You'll have to forgive my husband. He got into reading last year having never read more than the sports pages, and now you'd think he swallowed a dictionary! Always got a novel in his hands. Give it enough time and he might progress from youth-adult and read something meant for the grownups." She bumped past her husband and stood expectantly at the desk. "What is it, honey? A room for the night, perhaps two? Don't let our house of horrors display put you off!" she laughed. "Howard thought the hunters would like it. Most are purchases off eBay, or from trips down to Anchorage or Seattle's antique stores."

"I got that one right there!" Howard protested, pointing at an elk's head near the door.

"When you went out hunting for the first and last time with Big Brad Taylor and you cried for a week afterwards, didn't eat any red meat for a month!"

"Maude..."

"I don't mind hunting," said Stone. "We all got to eat and the meat's natural and sustainable. I just don't like vain people posing over the bodies of once beautiful animals, that's all."

"Go and check on something, Howard. I don't even care what..." The woman looked back at Stone, placing a well-thumbed register on the counter while her husband tutted and stepped back into the back office. "No computers here," she said proudly. "Not for the guests, at least. Most folk passing through tend to prefer it that way. We do take in a lot of hunters on their way up to the organized hunts. Howard gets a picture of them on their way back down for the wall," she explained. "Adds some theatre, I suppose. Anyway, all I need is a name and a vehicle license plate number... I won't be checking up on it either… but how many nights you would like is important. We're pretty much empty, so you can have our best room and stay for as long as you like. Stay for five nights and you can have a sixth night for free…"

"For god's sake, Maude!" Howard shouted from out back. "You're giving our money away, woman! A man knows how many nights he needs on the road."

"Shut your hole, Howard!" she shouted back at him, then smiled up at Stone and said softly, "What do you say, honey?"

"I may take you up on that," he replied. "Can I let you know later?"

"Sure thing," she smiled back at him. "Well, that's forty bucks and I do a good breakfast. Eggs, biscuits, and gravy with coffee. All in. Bacon's extra."

Stone smiled as he signed in as B. McKinley. The B being for Bill, short for William, and William McKinley being the twenty-fifth US President. He could not think why he had chosen the name, but then remembered that McKinley was one of four presidents who had been assassinated, so hoped it wasn't a bad omen. He smiled at Maude, already deciding that he would hit the road tomorrow. His beef with the two guys and their boss was done, and there was little he could do about the phone. He was not about to try ten thousand ways of opening the phone. Not every wrong needed to be righted and not every fight was his own. "Where can I eat tonight?" he asked.

"Right here, honey. We open to non-residents, too. There's the bar out front as well, but it's a drinking den. Best avoid that place. They judge how busy a night has been by how many eyeballs they sweep up off the floor. OK, I'm joking, but someone will start a fight in there for certain…" She shook her head disparagingly, but she had no idea how true that had been just a few minutes before. "Or there's the diner on the edge of town. I do all the cooking here, and it's what I call old fashioned and value for money."

"Thanks, but you've already been highly recommended."

"Ah, that's nice. Who was kind enough to do that?"

"Katy McBride."

"Such a sweet girl," Maude smiled warmly. "Done gone and taken on a bit too much to chew on with that mine of her father's and all, but she'll get there. She's from tough Alaskan stock."

"Mine?"

"Yes, a gold mine. McBride's Folly. Her grandfather and her father all made a fortune and went on to lose it there, too. They called it McBride's Folly when her grandfather hung on in there despite all the odds, and they've been calling it that ever since." She leaned forward conspiratorially and said quietly, "Her father, Hank McBride hit it big. Core samples, that's all. That's when they dig a hole out with something like a big corkscrew and sample the core and the depth. But he found the mother lode. He just upped and died before he told anybody, much less young Katy, where he had found it. Now the poor girl is searching three square miles of claim and running out of money fast, the poor dear…"

"Damn it, Maude!" Howard yelled from out back. "Too much gossiping, not enough work! Leave the residents be, woman…"

"I've already said it Howard, so shut your damn hole!" She looked back at Stone and shrugged. "I just hope the poor thing can keep the mine going until she finds where to make the next cut. I don't think she can afford any more mistakes. If she lucks out and goes bust, the next person to buy the mining rights is gonna hit the big time."

"That's rough," said Stone, but he was no more interested in gossiping with the late middle-aged woman than he had been when she first started talking. "What's the room number?"

"Twelve," she replied a little curtly. "Howard!" she yelled, then looked back at Stone. "Howard will show you the way."

"I've got it. Just point me in the general direction," replied Stone.

"Outside, turn right, that's the evens. Odds are left. So, you're sixth on the right."

"Got it. What time's good for dinner?"

She perked up again at the thought of some extra revenue and smiled warmly. Like most hospitality workers she could turn the charm on and off like a faucet. "Seven until nine, honey. Same for breakfast, but in the AM, obviously."

"Obviously," Stone smiled. "See you later…"

Outside, the light had faded, and the snow-capped mountains looked cold and uninviting. The sun had gone down, the air was cold and just a glimmer of sunset remained out over the tree-lined coast of the Pacific. Stone looked at the truck parked a few yards away, approximately outside rooms six and eight. He doubted anybody else would be occupying rooms tonight. Besides, he did not like to advertise which room he was staying in. Old habits die hard.

The room was standard American motel, the same as tens of thousands of motel rooms from New York to LA and from Miami to Chicago. A fifteen-by-fifteen-foot box with a queen-sized bed and a smaller double, a TV, a small fridge, kettle, microwave, and a mirror all clustered around, underneath and on top of the vanity dresser. A small but adequate bathroom completed the basic functionality, but it was all he could hope for or expect for the forty dollars. In most places it would have been closer to a hundred, but Stone suspected trade was difficult for the couple and winter would mean long, quiet periods. Better to open and get all of a little than nothing of a lot.

He ran a shower and pulled out some clean clothes. It had been quite a day, including a marathon walk and a bar fight. He was ready for something to eat, too. Stone emptied his pockets, took off his belt and kicked off his boots. He got into the shower fully clothed and used the shower gel to wash his clothes, stripping off to do a thorough job on them, then rinsing them under the showerhead. He rung them out and tossed them into the sink, before soaping himself all over and rinsing in the hot spray. When he stepped out and wrapped a towel around himself, he wrung out his clothes more thoroughly, shook the creases out and hung them on the heated towel rail before placing another clean towel over them to hold in the heat. He had done this more times than he cared to remember in the military and on the move with the Secret Service all over the world. Old habits die hard. By morning, the clothes would be dry, and the creases steamed out.

Once dressed in his clean clothes, Stone squared away the rest of his kit – a habit not only from his military and Secret Service days – but of being on the run. He was innocent, of course. But the FBI and Secret Service were not about to drop the charges before they interviewed him, despite him sending evidence of his innocence, and having an award-winning journalist corroborating his story. She had published the story with the Washington Post giving a full account of the dark web, conspiracy theories-turned-fact culminating in the assassination of the President's family in a pay-per-view bidding war. Stone had sent in the USB containing many offshore bank accounts, IP addresses and router services and within the information was a list of the users and their connection with international terrorism. But Stone was not coming in until he had a pardon or at least an agreement to turn state's evidence. He knew how the prosecutors in the Secret Service and FBI worked, and he wasn't going down that road. The problem with Washington DC and the law enforcement agencies keeping it safe was the ability for certain people to put political pressure on those same agencies and shape their own agendas.

Stone looked at the .45 on the dresser and decided to tuck it under the pillow. He was only going into the bar inside the motel, and it would be warm enough to remove his coat. There would be plenty of people around and he weighed up the likelihood of a local cop dining there, asking to see a conceal-carry permit he did not possess, on a gun he knew to be illegally attained. So many people were able to possess a firearm and open or conceal carry in Alaska, but he could not risk being run through the system. That went for when his truck had been stolen, and it would go for walking into a bar with a firearm. Stone would try to clear his name one day, but that day wasn't in sight just yet. Merely staying ahead of the search was all he could hope for, for now.

The restaurant was mom and pop style with half a dozen dishes on a specials board and the heady smell of percolating coffee in the air. Thankfully, for the sake of his appetite, the trophy animal heads had remained in the foyer. Stone took a booth and picked up the standard menu. He seldom ate from specials boards as he always suspected it was short-dated food made more appealing and priced for a quick sale. Maude bustled over with a smile and Stone suspected she was serving and cooking while Howard tended the bar and desk should the bell ring. There were no other customers, so they had it covered. Stone chose a plate of cheese nachos to go with his beer, and a ribeye steak done rare with fries and a side of coleslaw to put an end to the day's hunger pangs. He watched Maude hurry back into the kitchen, then looked up as somebody entered. He knew before he saw her face that it was Katy McBride. The way she carried herself, the oversized jacket. She glanced over and smiled, then headed to the bar and pointed to a booth two down from Stone's. Howard jotted down on a notepad and walked into the kitchen. He was back behind the bar and pouring a beer before Katy made it to the booth.

She smiled and said, "Are you going to look at me all night?"

"Depends which side of the booth you sit," Stone replied. "And whether you get whipped cream on your nose again."

"Well, I'm not ordering a hot chocolate, but I could share your booth, if it would make things easier?"

"Take a seat."

Howard hovered with the tray of beers and followed her to Stone's booth. "I'll get Maude to bring your orders out together," he said helpfully as he placed both beers on the table, then turned and headed back to the kitchen.

Katy smiled. "Well, *now* it's awkward..." She paused and smiled. "Can't just have a drink with you and leave."

Stone shrugged. "So, I hear you're a gold miner."

She smiled. "You've been asking around about me?" she asked coyly.

"It came up," he replied, taking a sip of his beer. "The lady that owns this place talks so much; she barely comes up for breath." Katy sipped her beer, leaving a frothy moustache over her top lip. Stone picked up a napkin and reached over, giving it a dab. "Must be a beverage thing," he said, watching her blush.

"I don't even know your name," she said. "Whether it's Rob, or John. Maybe I should check the register?"

Stone thought about the name he signed in with. It was a B, but he said, "I wouldn't do that, it'll only confuse matters further," he said quietly. He looked at her, saw something in her eyes that he liked, or trusted. "It's Rob."

She smiled and said, "It's OK, no need for a second name. You know there's probably not a real name in that register, don't you?"

"Well, I knew Alaska was the end of the line for many people."

"Is that why you're here?" she asked. "Are you running from something?"

"Are you?"

"I guess," she replied. "If running from using my law degree and having my own practice is reason enough."

"Why would you do that?"

Howard appeared with Stone's nachos and set them down between them. Katy dug right in and normally Stone would have been irked. He did not like sharing his food, but for some reason he didn't seem to mind.

"I guess it helps me to process my father's death. He wasn't just mining that ground; he *was* the mine." She paused. "My grandfather before him."

"McBride's Folly."

"My, you *are* well informed!" She laughed.

Stone ate some of the nachos and washed them down with the cold beer. "I'm curious about your gold mine."

"Well, you're not alone," she replied, sitting back in the booth, apparently done with his plate of nachos. "I'm under a damned microscope all the time," she added.

"How so?"

She looked around, despite the bar being empty. A man walked in and pulled out a stool at the bar. He ordered a beer and got busy with a bowl of nuts while he waited. Katy turned back and leaned forwards. "My daddy did some drill testing and hit it big." She paused, allowing the fact to sink in. "And I mean, really big. Normally you find gold as flecks and color the size of a grain of sand, or perhaps the size and thickness of an apple blossom or a small clover leaf. Sure, you get the odd nugget, but I haven't seen anything larger than a cornflake in years. My father used to keep the best of them in a jar and show me when I made the journey up. He always said the big ones would be his retirement." She shrugged sadly. "When I came up to sort out his affairs and take over the claim, I never found that jar. I don't know if someone took it, or whether he cashed it in early to pay the bills. But there was something special about that jar and the giant flakes of gold in it. Not that it makes a difference how big the pieces are; gold is gold, and the price doesn't reflect if your gold is the size of a golf ball or a grain of sugar. The weight is the weight. But my father's most recent find when he drill-tested was like coffee house sugar cubes. There was more value in those few core samples than he mined in ten years."

"When was this?"

"Last summer. He died in August, and

we closed the mine for the winter in September. We're snowbound all winter, and I got the mine equipment ready this spring, but it's been tough. We mine for a few days and get shut down. Equipment failures, labor issues, paperwork going astray just before site inspections. I can't get a damned thing done. We're getting into the season now and I still haven't got enough gold to pay for fuel. The workers have been paid this week, but I can't get a delivery of fuel until I pay for the last one." She wiped a tear away, then sat back in her seat as their food arrived. Maude smiled and placed Katy's basket of fried catfish and fries in front of her, then placed Stone's steak down and picked up the empty plate. She could see that their drinks were still half full and smiled before walking away. "I shouldn't really be spending money in this place, but I just couldn't face being on my own and opening a tin of something. Sometimes when you owe so much, the cost of a dinner can't possibly make it any worse…" she said, then added, "Sometimes it's just nice to drone away to a stranger…"

"I guess," Stone replied. "But we're hardly strangers now that we're having dinner together." He sliced off some of his steak. It was an inch thick and rare in the middle. The knife was not overly sharp, but it sliced through easily. Maude certainly knew her way around a griddle. "How did your father die, if you don't mind me asking?"

She shrugged, but he could tell that she had not become accustomed to the loss just yet and her eyes seemed sad and distant. "A car accident. He must have lost control of his truck and gone into the river. The point where he crashed is a deep and fast-moving part of the river. Hell, the whole damned river runs too fast, but on that bend it's like a washing machine." She sighed, then looked at him, her eyes sparkling once more. "I've never done this before," she said. "I saw you looking at me at the diner, and I liked the fact that I was the object of somebody's attention. I guess I haven't had much of that lately…"

"You're struggling at the mine," he said. He shrugged and added, "Look, it's common knowledge, you've even told me more than you probably wanted to, and we barely know each other. That kind of pressure is hard to escape."

"You know about pressure? Sorry, but I had you down as a drifter who uses fake names in hotel registers…"

"I have a past," Stone replied. "But this is Alaska, it's a prerequisite, right?"

"Well, that's the truth…"

"Pressure breeds mistakes. The thought process is muddled, and you can start to spiral. Like water down a drain. You need to clear your head. And whether that's getting away from here…"

"Not an option," she interrupted. "No time. It'll only get worse."

"Well, perhaps just relieving yourself of the burden with a stranger is a way to get the pressure out, like a vent."

"It *does* feel better to talk, I must admit." They ate in silence for a few minutes, and then she said, "Did you feel that?"

"What?"

"That moment when we just didn't speak, but it was OK."

"My mom and dad didn't speak for years…"

"No, silly. I meant that it felt OK because it just *was*." She smiled. "Really comfortable." She reached across the table and touched his hand gently. "I feel like I've known you for years, and we're just getting reacquainted." In truth, Stone could not remember having ever felt this comfortable and relaxed with a woman. His last real relationship had been with someone he had helped, the two of them bonded together by circumstance and fate, but after the demons had been slain and life had been returned to normal, their fire had extinguished, and life had taken them in different directions. Stone smiled. This experience was all new. "So, what are you running from?"

"Nothing."

"No, you're definitely running from something. Most people come to Alaska because it just didn't work out for them anyplace else, and then find *they* were in fact, only running from themselves. They didn't have problems. They *were* the problem."

"How'd that work out for them up here?" Stone asked between mouthfuls. "I'm guessing not very well."

"You'd be correct on that count. The same old shit happens because they were in fact part or all their previous problems. That is why Alaska is so full of lost souls, contentious people. Don't get me wrong, there are some good ones too. The best I have ever known. But largely, Alaska being the end of the line or the last resort, they end up bitter and twisted. That's my take on Alaska, anyway."

"Been far to get a comparison?"

"I studied on the east coast. Then, I trained in law and practiced in San Francisco." She paused and took a sip of beer. No moustache this time. "What about you?" Stone smiled, took a mouthful of steak, and chewed slowly. "Oh, I get it," she said knowingly. "Too soon?"

"Probably always will be," he replied. "I have a few things to work through."

"Don't we all?" She looked up as a man entered and stood at the bar. The man looked around and held up a hand when he saw her. The man had not seen Stone from his position at the bar and the angle of the booth. "Damn," she said quietly.

"Problem?"

"Duke Tanner," she replied. "He's been hassling me to sell my land and the mining rights to him."

"Sell your mine?"

"Yes." She paused. "Sorry, this won't take long."

Stone pushed his plate forward and looked up at Duke Tanner as he approached their table. Six-four, two-twenty and with hands like dinnerplates. Stone had seen him before, held a shotgun on him while the two men who had robbed him had been ushered away like naughty children.

Lame Horse. I need it done. No witnesses…

Chapter Four

"You…" Duke Tanner stared at Stone indignantly.

"Can I help?"

"I'm here to talk to the lady."

"Well, the lady is at *my* table."

"You were lucky earlier," Tanner sneered.

"Earlier?"

"At the bar," the big man frowned.

"The bar?"

"Near this place," Tanner snapped. "You know where the damned bar is!"

"Why was I lucky?"

"You had a gun on me, and you had cover."

"That was you?" Stone stared at him. "Sorry, you don't have any sort of presence that I would remember, or a distinguished face for that matter. I kind of looked right through you just then." He paused. "I guess you get that a lot. So, you're here to settle a score. Man to man, with fists." He looked at Katy and said, "I'm sorry, I've just got to step outside for two or three minutes with this guy, probably a bit less. I'll just finish my steak first…"

"Asshole…" Tanner glared at him, took a step forwards but Stone did not move. He looked down at Katy and said, "Who's your friend? I wouldn't go getting too close to him…"

"I'll do what I want, Duke. And the answer is still no. No, I won't sell. Not the land, not the mining rights and certainly not to you. Good night."

"Last chance, Katy…"

"Or what? The land is legally mine; I have the permits in place. So, you won't offer again? Great, then you can stop harassing me."

"I think she's made it clear," said Stone. "Go on outside, I'll be right out when I'm done here. Get some stretches in, I wouldn't want you pulling a hammy…"

Tanner shook his head at Katy, then turned on his heel and stormed across the bar and out into the motel foyer.

"Jesus, he'll be mad now," Katy said quietly.

"Who the hell was that guy?"

"Duke Tanner. He owns Macintosh Creek. It's one of the largest gold mines up here." She paused. "And it backs right onto my claim."

"How long has he wanted to buy you out?"

Katy pushed her meal away from her. She had lost her appetite. She looked at Stone and said, "Forever. And especially since my father took the core samples. They were life-changing, or would have been, had he lived long enough to mine the ground. He had labor problems, trust issues, so he never said where he had drilled the core samples. He just rented the specialist equipment and did it on a Sunday. Not many mines operate on a Sunday around here. The miners need a day a week to rest. But not my daddy. He mined seven days from April if the weather broke early enough, through to September. Duke Tanner has been like a dog with a bone since daddy died. He knows that I haven't got the money to mine unless I can get on the gold to recoup costs. But he has the resources. He just won't stop hassling me to sell."

"I know nothing of mining," said Stone. "But it sounds a great way to lose yourself. Head down, a target in sight."

"Many people come here to work a season. But only the fools stay and buy up gold claims…" she laughed, then looked at him seriously. "You're not seriously going to fight him, are you?"

"I'm sure I will," he said. "But not tonight. Tell me, is there an auto parts store near here?"

"Right here in Lame Horse. Fuel station and garage down near the river."

"The fast-moving one you told me about?"

"No, another one. We have plenty of rivers up here. This one is in Lame Horse and it's more of an estuary. The auto parts store is near the bank of the river. It's a good store and does repairs, too. It has a good selection of everything to keep a vehicle on the road."

"I'll pay a visit tomorrow."

"You have car trouble? Anything serious?"

"I hope not," he said. Between talking and eating and Duke Tanner's interruption, Stone had lost his appetite. He had cleared most of his steak, half the fries and a few mouthfuls of coleslaw. He put his knife and fork together and pushed his plate aside.

"You shouldn't underestimate Tanner," said Katy matter-of-factly. "He's a tough guy."

Stone nodded, but he had known tougher for sure. But he consciously checked himself, knowing that he had always had a side to him that people would describe as cocky. He had always thought of it as belief in himself. There was no stock to be had in self-doubt. Step into a boxing ring thinking you will lose, and you will be on the canvas looking up at the lights and hearing the count. Stone had never entered a fight doubting he would win. He had certainly been beaten in the past, but he had always got back up and carried on. He had served in the Airborne Rangers and a recon unit before being recruited into the Secret Service. And he had been in the company of enough tough guys to know that he *was* one. "The man's parting comment sounded more like a threat rather than that it was your last chance, and he wouldn't be offering again. How many men work for him?"

"A dozen or so."

"I think I met two more today..." Stone told her of his chance encounter, the theft of his vehicle and Duke Tanner getting between them. Katy listened intently, frowning as Stone described them to her.

"They don't sound like anybody I know on Tanner's team. I don't know why he would employ anybody who has shown dishonesty, let along blatant grand theft auto. I mean, when you're digging gold out of the ground, you want good people around you."

"Do you have good people?"

She pulled a face. "I have people I trust, and then there are a few question marks above some heads. My foreman worked for my father, but he also goes fishing with Duke Tanner when the salmon are on. It's a small community, spread over many miles. People have known each other for years."

"Do you live at the mine?"

She nodded. "Sort of. I sleep there in a basic cabin. But I have a bolt hole for when it gets too much. Many of the miners live in their RVs and trailers for the summer. There are a few guys who drive in most days, but it's difficult when they work twelve or fourteen hours and then face a hundred-mile drive on these roads. So, some of them camp a few nights a week in tents, then get back to their families when they haven't had such a tough day."

"And what about morale?"

"We work hard, and there's not much gold in the pan. So, I guess it's pretty poor," she replied solemnly. "I'm running out of time. I don't have much money left and bills need paying. The workers know there's not much chance of a profit share while we fail to get to paydirt." She paused, sighing heavily. "I've been coming into town to get away from it all. I should be sat in my cabin eating beans and saving every penny, but I just can't face it on my own..." She sighed again and looked at her watch. "This has been nice," she said. "But it's on me. I've used you like a therapist. Here you are just passing through and trying to lose yourself and I've bent your ear for more than an hour," she smiled. "It's getting late, and I don't like the drive at the best of times, let alone in the dark."

"I'll see you to your car," he said. "He dropped three twenties onto the table to include the tip and said, "But it's on me. No arguments."

Stone walked her through the restaurant and foyer and out into the chill Alaskan night air. Katy's truck was parked near his own. "Your tires!" She exclaimed. "They're all flat!"

"That auto parts store will come in handy now," he said.

"You knew..." She paused. "Who are you?"

"Why?"

"You clearly got the better of two guys and Duke Tanner this afternoon, and then again in the restaurant. You weren't scared, and he's a big guy. You seemed to enjoy antagonizing him. And you knew that he would damage your truck." She paused. "Trouble has followed you around, hasn't it?"

"I've seen my fair share."

"What will you do now?"

"I'll crawl to the auto parts place in the morning and get a new set of rubber."

"And that will be an end to it?" she asked somewhat dubiously. "I can't imagine that. So, you'll just fix the tires and move on?"

Stone looked at the tires and smiled. "Thanks for the company," he said.

She leaned forward and kissed him on the cheek. There was no sense in escalating it, it was meant as an affectionate thank you and he took it that way. "Maybe I'll see you again, perhaps on the way back down when you realize that you can't truly run away without forgiving the past or atoning for it."

"Maybe I'll grow a beard, wear plaid shirts and live in the woods."

She rubbed his day-old stubble and gave his cheek a little tap. "No, you look pretty good as you are." She walked to her truck and said, "Goodbye, Rob. And if you pass back this way, stop by and I'll definitely buy you dinner back."

Stone watched as she started up the big truck and trundled out onto the road. Right for up the coast, left for the lower forty-eight states. He looked back at the ruined tires and headed for his room. He had already figured he would stick around for a few days. At least until he had bumped back into Duke Tanner and worked out compensation for the tires. He headed across the dirt carpark and realized he would have words with Duke Tanner sooner than he thought. Standing in the shadows between rooms ten and twelve, the big man stepped out into the dim orange light from the covered porch running the length of the building.

Stone kept walking. Right up until three more men stepped out from behind the gable end of the building and lined up beside their boss.

Chapter Five

"You owe me for four new tires," said Stone.

"You just don't learn, do you?" Duke Tanner sneered. "What's your business with Katy McBride?"

"That's *my* business, and no business of yours."

"She's vulnerable after her father's death. I'd hate for someone to take advantage of her."

"Like you, you mean?"

"You know nothing. I'm looking out for her is all."

"She doesn't want to sell. Not to you, not to anybody."

Duke Tanner shook his head. "She doesn't know what she's doing. She's a rank amateur. She'll ruin herself trying to do what it takes people a lifetime to learn."

"So let her ruin herself. Let her fail and buy her mining rights when she's bankrupt." Stone paused. "But you don't want that because you know something, and you just can't wait to capitalize on that. And if she doesn't sell to you, then she'll sell to somebody else and that puts you back at square one."

Tanner stepped closer. At around six-four and two-hundred and twenty pounds he was a big man. And as a big man, he was used to getting his own way, but Stone could see in the man's eyes that he would normally have intimidated his opponent by now, and there was a level of uncertainty there. Stone himself was around six-feet tall and packed into a two-hundred-pound frame. He worked out daily and considered himself match fit. Tanner had weighed Stone up earlier and elected to bring along three friends. As far as Stone was concerned, the man had already showed his weakness. A fear of losing.

"I want you to leave town," Tanner said coldly. "Hit the road and keep on running from whatever the hell you're running from."

Stone nodded. "You're a big man, Tanner. And I'm sure you're tough, too. But you haven't got the smarts for this. You don't make a man's vehicle undrivable and then ask him to leave town. Just like you don't face off a man you know nothing about with three guys who need their arms and legs to pay next week's rent." He looked at the three men in turn and then said, "You've been warned. Your boss had better have four months' pay waiting for you and be as good as his word. Because you won't be working for the rest of the season…"

"Enough of this shit!" The largest of the three men shouted and charged forward.

The man leapt off the decking and covered the open ground in three strides. Stone dropped low and shot out a side kick, the heel of his foot connecting with the man's kneecap. The man's forward momentum met Stone's and the weakest point snapped cleanly, sounding like a thick twig being stepped on. The man howled and went down hard, but not before Stone straightened and sent a right hook into the left side of the man's jaw. The other two men had followed but stopped when they heard the snap. Stone stepped forward and stamped on the man's right hand. He stared at the other two men as he ground the man's hand into the dirt like a cigarette butt. The man was lulling between the two states of consciousness and murmured for Stone to stop, but Stone was in a fight four against one and he needed some shock and awe.

That was how battles were won.

"You bastard…" Tanner said, staring at his man and then turning his eyes to the other two men, who were both frozen to the spot, and sharing a look of uncertainty between them. Tanner reached behind his back and drew a large revolver. The gunshot rang out and Tanner froze, the gun limp in his hand.

"What in hell's name is going on here?" Howard racked another round into the chamber and the empty brass shell skipped across the dry earth. He stood with the hunting rifle held loosely in his hands, the muzzle moving between all of them, including Stone and Tanner. Maude stood at his shoulder with a cell phone in her hand. "Put the damned gun down, Duke!" Howard paused. "Right now, this looks to me like a stupid backyard brawl, don't turn it into something it ain't…"

"Am I calling the cops or what?" Maude asked.

"Not yet," Howard replied. He looked at Stone and said, "Now, that's some cold shit, Mister…" But he looked to Duke Tanner without waiting for Stone's reply. "And Duke, ambushing a man four against one, really? And then you go pulling a gun when it doesn't go the way you planned?"

"Don't call the cops, Howard," Tanner said quietly. "I guess it's done. But I'll remember this right around rent review time…"

"What about Will?" One of the men said, still staring at the man's ruined hand. "The fucking psycho guy was right; he isn't going to be working anytime soon… You got his wages covered for the season?"

"Shut your mouth if you still want a damned job in the morning," Tanner growled. "Will is going to be taken care of…"

"Are we done, then?" Howard asked impatiently, the rifle still drifting without prejudice between them all.

"I'm done," said Stone.

Tanner nodded.

"But I figure six-hundred dollars for four new tires," said Stone. "You can leave it as credit at the auto parts store in the morning." He paused, staring at Tanner coldly. "If it's not there by the time I get the bill, I'll be paying you a visit…"

Duke Tanner turned and walked towards a parked truck without saying a word. The other two men struggled with the dead weight of their companion and half carried, half dragged him silently to another truck.

Stone looked at Howard and said, "Thanks."

"Don't thank me, Mister. And you can be gone in the morning. We don't want troublemakers around here."

"Now, Howard…" Maude said. "The man was bushwhacked, outnumbered and just defending himself."

"Damn it, woman!" Howard snapped. "That man won't be working the rest of the season…" He turned and watched the two trucks race out of the carpark throwing up dirt and chippings which showered Stone's truck in a somewhat pathetic and infantile show of retribution.

"That man was one of four who thought they'd wreck my vehicle and then wreck me," Stone cut in. "His boss is intimidating Katy McBride, trying to force her to sell. Then, he turns up here with three heavies trying to force me to leave…"

"Well, if they wanted you to leave, then why the hell would they slash all your damned tires?" Howard shook his head. "It just doesn't make sense to keep you from leaving." Stone's face fell and Howard said, "What?"

Stone ran across the dirt and leapt up the stairs. He unlocked his room and returned with the .45 in his hand. "Give me the keys to your vehicle," he said. "Better yet, you can drive me."

"What?" Maude frowned.

"It was a case of misdirection," said Stone. "Where would Katy McBride be staying tonight?"

"Why?" Howard asked belligerently.

"Because you're right. Why make my truck undriveable and try to run me out of town? It wasn't a case of running me out of town, it was making it so I couldn't leave. Not until the morning, that is. Katy turned him down flat tonight, and Tanner said it was her last chance. I'm worried that while I was here with some smoke and mirror bullshit, Katy was the real target."

"Oh Jesus..." Maude said quietly and started to dial on the phone.

"Leave it! No time!" Stone snapped. "Get your vehicle and take me!"

He followed Maude, with Howard cursing and following behind him. As they reached the old pickup, Stone realized with sickening trepidation that he had underestimated Duke Tanner and had in fact played right into the man's hands.

He just hoped it was not too late.

Chapter Six

Howard drove with Maude up front. Stone rode in the back and had strapped himself in because the road soon became a dirt track and the big pickup slewed and bucked on the surface. Stone could not even decide what make and model it was, but it did not have four-wheel drive and handled like a tank. Once out of the town, small though it was, the darkness was entirely enveloping. There was little moon beyond the clouds, few stars to light up the sky. The pickup's headlights were poor, most likely they were dirty and needed a wash, because they did little to light up more than fifty yards in front of them. They had not seen what direction the other two trucks had gone in, but Stone suspected they would be following Katy as she made her way back towards McBride's Folly.

"Where does Duke Tanner live?" Stone asked.

"He bunks down at his mine most nights throughout the season," Maude replied. "But he has a big house on Madison Creek."

"Maude, God damn it!" Howard cussed at her.

"What?"

Howard glanced at Stone in the rear-view mirror, then gave his wife a sideways glance. "We don't know this guy, Maude. But we've known Duke Tanner for decades."

"And he's a liar, a cheat and a bully. Just because we know him and don't know this young fella, it doesn't mean we shouldn't believe him. Katy is a lovely girl and she's suffered since her father died. It's no mean feat running a gold mine."

"Running it into bankruptcy," Howard said sharply. "Maybe she should just take Duke's money and cut and run. Go back down south and practice law again."

"Howard…"

Stone pointed ahead of them. "What's that?"

Howard did not slow. "Just some debris. Most likely a fender bender between two vehicles and the debris hasn't got broken down with traffic yet. The haulage trucks grind everything into the dirt."

"There's more," said Stone. "Slow down!" he snapped, and Howard eased on the brakes. The big pickup slewed and skidded on the loose surface and more debris was visible in the road ahead. Stone got out and picked some of it up. It looked like part of a fender. There was both clear and colored glass as well. He tossed the piece of fender into the verge and ran back to the vehicle. "Drive! I can hear something going on up ahead!"

Howard glanced at Maude, his expression in the ambient glow of the cabin showed concern.

Stone had the .45 in his right hand. As they rounded the bend, rear lights were visible in the road ahead. When they drew closer a man was kneeling in the road. He looked up, shielding his eyes from what little glow the pickup's lights afforded. He was straddling a body. He stood up, then looked behind him as a vehicle's lights switched on. Howard hit the brakes and the truck skidded on the loose surface. Stone leapt out and the man started to run. Stone fired a round above the man's head, and the man ducked instinctively and bolted for the waiting vehicle. He leapt into the passenger side and the pickup slewed and fishtailed on the dirt road. Stone ran to the body, dropped to his knees, and checked for a pulse. Katy blinked up at him, confused. She had been on the brink of unconsciousness, close to death, and suddenly started to gasp madly for air. Maude and Howard appeared either side of Stone and stared down at her.

"I... I... couldn't breathe," she said. She attempted to sit up but winced and laid back down. "The truck bumped me several times from behind, then crashed into me and ran me off the road..." She paused, either finding the memory painful, or feeling pain from the incident. "I was dazed, and someone pulled me out of my truck and at first I thought they were attempting first aid on me, like resuscitation, CPR. But he blocked my mouth and nose with his hands, and I couldn't breathe... not even the tiniest amount of air..." she started to sob and Stone eased her close to him, smoothing a hand across her shoulder.

"Come on," he said. "Let's get you into the pickup." He gestured for Maude to lend a hand and she both eased her to her feet and comforted her. As they loaded her gently onto the backseat, Stone said, "Did you recognize him?"

"No. It was too dark," she replied quietly. "Thank goodness you all came; I was blacking out..." She started to sob. "Why would someone do that?"

Howard had backed up and turned in the road and they were now bumping back over the uneven road surface. "It wasn't Duke and those boys, though," he said. "It was a different vehicle."

"Duke?" Katy looked perplexed. "Why would you think it was Duke?" she asked, but it was already dawning on her. "Jesus… I know he wants McBride's Folly, but…"

"Like I said, it wasn't Duke or those boys," said Howard adamantly.

"We had a spot of bother back at the motel after you left, honey." Maude paused, glancing at Stone. "They tried to get the young fella here to leave town. He wouldn't have it and beat up one of Duke Tanner's boys…"

"What?" Katy looked at Stone. "Are you alright?" She looked at him, then shook her head. "Of course, you are. I'm so sorry," she said. "If you got hassled on my account. But why did you assume Duke Tanner would go after me?"

Stone shrugged. "Words were said, but it didn't make any sense. Howard here stopped it escalating, but it had already turned violent, and slashing my tires so badly, only made sure I wasn't going anywhere. Then I wondered if that was the play all along."

"You thought he might do something to your truck back in the restaurant, which was why you asked me if there was a garage or auto parts store in Lame Horse. I thought Duke was just getting back at you for your earlier stand-off, not as part of some plan to get to me…" she trailed off.

"Nonsense!" Howard protested. "What happened back at the hotel was down to pride, nothing more." He shook his head. "In the morning we'll get this all straightened out."

"Yes," Maude agreed. "And in the meantime, you can stay with us."

"Thank you," Katy replied gratefully. "But if it's all the same…" She looked up at Stone and said, "I'd like to stay with you tonight. I'll take the spare bed, or the couch or whatever you have, but I'd feel safer with you in the room with me…" She paused. "Would that be OK?"

Stone couldn't think of a reason not to spend the night with an attractive woman. Even if it was in separate beds. But more than that, his years protecting people had formed a need within him, a trait he just could not shake off. He looked at the vulnerable woman beside him and said, "Sure, I'd be glad of the company."

Chapter Seven

Maude had fixed Katy a large bourbon with ice and along with it, brought a tray of coffee to Stone's room. The kind reserved for diners and not the complimentary sachets in the rooms. Howard had called the police down in Emmerson and because Katy was not in need of medical attention, they had said they would dispatch an officer in the morning. They would assess the vehicle crash site, then meet up at McBride's Folly in the afternoon. Alaska was one of only two US states that did not have counties or parishes and therefore no local sheriff departments to handle regionalized crime, so the state troopers dealt with all law enforcement matters. With the nearest police department being just under three-hundred miles away, Stone could see why Alaska was a good place for people to run to. No search would ever find the truck or the man who had attacked Katy. Without a license plate, the trail would be cold by now, let alone morning. Any investigation would merely be an exercise in logging statements and the case would forever be open until a clerk deemed it no further action. Unless a conscientious mechanic recognized the damage he was paid to repair as a vehicle collision and reported it. But that seemed unlikely because cash talked in these parts and most people did not pry into another persons' business.

When Maude and Howard finally left them alone, Katy collapsed on the bed and said, "I'm sorry. I just felt safer with you, somehow."

"I get that a lot," Stone replied.

"I bet," she said. "A safe pair of hands. Were you a cop?"

"No."

"A soldier, then?" Stone nodded, but the devil was in the details. Talk of units or deployments created a trail and he had enough problems right now. Katy smiled. "I'm sensing a reluctance to talk about yourself." She paused. "I guess that's Alaska, right? Don't worry, I'm used to it by now. My grandpa had a checkered past all of his own. That's why he settled here from Texas."

"He was first to mine your family's claim?"

Katy nodded. "He was. He should have been the last, too. But after he died my father took over."

"What was the folly element?"

"McBride's Folly," she mused somewhat wistfully. "Grandpa was a bold man. Behind the claim is a savage waterfalls and gully which my grandpa dynamited and diverted. Because of some fissure or other, he ended up accidentally bringing down half the mountain and where the river once flooded across at least half his claim, it created a gully. He always maintained that the riverbed would be full of gold deposits, but it wasn't."

"And this was his folly?"

"And his end." Katy paused. "The falls is now called McBride's Falls, because in a fit of rage after years of failing to find decent quantities of gold, he went back up there and was going to dynamite the gully and redivert the river. This was welcomed by the local people, because further down the river course the water flows so fast that it can create heavy flooding in the spring thaws. Not just that, but it is a raging torrent for most of the way until it hits the Pacific. And even there it causes problems because the currents are treacherous for over two square miles from the shore. It's a boat user's nightmare." She paused. "Anyway, he wasn't seen again. Some say he slipped and fell and went out to sea. Others say a bear could have got him." She shrugged. "Who knows? But he was never seen again." She paused. "But the legacy of the Falls remains because up here people always heed this advice... Don't ever cross the river east of McBride's Falls. You'll end up washed away and lost forever..."

"That certainly sounds like a powerful river..."

"Too powerful by far. It was diverted to a gradient that simply could not cope. But there are stretches further down that are popular with white water rapid canoeists, but there have been many fatalities as a result."

"And then your father took over the mine," said Stone. "How well did he do?"

Katy finished her bourbon and shrugged as she put the empty glass on the bedside table. "Boom and bust. Some good years and some bad. That seems to be the way of the gold miner in Alaska. Canada, too. Except for the big concerns, I suppose. Hell, anywhere there's gold there's some guy close to losing the shirt off his back saying, 'next year will be my year...!' it's a fickle and unreliable process that leads to heartbreak and disappointment more than to joy and contentment." She paused and shrugged, as if accepting her fate. "Do you know who made the first million in the Gold Rush in the eighteen-hundreds?" Stone looked at her and shook his head. "The guy selling the shovels and pans and picks. True story. And therein lies the reality."

"It sounds like you're about ready to quit."

Katy looked someplace in the middle distance. Stone hoped it was somewhere she found some comfort, but he suspected it wasn't so. She looked tearful and rubbed at her right eye with the back of her hand. Stone thought it rather like something a young child would do, and he felt drawn to protect her vulnerability. He handed her a tissue from the box on his bedside table. "I can't quit," she replied quietly. "Too many ghosts. I need to put them to rest."

"Ain't that the truth…"

"What are you running from, Rob?" She lay back on the bed, pulling part of the cover over her fully clothed body. "I can tell you're a good man. I wouldn't be here if I thought any different."

Stone took a sip of coffee and shrugged. "I was set up," he said. "It's complicated."

"And you can't clear your name?"

"I thought I had. I sent USB drives full of information, even had the testimony of a guilty party, and that of a solid witness as well, but so far nothing has changed." Suddenly it felt good to share, if only in a vague outline.

"Would it help if you went to your bosses in person?"

Stone smiled. "I don't think you understand who my bosses are, and their lack of understanding."

"So, what are we talking about? Larceny, skimming, sexual harassment?" she ventured playfully.

"Sexual harassment?" Stone laughed. "You're sharing a room with me, so you'd better hope not!"

"Seriously, how bad is it?"

Stone could hear the recording of the speech in his head, the words he had woken to in the early hours for over eight months. *"I am former Secret Service agent Rob Stone. I have been the President's bodyguard and worked both on his security detail and on special projects for him during his two terms of office,"* the recording paused. Stone remembered bucking against his bonds, tethered to the chair in front of the bank of monitors. The President at the World Trade

Centre memorial gardens, the place where every year since the Twin Towers had fallen, the press and families gathered, in front of the eyes of the world to remember the fallen. Stone can see the President's family in those monitors, but also in the reticule of the three rifle scopes, all recording their sight picture. The internet biding, the deranged man – a former enemy – staring coldly at Stone as he counted down on that fateful day. *"On my first tour of Afghanistan I was taken prisoner. During my incarceration I came to sympathize with my captives, my Islamic brothers. I converted to Islam back on home soil. I have been committed to their cause ever since. I will strike at the heart of America, the Great Satan, at the September Eleven Memorial and Museum. And I intend to do it now, in front of the press and the eyes of the world…"* As hard as he tried – and he had thought of little else all these months later - he could not let the memory die until he had seen the three blood-splattered corpses on that stage, the sight of the President staring in disbelief, barreled into by his security detail and taken off the stage as his family twitched and bled and died in front of the world.

Stone had been drugged and hypnotized and even now, he was not sure what else he had divulged. The fantasy of him turning and sympathizing with Al Qaeda during his brief incarceration in Afghanistan had been well staged and even documenting the despicable venture, providing the FBI and Secret Service with digital money trails and both a solid witness and a co-conspirator, he was a long way from clearing his name. "It's pretty bad," he replied eventually.

"I'm still a lawyer. If we negotiated a small fee for a consultation, I would be bound by lawyer-client confidentiality and privilege. I could perhaps see a way through this for you." She paused. "Call it a dollar... Just to keep it legal."

Stone smiled. "Well, it's food for thought. But trust me, you don't want this on your conscience."

Katy looked worried for a moment, then smiled, "OK, but I doubt it's as bad as you think. People run when there are all sorts of ways that their innocence can be proven ..." Then she looked a little distant for a moment. "The police will be here tomorrow afternoon," she said tentatively. "Is that going to be a problem for you?" Stone's expression said it all. "So, I guess you'll be heading out in the morning..."

"I'll take you to your claim first." He paused. "I'd like to take a look, if you don't mind?"

"Sure, I'll give you the guided tour."

"I'll push onwards after that. Don't worry about me, don't leave anything out of your statement." He paused. "But don't hold back on Tanner, either. He showed his true colors tonight, and the guys that he met this morning are bad news. If you point a finger at Duke Tanner, then if he *is* behind your attack, then he won't try anything again. He'll be the number one suspect, and he's not *that* stupid."

"And if he is innocent?"

"Then it's no skin off your nose. It's an allegation, that's all."

"This has all gotten so very messy."

"Well, when you're in a mess, things tend to get a whole lot messier before you're through and out the other side."

Katy pulled the cover off her and started to undress. She smiled at Stone, looked somewhat gleeful at his expression which was somewhere between indecision and bewilderment. "Well, if it's that messy already, then this won't exactly make things any worse..." Stone watched as she stripped down to her bra and panties and knelt on the bed. He had not been with a woman for a long time. Eight solitary, dry months. And the anticipation was almost too much to bear. He tore off his shirt and tossed it aside, and she smiled as she straddled him, placed her hands on his firm, expansive chest and pushed him back down onto the bed. "Easy there, partner," she said quietly. "No rush, we've got all night…"

Chapter Eight

Stone was not a lover of biscuits and gravy, so he had upgraded to scrambled eggs and bacon and pancakes with syrup when he paid for Katy's breakfast. They drank a lot of coffee between them and chatted comfortably. The day after the night before usually told how things would play out, and Stone found himself wishing things could be different. That he could afford to stick around with the police investigating and did not have the threat of prosecution and incarceration hanging over him, like the proverbial Sword of Damocles. He liked Katy and he could tell that she liked him, too. They had clicked at dinner, clicked in bed, and clicked at breakfast, basking in the comfortable and satisfying afterglow that new lovers enjoyed. Stone had not felt so fulfilled in all manner of ways in years.

There had been no credit left for Stone at the auto parts store. He had not been surprised. He had paid for the four new tires in cash, choosing to get over-sized all-terrain tires while he had the chance, and both he and Katy had ambled around the carpark and watched the birds on the estuary while they waited for the tires to be fitted. Again, the chat had been comfortable, although neither of them had mentioned the antics in the motel room. Some things were better left unsaid, and this was not going to be the start of something new, but the end of something all too brief.

The drive out to where she had been run off the road had taken a little over half an hour and when Stone pulled up and parked at the side of the road Katy looked despondent. "You don't have to get out," he said. "But I want to have a look around."

"I'll be OK," she replied. "It's not the crash that's freaking me out. It's the fact that the man was trying to smother me…"

Stone nodded. They had barely talked about the attack, each time Stone had tried, Katy had been evasive. He wondered whether they would have slept together had she not been traumatized after the attack, and then he worried that he should have perhaps rebuffed her advances, given what she had experienced. He touched her arm and rubbed her reassuringly. "Can you remember anything about him?" he asked. "Anything at all would be helpful, and the police are going to want to know as much as you can tell them."

She shook her head as they walked towards the wreckage. "I guess he smelled," she said. "Yeah, he was pretty ripe. Body odor and unwashed. Cigarettes and beer on his breath, with strong potato chips, like *Cheetos*. Really cheesy."

Stone nodded. "Anything else? Hair, eyes, teeth?"

"I clawed at him… He may have scratches on his face. But he managed to pin both my wrists in one hand, then knelt on my arms so he could use both hands… It was too dark to see…" She frowned, closed her eyes, then opened them intensely. "When you all arrived in the truck, the dim lights lit him up faintly. I was passing out by then… But he had a tattoo on his neck. Like barbed wire…" She paused, stifling a sob. Her eyes were red and moist. "I thought that ugly tattoo was going to be the last thing I saw… He was looking your way, which was why I didn't see his features, I guess."

"You need to tell all of this to the cops," said Stone.

"You won't stay?"

"I can't."

"OK."

"I want to, though…" Stone turned and studied the truck. It was an old Ford Bronco and most of its engine had spewed out from the hood and into the drainage ditch. "You're going to need a tow truck and a hoist," he said.

"That was my dad's truck. I kind of liked driving it around. It reminded me of him."

"That guy with the tires this morning had a pretty handy looking shop. Would he mend something like that?"

"He would. He's the only guy for miles. He keeps all of Lame Horse's vehicles on the road. But it doesn't exactly matter," she said solemnly. "I can't afford to get it done anyhow, and my insurance won't cover me for that…" She shrugged as she saw Stone's quizzical expression. "OK, I let the policy slide…" She paused. "There's an old truck I can use at the mine. One of the maintenance guys can get it going for me…"

Stone nodded, then walked around the truck. There was sign of an impact on the rear left quarter. He recognized the technique. A hard contact from the pursuing vehicle on the rear edge of the target vehicle upset the balance and then inertia did the rest. Hit a vehicle on the left side of its bumper and it will generally force a hard left turn. The driver usually corrected it, but inevitably sent the vehicle into an opposite spin. "Most of the debris looks to have been from the other vehicle," he noted. "The State Police will be able to match the parts to get a clear identification of the vehicle. Then they need to search for vehicles of that make and model that are registered in the vicinity. The people who did this will have suffered extensive damage to their vehicle for certain. With few places to mend their vehicle and with the police putting out a watch, they have a good chance of catching them. It just relies on those places reporting them, and that's another matter entirely."

"Money talks." Katy shook her head. "And if the vehicle isn't registered in Alaska, then it changes everything. And then there's the fact that some trucks are here in their thousands. In their tens of thousands when you factor in Washington State, Idaho, and Montana. That's where most of the seasonal gold and fishing workers come from. Hell, they come from all over!" She paused. "People even make the trip up from Florida for a season's work and the promise of a fair dollar and a slice of the

American Dream!"

Stone said nothing. Katy was still clearly shaken and had resigned herself to the fact that Alaska's wildness, its rugged wilderness, and huge expanse was never going to see her attackers caught, tried, and sentenced. Alaska was as big as the entire Eastern Seaboard and every state that formed it. Perhaps that was what had made the place so appealing for people on the run, who Stone reflected, were people like himself.

"You were more than just a soldier," Katy said. "And you already said you weren't a cop. I can't imagine you working as a PI and tailing cheating partners or insurance scammers. So, I figure you were with another kind of law enforcement agency, or even intelligence agency, for that matter. An agent of some kind." Stone smiled. He didn't usually like questions, but then he didn't usually like the person asking them. "Hell, I could Google until I found your photo, the FBI's Most Wanted List…"

"Please don't," he replied. He shrugged. "You'll push me away…"

"You're leaving anyway," she said coldly.

"But I want to come back already," he replied. "I can't if I'm all out of options…"

"I'm sorry," she said and hugged him close. "I didn't mean to upset you, to back you into a corner. Christ, it's only been a day, but I've fallen for you…"

"And a night," he smiled.

"I don't usually do that," she said coyly, her face flushing despite the chilled air.

"I do," he said. "If a beautiful woman wants to be with me, who am I to turn them down?" He shrugged. "You never know where it will take you, or how much you'll enjoy it on the way."

She smiled. "You're quite the hopeless romantic," she said.

"Or just hopeless…"

"Certainly not hopeless, by any means…"

"Hopeful, then."

She smiled. "Come on, let me show you my life," she said. "Before you leave and decide you don't want to come back…"

Chapter Nine

"This is Marvin, my foreman," said Katy. "I'm just going to get Don to have a look at the old Blazer, see if he can get some life into the engine," she smiled and headed towards a group of men who were standing about smoking and drinking coffee from thermos cups. Stone watched as some of them straightened up and flicked their cigarette butts into the dirt. A few of them did not look overly concerned that their boss was heading their way and by nine-thirty, they were still on a break, or yet to start work altogether.

Stone looked at the man in front of him, shook his hand but he already knew he did not care for him, something about his eyes. Stone liked people who could hold his own gaze. Marvin was an old timer. Or he could have just been in his late fifties. Alaska was a tough place and gold mining was a sight tougher on the body and features. His face was weathered, and his stubble was as grey as the few hairs which remained on his head. The man's hands were hard and calloused. Stone's own were softer by comparison, toughened from years of weapon handling and gripping weight bars, but nothing compared to the man who appeared to excavate the dirt with his bare hands.

"You're the fella who done gone and ruined Phil's season…"

"Ah, last night." Stone shook his head. "No, I figure I gave him good and fair warning," Stone replied. "News certainly travels fast in these parts."

Marvin shrugged. "We're a tight knit community."

"If you're so tight knit, how come you don't recognize loyalty?"

"What?" Marvin turned and glanced at Katy talking to the group of men. He glared back at Stone but was met with Stone's thousand-yard stare. Marvin looked uneasy. But he pressed on. "What the hell are you talking about?"

"Well, your friend Tanner is putting a great deal of pressure on your boss to sell. You need to work out what and who is more important to you. Your friend, or your livelihood."

"I've known Duke Tanner for years," Marvin replied indignantly. "And I worked with Katy's father. I did odd jobs for her grandfather when I was a kid."

"She's having a tough time. Her season was a bust last year because of her father's debts and this year it's make or break. You should tell your buddy to back off, get behind your boss and drive this season forward. Duke Tanner should back the hell off. If not because of Katy persistently turning down his offer, then because you should be telling him to leave her be."

"Why don't you mind your own God damned business?"

Stone stared coldly at him and said, "Right now, I'm looking out for Katy. I'm just passing through. When I come back, I don't want to see her still being hassled by Tanner. Perhaps you should have a word…"

"You think you can intimidate me?" Marvin grinned. "You don't know me, boy."

"And you don't know me. Or what I've done. Now, I'm giving you the chance to play nice. I'll be talking to Duke Tanner, too."

"Well, good luck with that," he sneered. "I'm going now. Got to go and make a cut. I wouldn't want to let my *boss* down, would I?"

Marvin walked towards a large bulldozer, barely acknowledging Katy as she walked past him and back to Stone. Katy didn't miss a beat and Stone figured she was used to not having her manager's respect. Or showing common curtesy for that matter.

"Don will have the old Chevy Blazer up and running by the end of the day," she said. "What's wrong, didn't you get along with Marvin? He's tricky, but he knows gold mining."

"That's what concerns me," Stone replied. He sighed and said, "Come on, I thought you were going to show me your life?"

Chapter Ten

The ground stretched out before them, the mine waste making it look more like a lunar landscape than a gold mine. Stone could see the trees in the distance, but there were piles of broken trees poking out of what he had learned was called over burden – the topsoil that needed to be removed before they got down to the bedrock. The bedrock itself held the gold deposits in pockets, that would once have been riverbed or glacier.

"We are bound by contract to bulldoze the over burden back afterwards, which allows new trees to grow back, eventually." Katy paused, shielding her eyes from the sun with her hand as she pointed to the most desolate area at the foot of the mountain. "You'd be surprised by how quickly the trees regrow. A few summers' worth of seed dispersal by the wind and this place will be green with saplings, after another few years the trees will be head high. There are mines throughout the valley that have been mined out ten years ago, and they are all forest again now."

"I guess that's a good thing," said Stone. "Because this place looks like one of Dante's Seven Circles of Hell."

"Yeah, it's not pretty. I get that." She paused. "But I think of it as a short-term thing. The land *does* get returned to nature."

"Not so much raped, as briefly fondled…"

Katy sniggered. "Oh, OK. That doesn't make it sound so great, I admit." She paused. "Are you an environmentalist?"

"It's on my mind more these days," he admitted. "But in a past life I was a gear head, I guess I would be again if I had the chance."

"Cars?"

"Cars and motorcycles."

"Well, we use a lot of fuel with our excavating and hauling, and generators. I'm not all that comfortable with it, but I need to get this done before I go back to practicing law, drive a Prius and start recycling my coffee take-out cups…"

"You'll mine the ground until it stops giving up the gold, then just quit?"

"I'm finishing what my grandfather and daddy started."

Stone nodded. "There's nothing like

finishing unfinished business."

"You have experience with unfinished business?"

He nodded. His brother had been in the FBI. He had been a hell of an agent by all accounts. An assassin had cut his throat and left him to die in the gutter. He glanced at his Rolex. It had belonged to his father, then gone to his older brother when his father had passed away. Stone had been given the watch at his brother's wake. It was the only possession he had that meant a damn. "I do," he replied. "But unfinished business eventually gets finished, and you just have to hope it hasn't cost you more than it was worth along the way."

"I think I know what you're saying," she said quietly. "Is it like the Chinese proverb that a man seeking revenge must first dig two graves?"

"In a way," Stone replied. "You want to find the ground where your father took his samples, but you risk losing everything in doing so. Sometimes you need to know when to hold and when to fold…"

"And when to walk away and when to run?"

"It's a great song…"

"But I guess it's a valuable life skill." She sighed. "Perhaps I should just sell."

"But not to Duke Tanner."

"Nobody else is forming a line."

Stone nodded. A bulldozer was making its way to an area of ground in the lee of the mountain. Behind it an excavator followed. "You know, when I heard gold mine, I pictured a cave, or a mineshaft dug into a wall of rock."

"Like the old timers prospecting?" she smiled. "All battened up with wood, like in the old Western movies?"

"Yep."

"I guess they worked with what they had. Dynamiting into the mountainside made up for their lack of digging technology. Until the Chinamen of the Old West were put to work."

"Another of America's less than desirable moments in history." He paused. "And there's been more than a few. Lieutenant Colonel Custer had been ordered by President Ulysses S. Grant not to do anything that might jeopardize the peace treaty with the native Americans, but Custer sent a letter to the New York Times and declared that he alone had discovered gold in the Black Hills in South Dakota. It sparked the US Gold Rush. The country was in recession, and everybody wanted to get rich. It meant the Sioux and Cheyenne Indians being pushed off their land, which meant war. And all for gold. I guess it's fitting that Custer will always go down in history as self-serving and arrogant and dying in such a memorable manner. So confident of success was he, that he ordered his company to box up their sabers before they left. He thought he could gun the Indians down at a distance. They literally ended up in hand-to-hand combat against knives, spears, and tomahawks with nothing but empty guns to use as clubs. Eventually, the Native American people would be forced onto tiny reservations."

"I guess we were built upon slavery and exploitation. These days the gold is taken out of the ground by a never-ending line of people looking for good money and a share in the American Dream." She paused. "Anyway, that old gold mine picture you have was the case in the Black Hills in South Dakota or in the mountains in Colorado and California, then they learned more about deposits in dried-up riverbeds. Sure, there were mines like that up here, but it's mainly about scraping off the over burden on an industrial scale and getting down to pay dirt, which is a layer just above the bedrock. The gold sinks over time, until it can sink no further. It starts off in seams up in the mountains, then over millennia, it is pushed out by erosion, glacial movement, and rivers. It gathers on the bends in the rivers, sinks into what we call deposit pockets. Over time, the course of the rivers change, and soil builds on top from waste matter such as trees, dust, leaves and mud."

Stone looked at the bulldozer as it started to carve out its path. He tried to estimate how many football fields would fit into the ground. He used the size of the two vehicles to get some sense of perspective, watched a third vehicle make its way over to the other two. After he laid the football fields out across the bottom and down one side, he estimated a thousand stadiums worth of grass. Probably a whole lot more. Much of it had already been scraped to mud. "It looks like you only have a few patches left to mine," he said pointedly, looking out towards the far end of the claim.

"That's right."

"So, if Duke Tanner wants your land so much, then what would be left for him to mine?"

"Not so much," she replied. "Just what

you see here and going back another two hundred yards into the trees. But Tanner maintains he is the better miner and that if he re-mined the ground and the tailings... that's the waste after going through the sluices... then he would find more gold. He basically wants to re-mine what three generations have spent blood, sweat and tears over."

Stone looked way to his left. There was a belt of trees and then a similar moonscape sight for almost as far as he could see. "What's out that way?"

"Duke Tanner's claim."

"His claim butts right up to your own?"

"We're neighbors," she said sardonically.

Stone watched for a while. The machinery had a hypnotic, almost calming effect. The bulldozer tore off the top layer and the excavator filled the truck, then when it drove away, the excavator made a large pile of earth for moving. "If I were you, I'd concentrate all your efforts over there." He pointed to the boundary of trees between the two claims.

"You're a prospecting expert all of a sudden, Mister Old West Movie...?"

Stone checked his watch. The State Police would be here soon. "Duke Tanner has an agenda. I think he stumbled across your father's core samples."

"I had thought that, but Marvin assured me the ground is untouched."

"Take a hike down there and have a thorough look," said Stone. "And don't tell Marvin."

"You don't think I can trust him?" she asked, clearly wounded by the insinuation. "He was with my father for years. He was here briefly with my grandfather, too." She shook her head. "No, I trust him implicitly."

"OK, I'll let you be the judge of him. I'm just passing through. But the rest of your crew look like they're swinging the lead."

"Swinging the lead?"

"One of my mother's many sayings. It means taking it easy on your dime."

Katy shrugged. "Short of cracking a whip across their backs, I don't see what else I can do." She paused. "I'm sure they will get more enthused once there's gold in the grates."

Stone nodded. He could see she was struggling, but he was no expert on this type of work. He was a good motivator and had led men into combat, but like he said, he was merely passing through and had never even seen a gold mine before this morning. What did he know about manual labor and the way men took smoking and coffee breaks before working? "Well, I'm out of here," he said. "I don't want to be around when the police come here."

"I hope you can stop running soon, Rob. I really do." She reached out and hugged him close, and he responded by holding her firmly. It felt warm and comfortable and right. She smelled good, too. "It was lovely getting to know you. However briefly. Hopefully, you'll look back in someday?"

Stone pulled away and smiled. "You can count on it."

Chapter Eleven

North was right and south was left. Stone took the left and after thirty-minutes he was in Lame Horse and handing over two-thousand bucks to the guy who owned the auto parts store. He instructed him to tow Katy's truck and get it fixed up enough to run. The guy had been confident he could get the engine mounted back in the vehicle, running as sweet as Ford had intended all those years ago and that any structural compressions could be straightened out on the jig. He liked Katy McBride, did work for both her father and grandfather, and would get the job done on his two big ones. If there was anything left over, he would work on what needed doing next. The truck was old, and Alaska was tough on trucks.

Stone turned around and headed back up the highway. When he reached the sharp right-hand turning for McBride's Folly, he slowed the truck and stopped in the middle of the road. Ahead would take him north and away from Lame Horse. He knew he could not be around when the State Police arrived. But he just couldn't let it go. A nagging at the back of his mind. Stone had never walked away from a fight. And he was not about to do so now. He floored the gas pedal and when the truck hit the dirt road, the rear end slewed on the loose surface. Stone kept his speed to around forty. When he reached the site where Katy had been forced off the road, he slowed watching the police cruiser and the two officers beside the wreckage. They were shooting the breeze, doing no more of an investigation than looking at a truck with half its engine hanging out. Stone recognized the expressions on their faces and knew that they would be no closer finding the men who had done this to her in a week, a month, or a year. The police officers barely looked up as Stone passed them by.

Stone took the left and settled in for the unfamiliar ride. There were the wrecked carcasses of mining equipment from trucks to backhoes to trommels littering the sides of the dirt road. Stone could see it was a make do and mend operation. Entire vehicles stripped out to cannibalize other equipment and keep them working. Some of the rusted hulks looked decades old and all had taken on a patina of red and brown, a trace of logo or sign writing only visible when it caught the light.

Stone checked the .45 as he drove, tucked it into his inside jacket pocket. He now had two pump-action shotguns and one was in the footwell beside him. He was not sure about Alaska's laws transporting firearms, but he figured it would be more casual than unloaded and locked inside a carrier. But he also figured that if it took a pair of nonchalant cops until midday to get here from three-hundred miles south, then he wasn't going to be running into many patrol vehicles. Which worked out fine for what he had planned. If the term planned could be used, even loosely.

Tanner's mine mirrored McBride's Folly in every way except one. There was the same equipment, the same mud and dirt and traces of ice and snow that had remained in the shade. The same lunar landscape, the same broken and felled trees bulldozed into heaps. The same cabin acting as an office, another for the gold room and another for what Stone assumed was a mess hall and recreation room. The only difference was that there were no groups of men standing around and shooting the breeze, sipping coffee and smoking. The vehicles were all in motion and the only man not digging, hauling, or bulldozing was Duke Tanner, and he stepped outside of his office cabin and watched as Stone pulled up front and switched off his engine. He wore a revolver in a holster on his hip.

Stone got out, eyeing the openly carried handgun. "Expecting trouble? Just as well."

"There are bears all over. And people fixing to steal my gold. That's reason enough." He paused, looking around, then back at Stone. "You're either brave or stupid."

"I've been both in the past, but today I'm just collecting what's mine. It should be simple enough."

"I'm thinking… stupid." Tanner's hand neared the revolver. "There's nobody around and no witnesses. Maybe I just thought you were fixing on stealing my gold."

"Suits me fine. I'm carrying, too."

Tanner spat on the ground and said, "Then, I hope you're fast on the draw."

"The only thing faster is light..."

Tanner frowned, looked around again, but there was still nobody else nearby. He had the look of a man about to make an irreversible decision, but still wasn't quite sure whether he could do it. "What do you want?"

"Four tires. Six-hundred bucks."

"And that's it?"

"Then I'm as good as gone."

"But you can't let it lie," said Tanner. "Six-hundred dollars is really that much to you?" He laughed. "Of course, it is. Look at your shitty truck, your shitty life…"

It wasn't just six-hundred dollars to Stone. He was on the run, but he hadn't given the FBI everything. There was twenty-million dollars in various locations at his disposal and that gave him twenty-million ways of staying ahead of the hunt. No, to Tanner it was just six-hundred dollars, but to Stone it was letting a bully have his way. Stone couldn't care less about the money.

"It's six-hundred bucks today," Stone said quietly. "Or it's more than you can afford another day."

"Just how do you figure that?"

"Every now and then in life you meet a guy who you don't push. Who you won't get the better of, and who you don't beat, no matter how hard you try." Stone paused. "I'm that guy…"

"Well, that makes two of us, I guess." Tanner paused. "I figure you owe me a season's pay for a man who can't even wipe his own ass now."

Stone grinned. "No, that was on you." He paused. "It's all on you." He looked at the earth mover near them. Six wheels and all of them over six feet high. "What do you figure one of those tires cost?"

Tanner regarded him closely. "Two thousand bucks a piece."

"Wow. And there's six of them, right? That's going to get real expensive, real quick."

"You really like trouble, don't you...?" Tanner stated flatly.

Stone glanced to his left where two men were getting out of a small ATV which looked like a modern version of a Willys Jeep. Behind them, two more men ambled towards one of the cabins. Lunch break time. They watched Tanner and Stone as they fired up cigarettes and worked on them voraciously. Stone looked back at Tanner and said, "Looks like it's chow time. Do it now, Tanner. Get six-hundred bucks out of your petty cash tin and give me what you owe me before your guys get wind that something's going down. Better to bite the bullet and lose face with me, than with your entire crew..."

"And you're gone?"

"Like yesterday." Tanner looked over to the men as he considered his options. "People steal gold all the time," he said. "Maybe you came up here fixing to get some easy money. I could talk the guys around real quick. It's their gold in the grates as well…" He looked back at Stone and froze. Stone held the .45 in his right hand. The hammer was back, and Stone's finger was close to the trigger. His leg shielded it from view, but not to Tanner. He had a close-up view, and his own revolver was in its holster, with a safety strap over the hammer, buttoned in place. "It's all about situational awareness, Tanner. When to hold firm, when to look and when to draw someone's attention. I've been here before. Many times." He walked forwards, closing the gap between them, and edging the muzzle of the .45 up slightly so that it lined up with Tanner's balls. Then Stone said, "Let's go and get my money…"

Chapter Twelve

Duke Tanner sat back heavily in his leather swivel chair behind a desk he had made from old pallets and some reclaimed doors twenty-five years ago. He had no idea why he had kept the desk when he built the cabin ten years ago to replace his portacabin, but it was solid, and he thought it added a rustic charm.

If it ain't broke, don't fix it…

But something was very broken. Something had changed and he did not like it. He had been here all his life. He had made a success of himself. He was the big man and if the town was classed as a parish and required a mayor, then he would be it. He pulled gold out of the ground and employed twenty men and what he said was word. No question. He had his fingers in pies all over town – practically owned it as well as the people. And then a man had shown up, shown an interest in the one person standing between him and an unimaginable fortune and when he had tried to move the man on, he had been met with an immovable object. Was Tanner himself irresistible force? Because when irresistible force met immovable object, there was only room for destruction.

But Stone was gone. He had paid the man what he had sought for the tires. It was done. Although the nagging feeling Duke Tanner was experiencing felt like defeat, and the one thing that could make defeat more palpable was victory. Without her protector, Katy McBride would fold. He just needed to exert more pressure. And he would do that in spades.

"What the fuck did that guy want?" the man asked as he walked into the cabin, his footsteps echoing off the wooden floor and walls.

Tanner looked up, watched the man's brother follow him through the door. Both men were tattooed, sported shaven heads with more than a week's stubble on their faces, and wore chunky gold chains around their necks. Big links, Cuban style. Tanner estimated a couple of pounds in weight each. More gold than Katy McBride was getting out of the ground for certain. Faded jeans and mid-length black leather jackets finished their look, and they certainly looked at odds in the Alaskan landscape. Or like they had lost their Harley Davidsons in a bet at Sturgis. He had sought out of towners, recommended by an acquaintance he had once done business with. The two men were working as casual labor, but if they stayed too long, with no discernible skillset, the other miners would start asking questions. They needed to get the job done and leave.

"You boys fucked up," Tanner said tersely. "Another mile and you could have run her right off the road and into the river. That was the plan. The same place her daddy met his end. The idea was that she would be scared witless, see how close she came to meeting her daddy's fate and rethink my offer. If she died, she died. I will get the mine somehow, but you boys did a half-assed job making her crash on a straight stretch of road and then trying to finish her off by suffocating her. What the hell was that about?"

"How did you know?"

"Guess what? It's a small fucking town…"

"We got lost…"

"I'm not paying you fifty-grand a piece to get lost. I'm paying you to do a job for me. I want the deeds to her mine and the mining rights signed over to me. So, I want her willing to accept my offer. She needs to be softened up." He paused. "Now, it can't be a damned car accident again. It will look too suspicious. I want her to sell to me. I want her to run back down south and never look back. Understand?"

"Got it," the older brother replied.

"Now, get the hell out of here. You're stinking the place up…"

Both men turned and walked out of the cabin. When they were outside, the older brother said, "What the hell *were* you doing with her?"

The younger brother gave a crooked, grin. His teeth were blackened and chipped and he had escaped even the most basic of America's dental plans his entire life. "She's a sweet piece of ass," he said. "And I bet she's got tits and a pussy sweeter than a candy store window. I was just seeing if I could make her go night-night before I got myself a piece of it."

The older brother punched him playfully on the shoulder as they walked. "Shit, bro. I thought eight years in the slammer would have taught you that if you can't get some and you need to play, then it's better to pay…"

"Not exactly going to find me a hen house around here, am I?"

"Damn, brother. Just keep your dick in your pants and think about what you can do back in San Fran with fifty gees in your pocket." He paused. "Don't go getting all weird and shit on me, we got a job to do."

"And then we're out of here?"

"Damned straight."

Chapter Thirteen

Secret Service Headquarters
Washington DC

Max Power had faced several interviews like this one. Opposite him sat the District Attorney William Kassel, the Chief Prosecutor (Secret Service) Andrew Clearwater, the Director of the FBI Cassandra Burrows and the Director of the Secret Service Richard Armitage. There was a lot of power in the room, and each person had shown a degree of amusement or rather, bemusement at the name of the technology expert seated before them. Max Power was born John Maxwell Power and Maxwell was a family naming tradition for the men in the Power family. John Power had changed his name to Max Power in his freshman year in a bid to get laid. It had not worked. But it had always been a great conversation piece or would have been had he not been the same geeky man he was ten years ago. As usual, his hair was untidy, and he had attended the meeting in *Simpson's* socks and a black tie with a geeky statement about MS Dos commands written in white:

Keyboard Failure: Press F1 to Continue.

Bad Command or File Name: Go to Your Room!

COMMAND.com not Found: Should I Fake it? (Y/N)

Must Specify Destination: Start TRAVELAGENT.exe? (Y/N)

Out of Memory: Run ALZHEIMER.com? (Y/N)

BREAKFAST.exe Failure: No Response from Cereal Port.

An agent from the internal security team finished rigging Max Power to the polygraph machine and started to check the reading. The man had studied Power's tie with interest but did not get the jokes as he was probably quite normal, despite what he did for a living. "I'm going to ask you a few test questions before we start, just to check the machine's readings. Please answer truthfully in either a yes or no response. "Do you understand?"

"Sure."

"Again, Mister Power, in simply a yes or no response…"

"OK."

"Yes, or no?"

"Yes, or know to what?"

"Do you understand?"

"I do…" Power shook his head. "Sorry, I didn't know we'd started."

The agent sighed and said, "Simply answer yes or no to my question. Do you understand?"

"Yes."

The agent frowned. "The polygraph shows that was a lie."

"Sorry, I think it must be in response to whether or not I understand. I don't understand the situation, so understandably, my response is deep seated. I therefore haven't given the appropriate response to which you were projecting your expectations." He paused, watching some of the most senior intelligence officers in the country becoming impatient. "OK! Good to go!" Power took a deep breath and exhaled long and slow.

"Is your name Max Power?"

"Well, yes and no. It was John Maxwell Power, but I changed it in college…"

"Yes, or no…"

Yes, er no. Well, yes, sort of…"

"For the purpose of the test…" the agent sighed and said measuredly. "I will continue and try to ask a question that you can give a yes or no answer to…"

"OK…"

"Are you thirty years of age?"

"Yes, well my birthday is next week, so I suppose generically, with my mother going into labor ten days overdue, I am in fact, already thirty-one." He looked at the rest of the panel and shrugged. "Yes. Thirty on a form, I guess…"

The agent sighed. "Do you work for the Secret Service?"

"Yes." Power smiled. "I did it, a one-word answer. Yay, go me…"

"Mister Power!" Chief Prosecutor Andrew Clearwater snapped. "Your behavior can be construed as evasive at best."

"I think I should probably have legal representation," Power said matter-of-factly.

"Do you think you need legal protection?" Clearwater asked.

"Is a one-word only answer response for the purposes of the polygraph required or expected for that question?" He shrugged. "I think any response would be inadmissible in a court of law as the polygraph test is being run by an agent of internal security, and therefore an expert in polygraphy and not, with respect, the panel of senior figures before me." He paused. "I have attended three of these tests previously, so could someone please tell me why I am being subjected, unfairly in my opinion, to another test, when previous polygraph readings have shown that I am not in contact with Rob Stone, have never been in contact with Rob Stone after the assignment where I was called upon to provide technical assistance and that I have no idea of Agent Stone's whereabouts. I do not have, nor ever have had access to assets seized by Stone during his assignment and other than a rented apartment, a modest vehicle on a zero percent payment plan and two cats waiting for me to arrive home, have no financial commitments, dependents, or debts. I do not have more money than my means allows." Power stood up and tore off the adhesive patches holding the sensors and wires in place and adjusted his tie. It would have been a more credible gesture had the MS Dos jokes not wafted in the panel's faces, but the man was not working with much to start with.

"Do, please sit down, Mister Power," said Clearwater. "We haven't finished here, yet."

"No," said Power. "We're done. Each time I have been requested to undertake this procedure, I have done so in good faith and foregone any legal representation, despite it being your legal and moral obligation to advise me counsel." He walked to the door, and nobody tried to stop him, but he turned and said, "I hope you catch him. I hope you do whatever it takes so that I can move on with my life and my career and this dark cloud above me is lifted." He closed the door behind him and made his way down the corridor. He paused at the water fountain and bent down to sip but spat out the nicotine gum he had been holding under his tongue and drank heavily. He was not a smoker, but the flood of nicotine had stimulated his resting heartbeat further to the amphetamine he had swallowed on his way to the unmarked office on the top floor. He was used to their questions now, and not only did the amphetamine and nicotine shot make his heart race – something that had always been attributed as a severe case of nerves, but the act he put on made his readings unreliable at best. Max Power was a geek, and he wasn't a field agent, but he had a higher IQ than anybody else in that room, and he had seen enough of Rob Stone, and enough of the evidence to know they were only interested in a witch hunt and had no intention of clearing a framed agent's name.

Power glanced at his Casio digital watch. It was a calculator model, and quite valuable in today's market, despite having worn it all his adult life and not in an ironic gesture. Geek was finally in style, and he was even considering a beard and man-bun to up the ante and gain some credibility with the women in the secretarial pool. But who was he kidding? If his name change had changed nothing ten years ago, facial hair and a questionable hair style was not going to help him now.

He had another hour until the end of his shift. The water was helping with the voracious thirst caused by the amphetamine, and he could feel his heart rate slowing, his blood pressure lowering. He did not feel himself and he was light-headed, felt drunk. He had never experimented with drugs, not even in the early Max Power years on campus and would not take any more once they were finished with him. He carried them in a signet ring with a screw-down cap. There was room for six of them as they were LSD-soaked rice paper squares. Not a heavy dose, but enough for him and as much as he'd ever want to risk taking.

"Max Power?" the woman asked from behind him. Power turned around and stared at her. "Are you OK?"

"Sure."

"Your eyes look dilated, are you sure you're not ill?"

"I'm fine," he replied, wiping his mouth with the back of his sleeve. "Who are you?"

"Liz Roper," she said.

Power smiled. He was quite sure she was one of the most attractive women he had ever seen. Porcelain skin and auburn hair, with the most penetrating and intense green eyes imaginable. "How can I help?" he asked.

"Can we get a coffee?" she asked.

"Absolutely," he beamed back at her. "Just say where and when and I'll be there…"

"That's great. But I'm kind of talking about now."

"Oh, sure. Well, there's the coffee shops in the building."

"Let's take it outside," she said. "Can you spare the time?"

Power glanced at his watch, but he barely registered the time. "Yep, nothing else on for the rest of the day. Java Joe's? It's right across the street."

"Sure," she replied.

They headed downstairs and went through the security gauntlet. Keys, wallets, and pens in the box and x-rayed while they walked through the metal detector. Liz Roper declared her firearm and Power watched as she placed it along with two spare magazines in the box. They were given a once over with the metal detector wand before the guard pointed them over to collect their possessions.

Max Power watched her holster her weapon. "You're a field agent?"

"Treasury," she nodded.

"I thought you were in the secretarial pool."

"Wow." She fastened a single button on the jacket of her trouser suit and said, "That's quite a generalized assumption on gender."

Power stared at her and said, "I didn't mean it." He paused. "I just…"

She started walking and gestured with a flick of her head for him to follow. Her hair swung loosely over her shoulder. Power was mesmerized. He had never been in the company of a woman in this league. He checked his watch again. He was leaving an hour early but had already decided he would arrive at dawn tomorrow to compensate. He started to head right, but Liz Roper headed left, and he did a sort of half skip as he changed directions, hoping she had not seen.

"The coffee's better at Bean Around the World."

Power knew that it was on 9th Street NW and Palmer Alley. A corner location, but too far for a quick break. He had never been there, but he had driven past, and it had a good deal of outside seating and always looked busy. They crossed over on 9th Street and Liz stepped around and walked on his left. Power had the road on his side, but he did not resist as she brushed against him and his heart raced at the notion of a beautiful woman being so forward as to ask for... what, a date? He couldn't exactly process that it had happened, but he figured this was how the acorns of love took root. He had no experience in such matters, but he was more than willing to go with it.

"How long have you been with the Secret Service?" he asked.

"Ten years," she replied. "Just got transferred from Los Angeles."

"Right, that explains it."

"Explains what, exactly?"

"Why I've never seen you around."

"How can you be so sure?"

"Are you kidding?" He laughed. "No, trust me, I'd have remembered you."

"I think you probably will for some time to come…"

It all happened at once. They walked past the black van, the side door slid back, and rough hands grabbed Power as Liz Roper pushed him inside. The door slid closed, and Roper turned and opened the passenger door and hopped up into the seat. The two men in the rear of the van had Power pressed down on the floor, the chloroform-soaked rag pushed into his face. By the time they were fixing the cable ties around his wrists, Power was unconscious, and the van was already pulling out into the beginning of the rush hour traffic.

Chapter Fourteen

He slowly came round, the heat inside the hood stifling and the air heavy with his own breath. He could not see, could only hear background noises and he struggled to breathe. His hands were way beyond feeling, the sensation of pins and needles long turned to a dull ache that ebbed and flowed with his heartbeat and ended in excruciating pain at his fingertips.

If he was a field agent, then it would have been time to remember his training and draw from experience. Subtle sounds, smells, the feel of the floor beneath him, temperature, the regional accents, and gender of the voices in the van as he had been subdued and drugged; whether the van ran on diesel or gasoline – it would all be valuable intelligence if he managed to escape. However, Max Power was not a field agent. He had never even fired a gun. Not ever. Not even a BB gun as a kid. When the kids on his block had been doing that and knocking out panes of glass on the derelict house in their street, Power had been inside playing *Warhammer*. He was merely a gifted technology and communication expert who worked for the

Secret Service. He had no training for this.

He wasn't a big man and was dragged to his feet by two pairs of rough hands that were used to lifting heavy weights. They pressed him down into a chair, then secured his ankles to the legs of the chair with the dreaded cable ties. He felt them cut into him, heard them ratchet tightly together. He tried to ask for his hands to be released, the feeling now completely gone, but it was only then that he realized that his mouth was taped over, that something dry – a ball of cloth - was inside his mouth. The sudden realization made him gag.

"You don't want to be doing that," a man said. "You'll choke and drown, for sure."

Power suppressed his gag reflex, breathed the hot, stale air through his nose. He felt the cable ties around his wrists loosen, heard them snap as they were snipped by something sharp. His arms were pulled apart, and he tried to resist, but put up embarrassingly little fight. He doubted the two men even noticed. But they tugged at the hood and when he blinked against the bright light of the single bulb hanging from the ceiling, he looked up into two faces he did not recognize, but who looked frighteningly at ease with their actions. One of them tore at the tape around his mouth, and Power tried to move his arms but realized that they had been tethered to his own belt with more cable ties. He had not felt them do it, despite the feeling slowly flooding back into his wrists and fingers. The other man ripped out the ball of cloth that had been put into his mouth. The dry material tugged at the soft skin on the inside of his mouth, and he tasted the metallic essence of blood.

"Who are you?" Power asked. "I..." He was cut short by a sharp slap across his cheek. He smarted at the blow, blinking, and opening his mouth to test his jaw, which felt like it might have been dislocated by the force of such a slap.

His abuser said nothing, but he tapped his partner on the shoulder and the two men left the room, closing the wooden door behind them. Power looked around him. The walls were stucco and lath, but long in need of patching. There was a small, boarded up window. Beneath him, a patchy cement floor. Power was no home improvement expert, not even a novice because he had always lived in rented accommodation and never thought once about the jobs that kept a building from crumbling, but he suspected that meant he was on the ground floor. Stucco and lath seemed a residential material, and residential homes had floorboards on any floor above ground level. He wasn't sure how this could help him, but if he could get free and remove the boards on the window… He shook his head, the notion leaving as quickly as it had arrived. Such nonsense was for the cinema screen. He had no way of breaking the cable ties, no knife, or tools to pry off the boards at the window and he was not a physical man. He already knew he would not have the strength and if his escape involved a climb, he doubted he would be capable of holding his own weight for more than a few seconds.

His attention turned to the door as it cracked open on a poor-fitting lock, or rusted hinges. Liz Roper walked in with a coffee in a go-cup. The irony. Power watched her, mostly fearful, but with a great deal of anger as well.

"Wow, intense. Now there's an expression which goes with the ridiculous name." She purred. Her auburn hair looked darker somehow. The light and shadow of the room made it glow more vividly. She sipped some of the coffee and said, "Now that's a good roast…"

"What do you want?" Power asked subduedly. "It's not what I had in mind when you asked if we could go for a coffee."

"Not your best date, huh?"

He shrugged. "Sadly, it's not my worst, either."

"That remains to be seen," she replied, still savoring the coffee. "Tell me what you know about Special Agent Stone." Power's face dropped. "Ah, this should be interesting."

"I've told you all I know!"

"You haven't told *me* anything."

"I just came out of a polygraph session!"

"Polygraphs? Don't make me laugh," she scoffed. "They only work if your heart rate can be steadied. What did you use? Ketamine? Speed? LSD?" She shook her head. "I'd have thought better of the Secret Service."

"But *you're* Secret Service," Power frowned at her. "Aren't you?"

"No. I am not," she replied derisively.

"But your ID, your weapon…" He shook his head. "How were you even in the building?"

She smiled and said, "The US Government have over fifty law enforcement agencies, and all operate their security protocols on a similar level. There are eighteen thousand police departments and a hundred other federal agencies with the power of seizure and prosecution. With the right ID and knowledge of procedures, they're a walk in the park to get into." She paused, taking the lid off the go cup. "The Secret Service provide the best security for a world leader and their subsequent political and diplomatic charges, but as an agency office, it was no more difficult to penetrate than the Department for Fish and Game."

"I don't buy it," Power said. "You can't walk into the building with a homemade identification card and clear security."

"I'm not here for an interrogation," she said coldly. "But you are. I will ask the questions and make the statements. All I want from you are honest answers. And I will not be using a polygraph. I will know when you're lying to me. Because I have a lot of experience in these matters, and I can spot a liar. I can spot someone making up shit just for the pain to stop, and I know when a person has reached their limits…" Power stared at her, horrified by her words, but when he saw her rapid movement, he couldn't do anything except brace himself for the pain. The coffee left the cup as she casually upended it into his lap and the hot liquid instantly burned through his thin suit trousers and scalded his skin. He screamed and panted in agony as the tender, sensitive skin in the region was flooded with steaming liquid. "Extra steamed milk. Full fat. And plenty of sugar. Makes it stick to the skin…" she told him calmly. "I'll leave you alone for a while to think over your situation. When I return, you'll start talking and I'll know if you're lying." She headed back to the door, turned as she crossed the threshold and remarked, "It's in your best interest to tell me the truth, Mister Power. But I've got as long as it takes, and you're not going anywhere."

Chapter Fifteen

One week later
Langley, Virginia

It was a curious location, but they had used it before. On the shore of the Potomac River, the park bench was in Virginia and the shoreline not fifteen feet away was in Maryland. Tossing litter into the river from here would be a federal offense, crossing state lines and the FBI would be dealing with your case.

The spring weather had turned the grass lush, the blue sky and sunshine belying the fact that the wind funneling up the Potomac River from the Chesapeake Bay and the Atlantic Ocean beyond was bone-chillingly cold. Liz Roper tucked the collar of her coat up and shivered involuntarily.

"Cold today," the voice came from behind her, and she glanced around to see a severe-looking man in his early sixties watching the slow waters of the river that flowed through the nation's capital city. He stepped around her and sat down on the bench. "So, tell me where we are on this."

Liz Roper looked at Mike Rogers, deputy director of the CIA and said, "Our asset has talked, we are in the process of organizing a sting."

"As I would have expected by now."

"He's tougher than he looks."

"Seriously?"

"He's a techie nerd, but he has resolve."

Rogers nodded. "So, we underestimated him. I hope to God, I didn't underestimate *you*."

"You haven't, sir," Roper replied. She glanced up and could see both members of the deputy director's security detail. One with his back to the river, the other staring at the slow-moving water. A third was seated in the black Chevrolet Suburban. "I'm confident that I will get what we want from him. Stone and Power are in occasional contact via a Hotmail account. They sign in and leave a message in the draft folder, then edit it and save, that way they can communicate without a single email being sent into the ether."

"Clever." Rogers nodded. "And the money?"

"Stone got enough from the internet enterprise data to keep twenty-million dollars US. He hasn't used more than around thirty-thousand dollars being on the run. Most of the money is in offshore accounts, but some of it was drawn in Panama and is hidden around the mainland US in deposit boxes or lockers. Several million dollars at least."

"And Power doesn't know where?"

"No. But I know we can get to Stone through Max Power." She paused. "And once we have the information, Power can transfer the funds in those accounts electronically."

Rogers stared at the water, his eyes transfixed. He sighed, and even in the early May sunshine, his breath near the icy water was visible. "Don't underestimate Stone," he said sagely.

"He hasn't been cleared of any charges. And he won't be for as long as the CIA can still fan the fires and put pressure on the attorney general and justice department. Stone has nowhere to go and with his only link to inside information regarding his status as a wanted fugitive under our control, and the progress the United States Marshal Service and FBI are having in his search, we can force a mistake." She paused. "Trust me, sir. I've got this. *We've* got this."

Rogers nodded. "You'd better had, Liz. When this is finished, I want the bulk of that twenty-million dollars in my hand and that damned computer geek lying six feet under," he said coldly. "And you'd better make damned sure Stone is lying next to him."

"I understand, sir. But I do have a problem with a part of that brief…"

"You'd best spit it out, then," he replied somewhat impatiently.

"Max Power isn't a problem," she explained. "The two knuckleheads you've given me will have no problem killing him."

Rogers smirked. "But Stone troubles you," he said wryly. "You could do it yourself, Miss Roper."

"I'm not a trained killer," she said irksomely. "And those Virginia farm boys aren't up to taking out a man like Stone. He's ex-special forces, and an ex-presidential bodyguard. Seriously, you want this done, you have to help me out here…"

"You are right not to underestimate the man," he replied wistfully. "You've seen his record, Miss Roper. But do you know how he came to be in the special forces?"

Liz Roper shook her head. "No, I figured ego. You know, like being the best of the best or something?"

"Not a bit of it. Not even close." He paused. "You see, Stone was a master sergeant in an artillery unit. Rear echelon, raining hell on Al Qaeda and the Taliban with explosive shells. Never too close to the action, but always there for support. And then one day, his Humvee rolls right over an IED and his entire unit is cut down by machine gun fire and RPGs. All but two men. Stone and a young private. They were taken prisoner and held for more than a week, in which time, and I'll leave it to your imagination, but it's fair to say they endured hell. Then came the ubiquitous beheading video to be filmed for *YouTube*. They started off with some aid workers, some Afghan regulars and sadly the private that had been taken prisoner alongside Stone. Stone was forced to watch. And then it was his turn. He later reported that he saw the sword raised high above the executioner's head in the shadow…"

"Jesus…"

"Allah and Buddha combined…" Rogers shook his head. "Bang… bang… bang… and special forces are in the compound. Seven seconds from start to finish, and every Taliban son-of-a-bitch is dead. Stone gets evacuated and sent home for some R and R. Only he can't rest. He applies for Airborne Rangers and a year later he's out in Afghanistan. He did cross-over operations with Delta Force and SEAL Team Six, ended up heading a Recon unit. That takes some balls. To go through what he did and turn it around. He was recruited by the Secret Service at the end of his final tour."

"I didn't know," she said quietly. "That's quite a driven character."

"Like I said, you're right not to underestimate him." He took out a business card and handed it to her. "So, consider the matter resolved."

Roper looked at the card and read the telephone number. That was it. Nothing more. She frowned and said as she put the card in her pocket, "What does that get me?"

Rogers smiled as he watched the water, turning his eyes towards Snake Island more than halfway across the river. "That gets you a cleaner. He prefers to text. I'll call him and tell him to expect your call soon. I hope…"

Liz Roper stood up and nodded. She walked back across the grass to her BMW. Rogers was waiting for her to leave before he made a move. His two bodyguards were still watching each other's backs, and the cold waters of the Potomac looked deep and unforgiving. She exhaled a deep breath as she drove her car over the loose surface and back onto the road, and she reflected on the feeling inside, like her gut had twisted, and she found herself wishing that she had not become involved in this. And more importantly, praying that she would come through unscathed.

Chapter Sixteen

One week later
Alaska, 200 miles North of Lame Horse

Stone had taken the cabin for a month. It was twenty miles outside of town and close enough to the river to be a convenience, but far enough away and elevated enough to avoid spring floods during the snow melts and summer surges as the glacier thawed. The town of Brown's Landing had a couple of bars, two motels, and a large grocery store as well as an extensive general store and hardware supplies depot. A gas station, and a hunting and outdoor supply store completed the town's independence and although Stone had only been through it once and visited twice more for groceries and some fishing tackle, it had seemed a busy place catering for the many homesteaders in the vicinity and the townsfolk living there.

The cabin was basic, but intentionally so. Catering for city-slickers who wanted a taste of the Alaskan wilderness, if just for a week or so. Downstairs was open plan with a wood burning stove providing heat and cooking facilities, although there was an electric oven and stove for the hotter months. Stone would not be cooking inside much, so it wasn't any concern for him. He had used the large kettle barbecue on the deck to cook some burgers he had made from ground chuck he had bought in the grocery store and to hot smoke the fillets of two large rainbow trout he had caught in the river on a pole and line that had been propped up under the porch. Other than that, he had broiled canned hotdogs on the grill and gotten through a half wheel of Monterey Jack cheese. He had spent his days walking the paths through the forest, up to the foothills of the mountains and along the rocky shores of the coast. He had returned each evening exhausted and despite feeling ready for sleep in the loft sleeper upstairs, had slept fitfully as he thought of Katy McBride and her endeavors at McBride's Folly. And his thoughts were not only of her endeavors and what she was trying to achieve at the mine, but of the night they had spent together. The scent of her, the taste of her, her soft groaning in his ear as they had made love, the way her tone had changed as she had climaxed, the way she had writhed underneath him, on top of him. The memory was almost constant, distracting him from every task he pursued, every moment he stopped to take stock.

Katy McBride had gotten to him. He knew he wanted to see more of her, learn more about her, and share himself with her. It was so much more than a physical desire and he knew that he was falling for her hard.

Stone had traipsed a hunting path to the base of a mountain, where he sat down to eat some of the smoked trout and bread that he had brought with him. He estimated he was six miles from the cabin and pushing at least four thousand feet in elevation. In front of him the Pacific Ocean looked cold and uninviting. He had not expected the water to look black, but it did. He figured the sand and rock beneath the surface was volcanic. The beaches were a curious mix of yellow and black sand, that looked darker at the shoreline or where fresh water had sprung from the rocky shore and flowed across the beach. He had been warned about bears foraging for oysters and clams on the shore and he carried one of the shotguns with him on his hikes through the woods. The weapon was heavy, and he had fashioned a shoulder sling from some rope he had found and kept it strapped to his back. It was a strange notion to be armed while out hiking. Not something he had been used to in Virginia and Maryland. But he doubted he would ever return there willingly again. His life was so uncertain, had been for the nine months he had now been on the run.

After shutting down a deadly internet game of pay-per-view killing, a gladiatorial style contest hosted on a previously unpopulated Panamanian island, Stone had found himself framed for the killing of the President's family, as part of a biding scheme made available to international terrorist organizations who could claim responsibility if they won the bid. Stone had given the information he had stolen to the journalist who had helped him to uncover the dark web enterprise, and Max Power had delivered Stone's findings to both the FBI and the Secret Service. Stone had kept the details of one of the offshore accounts, a sum totaling just over twenty-million dollars, recognizing the need for leverage, as well as funding his hiding until he could clear his name. But neither the Secret Service nor the FBI seemed any closer to recognizing that Stone had been a pawn, unwittingly made the scapegoat to these despicable acts, despite the evidence of his innocence at their disposal.

Stone sighed as he surveyed the view. He was in purgatory. No vista appealed to him; no act excited him. His food had little taste and alcohol merely numbed the void he had been lulled into. But the only thing that had lifted his spirits for over eight   long months had been meeting Katy McBride. She excited him and he was interested in her. She had lifted his spirits, for however short a time, and he could not stop thinking about her, nor the wonderful night they had spent together. Intimate and complete. The weeks since their meeting and him leaving had been tough.

"Fuck it..." he said quietly. And then he got up and started to trudge back down the mountain.

Chapter Seventeen

Virginia

Max Power worked at the laptop, his fingers skipping across the keys with the dexterity and familiarity of a concert pianist playing at *tempo prestissimo*. As usual, one of the men stood behind him, but Power no longer feared him. He was the muscle, and he had a job to do. Liz Roper sat to one side, her shapely legs crossed elegantly, the slit of her skirt open just short of impropriety. But he no longer felt attracted to her. She was a cold, cruel bitch and he loathed her.

"I don't want to think you were lying to us," she said. "But Stone hasn't checked in for your updates since before you... er, came to work for us."

"Before I was abducted and tortured. Go on, you can say it," Power replied tersely. He ducked as the man behind him gave him a rap on the skull with his knuckles. "Hey!" Power turned around and snapped, "Hey, fuck you, Bob..."

The man shrugged and said, "Eyes on the

screen, fingers on the keyboard, geek."

Power turned around and got back to work. "You say geek like it's a bad thing. Notice you're not doing the skilled work, jock. And a coffee wouldn't go unappreciated, you know?"

Liz sighed and looked at the man standing watch behind Max Power. "Make mine a cappuccino," she said. "See what Ted wants while you're on the Starbucks run."

"A Danish wouldn't hurt either," said Power, but he ignored the man's crude retort. "And some *Imodium*, my IBS is flaring up again…"

"For Christ's sake!" Bob rolled his eyes. "The fucking Amazon rainforest is taking a hit for the amount of paper you're using…"

"Well, that's what you get for abducting a guy and waving your fucking guns around him all the time…"

Despite being held against his will, Power had become used to his captors and his surroundings. He did not like them, but he no longer feared them constantly. Not like a few weeks ago. He tried to put that unpleasantness to one side. Especially as he had fleetingly found Liz so attractive and now despised her. Power had not needed much softening up. The hot coffee landing in his crotch had done its job, and a beating at the hands of Ted and Bob had shown him what could be expected if he refused to cooperate. And now, all he had to do was contact Stone through their shared email account, where they would edit and save an existing draft message, and no trace of their conversation would be recorded or discovered. Until Power had divulged everything under interrogation. It had been a fool-proof plan, but for human weakness.

Chapter Eighteen

McBride's Folly Claim, Alaska

The truck bounced and juddered over the rutted ground and came to a welcome rest in front of the cabin-come-office. Stone was relieved. It had been a long drive. As he stepped out, he saw Duke Tanner and Marvin wander out of the office. They stood and watched Stone, and as a precaution Stone reached in for the .45 and made a show of tucking it into the front of his pants.

"No need for guns here, Mister," the site foreman said bluntly. "No predators come around here with all the machinery."

"I see plenty from where I'm standing," Stone replied, ignoring Marvin, and staring directly at Tanner. He walked forwards, closing the gap considerably. "Where's Katy?"

"Mister, you'd better get out of here," Duke Tanner said, stepping down the steps and standing in front of Stone. "We're running a mine here."

"We?"

"I'm helping out," he said. "While young

Katy gets well."

Stone stared at him. "What's wrong with her?"

"Nothing some rest won't cure," said Marvin, taking the steps and standing beside Tanner. "Now, as site foreman, I'm ordering you off the claim."

"Where is she?"

"The foreman said for you to go…" Tanner said, his hand lowering toward the revolver on his belt. He turned to Marvin and said, "Katy McBride is in Carlsson Sound hospital, isn't she?" When he turned back to Stone, the revolver was halfway out of its leather rig, but he froze when he realized Stone's .45 was not only aimed at his gut, but he had taken a step closer to dissuade all doubt he would miss.

"That's twice I've got the jump on you trying to sneak a gun on me," said Stone, smiling as he watched Tanner freeze. "Do it a third time and I'll empty the magazine into you." He paused. "Now, take out the gun… slowly… and hand it to me. Butt first."

Tanner scowled, but he did as Stone ordered anyway. "I've got plenty more guns," he said.

"No doubt," said Stone as he took the revolver carefully between his thumb and forefinger. "But it doesn't hurt to have a gun with somebody's prints on it…"

"What do you mean?"

"Stick to gold mining, old timer. You've just gotten out of your depth," Stone backed away and when he reached the truck, he tossed the revolver onto the passenger seat, still keeping the .45 on the two men. "Now, what the hell happened to Katy?"

"She can tell you," Tanner said coldly.

"If you've hurt her…" Stone did not finish his sentence. He was done with threats. Now wasn't the time, and he wanted the story from the horse's mouth. More than that, he wanted to see if Katy was OK. He climbed up into the truck, ignoring the smirk on Duke Tanner's face. When he swung the truck around and watched the two men in the rear-view mirror, they watched him go for a moment, then walked back into the office. Stone could only guess at what the two of them were planning, but he had noted that Duke Tanner had not denied a thing when Stone had implied that he had hurt her.

Chapter Nineteen

The hospital was small and built on a single level. There were many rooms off the corridor and the building was built like a donut with a garden in the center of the ring. The wards were configured in rooms of four or six beds and Katy occupied a room all to herself with three empty beds that had not been made up. She looked up as Stone walked in, a lame bunch of flowers that had cost him twenty bucks in his hand and wearing a look of concern upon his face.

She looked shocked to see him, but that was not all she looked. She looked terrible and had clearly been savagely beaten. Her eyes were black and both her top and bottom lips were swollen and split. Stone could see that her right wrist was bandaged, and her left arm was in a sling.

"Jesus Christ… Who the hell did this to you?"

"I fell…" she said quietly.

Stone scoffed, "I've spent my entire adult life either getting my ass kicked to look like that, or making some other guy look that way…" He paused. "Who did this to you?"

She looked annoyed, shifted irritably in her bed. "I fell," she said adamantly.

"Onto somebody's fist?" He walked over and handed her the flowers, but she struggled to move, and the effort clearly hurt her. Stone looked around, then settled on a water jug on a single cupboard unit beside her bed and dropped them into the water.

"Great, let's hope I don't get thirsty…"

Stone smiled. "I'll get you a clean pitcher before I leave." He paused, sitting down on a chair beside her bed. "What happened?"

"You're a man of action, aren't you?" she said sadly. "You could have asked how I was, whether I was in pain, but no. You go straight for the fix. You want to know, so you'll get whoever did this, right?"

"Well, at least you're no longer talking bullshit about falling…"

Katy shrugged, but even the merest of movements caused her discomfort. "It's good to see you," she said softly. "To be honest, I never thought I'd see you again. I thought you'd be going the full Grizzly Adams and would at least have a two-week-old beard by now." She paused. "You're not even wearing a plaid shirt."

Stone smiled. "Well, now that I'm here, are you pleased to see me, or do I go back to my cabin and train a bear cub, or something?"

"Are you getting a lumberjack shirt?"

"Probably not."

"Then it's good to see you," she smiled. "But what brought you back?"

He shrugged. "I just wanted to see if there was something worth chasing," he replied. "I'm not sure if it can go somewhere, but it must be worth the ride."

She looked up at him sorrowfully. "Maybe it would be better if you just kept on moving," she said. "I'm in too deep with the mine, have too many decisions to make money wise. I am in a financial mess, to be honest. Not the greatest start to something..."

"You'll get there," he said. He stood up and leaned over her, but she flinched away, and he frowned. "What? I thought…"

She clasped his hand and said, "Let's just take it slowly."

He shrugged, "OK," he said and went to kiss her, but she turned her cheek, and his lips brushed her soft skin instead of her lips.

"They're too sore," she explained. She squeezed his hand more tightly, then said, "What in God's name did you think you were doing with my dad's truck? Scooter came by with it all put right, the engine reconditioned and new brakes and tires all round."

"I thought I'd help," he said. "I don't want anything in return."

"I can't accept it; I'll pay you back."

"Get yourself well and find that gold, then you can talk about paying me back. But I really don't mind."

"I'm probably going to sell out to Duke Tanner," she said suddenly, her face dropping. "It's the right thing to do. I'm no gold miner, I suck at it. I need to wash my hands of it and return to practicing law."

Stone shook his head. "Not to him!" He paused. "He did this to you, didn't he? Or had it done?"

"I fell!"

"Bullshit. Your eye sockets are blackened in only a way that a fist can do. You've suffered a backhand swipe across the mouth, and I would say that whoever did this to you twisted your wrist in an arm-lock…"

"Stop it!"

"Well? I'm right, aren't I?"

"Just get out!" she screamed at him and a second or two later a nurse hurried in. Katy looked up and said, "My visitor was just leaving," she explained. "Please see him out…"

Stone looked at Katy, and then back at the nurses. "OK," he said, holding up both hands in a passive gesture. He looked back at Katy and said, "I'll help you…"

"Sir, if you don't come with me, I will have to call security," the nurse told him.

"Katy don't do anything rash," said Stone over his shoulder, making his way towards the door. "I can help you deal with this. You're a lawyer, give me power of attorney and I'll run the damn place until you're back on your feet…"

Katy held up her hand, wincing with the effort. "Wait," she said calmly, then shook her head, unable to process the thought. She looked at the nurse and said, "I'm sorry, I need a minute."

"Are you quite sure?" the nurse replied, eying Stone hostility. "I'll be right outside, honey…"

Stone walked back, pulled out the chair and sat heavily. "Jesus. A man mends your truck, halts his plans for merging into the landscape, and declares his feelings for you, and you go and get him thrown out?" he said mockingly.

"Not exactly thrown out," she smiled, and it was the first time he had seen true warmth in her expression. She reached across and gave his hand another squeeze. "What the hell do you know about gold mining?"

"Well, I'll know a damned sight more tomorrow than I do today, and I guess I'll know a hell of a lot more than that by the end of the week…" She smiled, but her lips were dry and cracked and it made her grimace. "I'll get you that water," he said and made his way outside. He searched for the nurses' station, then caught sight of someone watching him from the far end of the corridor. As far as he could see against the curvature of the building. Shaved head, neck tattoos and a biker jacket of denim and leather mix, held together with badges. He knew the face, had cracked it with the barrel of a shotgun two weeks earlier. One of two men who had stolen his truck and gone off with Duke Tanner. The night Katy McBride had been run off the road and attacked.

Lame Horse. I need it done. No witnesses.

Stone stared hard. The man hesitated and it was enough to show his intent. He wasn't here for a check-up or to stick a band aid on something. He was here to see Katy McBride and that could only mean one thing. He was finishing what he had started. Stone did not believe she had fallen, but he was certain that if the man had not been involved in that, then he had certainly been involved in running her off the road and that meant the cold and calculated method they had chosen to either kill or subdue her by smothering her. Stone was pacing towards the man hard. He saw the hesitation turn to panic and fight or flight kicked in. The two instincts are often determinable by guilt and context and the man ran. Choosing not to flee in a bar fight was an entirely different matter, but then again, he had already lost out to Stone once before. Two for two. Guilt and history. The man was in a full-on sprint and barged between two nurses, sending them both sprawling to the floor. He dodged an orderly pushing a gurney, then paused to grab the gurney from him and upturned it sending it clattering into the two nurses, and the mattress and cover bundled onto the floor. Stone looked at the two nurses, realized they were just shaken, and hurdled them landing on the mattress. His feet became caught up in the mattress cover and he steadied himself as he kicked the cover free. The orderly was getting back to his feet and cursing loudly, Stone bypassed him and sprinted onwards, but the curvature of the corridor meant he could not yet see the man he was chasing. The look on the face of one of the medical staff as he approached him told Stone the man had not come this way, and he stopped and jogged back down the corridor to the first room on his right. It didn't make any sense to Stone, as he was entering the center of the donut, and escape could only be achieved on the outer ring. He pushed the door open and was immediately met with a bed wheeled with terrific force. Stone crashed back against the door and sprawled into the corridor. He realized to his horror that an old and frail-looking woman was still in the bed, and her drip was trailing, sluicing a clear liquid onto the floor as if it was a hose that had been left switched on. She was screaming and the man he had been chasing pulled the bed back towards him, then got his shoulder behind it and charged forwards again, the bed hitting Stone like a medieval battering ram. Stone, who had been getting back to his feet, was cannoned backwards and the bed continued to roll over him. The man saw his chance and stepped around the bed, kicking Stone in the face as he took off back up the corridor.

Stone felt the impact, was aware of the sensation of numbness, his hearing replaced merely by an overwhelming ringing in his ears. His vision blurred, replaced by white light and stars of gold and red. He had fallen onto his side, and he shook his head, objects gradually becoming clearer, the white light ebbing and the stars moving in circles. He blinked profusely, struggling back to his feet. He was aware of voices, some of outrage, others of concern, and above all of these, the screaming of the woman in the bed, who had now been prioritized and was receiving attention from onlookers.

Stone started after the man and pushed his way out through the doors and into cool Alaskan air. He looked around him, but oblivious to what had just happened inside, the outside world was in full swing. Paramedics were unloading a patient under a covered area to the side of the main entrance. A couple were walking together, the woman way past her due date. He imagined they were waiting for the baby to decide when they were ready. He looked to his right and a couple of vehicles were parking, while another truck was gently pulling clear of a space, the driver pre-occupied on his phone. Stone walked onwards, scanning the carpark, the other doors of the building. He saw a police cruiser and his first instinct was to rush forward and requisition the cop and aid his search but remembered in time that he was on the run.

Questions and answers.

Stone kept walking, his senses slowly coming back, and the pain of the savage blow to his face becoming prevalent. He was no stranger to pain and injury, from the football field as a star quarterback he had experienced more than his fair share of tackles, to the battlefield and beyond. He knew he had taken a blow that would have felled most people, people who had not been taken to the edge. He could feel the ligaments in his neck protesting, feel the bruising coming out. He touched his forehead and felt a sizable bump. At least that was a good sign, the swelling going in the right direction. Stone knew he had been lucky, but you made your own luck. His forearm was throbbing, but he had gotten his block in first, the man's shin connecting and taking some of the speed and energy out of the kick. He figured he could have ended up with a broken arm, or a worse head injury if he had not reacted accordingly, but his block had done its job.

Nobody gunned their engine in a hospital parking lot. But someone had. Stone could hear the warble of a V8. Not tuned for speed. A solid-sounding truck engine, torqued down for towing and hard work. A gear change, and then another through an automatic box. Too much speed for a carpark in broad daylight. Stone started to run towards the noise, but it gained quickly and as he charged out from a row of parked cars, he saw the old Chevy Tahoe coming towards him. Both men were clearly visible behind the windscreen. The two men he had given a ride to and who had stolen his truck. One of the men was reaching for something and instinctively, Stone dived onto the grass as the younger of the two men fumbled and pointed a revolver out of the window. Stone rolled and the gunshot rang out, the bullet going wide and throwing grass and mud into his face. He rolled behind the hood of a parked car, then kept rolling as he heard another gunshot and then the sound of the truck mounting the sidewalk and then the grass. The truck collided with the last two feet of the car's hood and fender and the car was knocked out of its space a full forty-five degrees and rested in the road, rocking on its springs, and blocking the lane. The truck slammed on its brakes and the younger of the two men waved his revolver from side to side, fully expecting Stone to still be there. But Stone was long gone. He had rolled and sprinted and flung himself behind a soccer mom SUV. He kept his head low, dared not move as the man checked in vain, struggling to come up with a plan B. The engine of the Tahoe revved above the noise of the crashed car's alarm and the man got back inside. The truck took off at a terrific pace and its engine and exhaust reverberated off the parked vehicles and became ever more muted. Stone got to his feet and brushed the dirt off his clothes but stopped when he heard a siren and then several gunshots. Two short, sharp reports of an automatic, and then three more that sounded louder, echoey and less sharp, which he knew to be that of a more powerful caliber revolver. He could tell that the gun fired at him had been something like a .357 magnum or a .44. A powerful, but standard trail gun in these parts, with plenty probably riding around in vehicle glove boxes for bears and 'just in case'.

He started to jog in the direction of the gunfire and when he rounded the building back to the entrance, he could see paramedics working on the cop. There was a lot of blood on the ground, and onlookers were gathering sharing their accounts of what they had just witnessed. Stone fought his instinct to lend assistance, even take control of the scene, and slinked back in through another entrance.

There were medical staff, orderlies, and security officers in varying states of panic attempting redress, but Stone recognized the headless chicken scenario and the fact nobody confronted him meant that the situation was fluid, with nobody establishing control. When he reached Katy's room, she looked up her expression full of concern. "Where have you been?" she asked, then she exclaimed, "… Oh my god! What happened to your face?"

"You should see the other guy…"

"Really?"

"No, he got away," Stone conceded. "But I think he was here to see you…"

"What do you mean?" she sat up, or at least tried and she grimaced and sunk back down in the bed.

"Here, let me help…" Stone went to her, and he gently slipped a hand under her and eased her up closer to her pillows.

Katy winced and used him as a frame, taking her weight as best she could as she shifted.

"What did I tell you?" The nurse appeared, frowning. "If you need to move, press the alarm. I will help you; those stitches will tear…" She looked at Stone, not noticing his bruises, she was only concerned for her patient. "Stand back, sir," she said firmly, and Stone detected, somewhat rancorously. Then she eyed him more closely, and said, "That's a mighty fine bump and bruise you have there…" She looked at Katy and said, "Is everything OK, ma'am? I can get security and the police if you want me to."

"No," Katy replied sharply. "No, he's a friend…"

"Well, OK," the nurse replied. "Now, just sit tight, we have security on the corridors and the police are on the way. There's been an incident outside, but it's all under control." She looked at Stone and said, "Well, seeing as you're a friend, I suggest you sit here with the young lady and look after her until everything is settled outside. And that includes letting anyone in here, who isn't her friend. If you catch my drift…" She looked every bit as stern as she sounded, and Stone nodded dumbly as he watched her leave.

"I never did get that water," he said.

"Don't leave me," Katy replied quietly, squeezing his hand for comfort.

Stone looked down at her and said, "I won't. You're quite safe with me."

"I know I am," she said, her voice almost drifting. Her eye lids looked heavy, and she looked as if she was about to go to sleep. Stone sat down, keeping hold of her hand. "I know I'll be safe with you…"

Stone watched her as she dozed peacefully, but there was something about the tone and expression of the nurse that made Stone uneasy. And the more he thought about it, the more questions he had and the more he knew Katy McBride was not telling him the truth. It had been no accident, and the man in the corridor had confirmed it. He had been coming to finish what he had started, and Stone swore then and there that the man would not get another chance.

Chapter Twenty

"You'll want your old room," Maude said. "For the memories…"

"Any room is fine," Stone replied irritably. In his experience hospitality staff delighted in knowing their guests' business and stood in sanctimonious judgement at any opportunity.

"You've seen her, then?"

"I have."

"She was in quite a state, when they found her."

"When who found her?"

"Don discovered her in the morning, then Marvin called for an ambulance. They sent a medical helicopter and took her down to Carlsson Sound." She paused. "She didn't tell you?"

Stone shook his head. "There was a problem with security down there, we didn't get to talk about much."

"Yeah, active shooting, or some such."

"A guy shot a cop. I don't think it is classed as an active shooter scenario." Stone picked up his key, but Maude kept hold of the tag.

"Don's a good guy," she whispered. "They're cousins and he takes care of the maintenance for all the machinery at the mine. Marvin has been with the McBride's for years…" She looked around for any sign of Howard, then whispered. "But I saw a side to Duke Tanner that night and it's got me thinking he'd stop at nothing to get his hand on McBride's Folly. And he and Marvin have been friends for years…"

Stone smiled. "I usually trust a woman's instinct," he said. "I hear Katy's father had his problems out there, his father before him. I understand Marvin worked with all of them, at some time or other."

"A lot of guys work for a lot of mines," she replied. "It's a big state, but a small community. I guess most people have worked for Duke Tanner, for that matter. Marvin did too. There were times when he helped out in other mines, as well. He went back to work for Katy's father, but there was the tragic accident soon afterwards, then Katy took over and Marvin stayed on to help her through." Stone nodded. He tugged at the key and Maude released her grip. "Table tonight?" she asked expectantly.

"I'll let you know," he said.

Stone headed outside and to room twelve. It was getting dark, so he did not have much time to lose.

Chapter Twenty-One

Paris, France

He lived alone by choice. He had no sexual orientation or persuasion, but he was open to the fact that he probably once had, although he could not remember what that had been. But that would have been a long time ago, and he knew there were blockages in his mind, barriers by which he knew little of anything before his training and certainly no more than snippets from a childhood that was devoid of both compassion and comfort. Bereft of love. What memories he had presented only in dreams, and he was aware that they may not be memories at all, because as hard as he had tried, he could not conjure a memory at will. No mother, father, sister, or brother. No best friend, no bully. No school, no college. Nothing. Apart from the farm. That had been where the initial training had taken place. The training, the classroom, the scenarios. And then the training in the field. The killing in the desert, the plane ride home. Just a small private jet and two pilots up front. And then the missions. Blooded, tested, then utilized. He had worked all over the world and he had killed politicians, organized crime leaders and oligarchs alike. He lived frugally, just four apartments leased in his name – or his legend – in Washington, Paris, London, and Berlin, all chosen strategically, and all sparsely furnished with no personal possessions, and sanitized before he left for his next assignment. His salary was paid monthly into an offshore account, although he never used any of the money – his company expense card would take care of all he needed – and he had not been given access to the account for security reasons.

The apartment was above a boulangerie and a bar, which meant early starts for one business and late finishes for another. Hence the inexpensive rent. But it did afford a clear view of the Eiffel Tower and the Seine, which he reflected looked different from one day to the next. There was a reason so many artists had honed their craft in the city, the light, the dark, the thunderous clouds that could close a lid on the city, and the exquisite light on a fine day that could set it free. The noise factor did little to detract from the view. And views were important to his being, almost treating him with a mindfulness he could not find elsewhere. Not that he would ever talk about such feelings with his handler. He already knew that what he did, what his services provided, was neither socially nor morally acceptable. They had drilled that into him repeatedly at The Farm. But he also knew that what he did, reprehensible though it may be, was utterly necessary. He helped keep the world in check. Without him, and for all he knew, others like him, the United States of America, and its allies, would not be safe.

The text sounded and he took his eyes off the reflection of the early dawn sun on the Seine and looked towards the dresser. It was the only item on there and it vibrated and started to spin. As he stood up from the hard, wooden chair, he already knew who it would be. He had no other contacts and nobody else who would call. The text simply said, *Washington ASAP.*

He had the means to buy a ticket and he would reply to the text once his travel arrangements were in place, and then again when he arrived at Dulles Airport. He would then be given three hours to first run through anti-surveillance drills to check for a tail, then freshen up before meeting at one of five prearranged rendezvous points that were used on a rotation basis. And then he would go to work and an enemy of the state would die.

Chapter Twenty-Two

Stone had found an area of ground to park on fifty yards off the road that had alder and willow and young spruce to hide his truck from view. He cut a few switches with his folding *Spyderco* serrated-blade knife, the razor-sharp blade slicing easily through. He spread them over the roof and hood, more to stop the shine of a flashlight or headlights from the road, than to hide it from sight. He then cut a switch and pressed it into the ground on the edge of the road to act as a marker. He lined it up on a telegraph pole and a road marker opposite. That gave him a triangle of markers, so he would not struggle to find the truck later.

It was a three-mile hike to McBride's Folly, and another mile to Duke Tanner's claim. He had the .45 and a spare magazine in his jacket pockets and hung the shotgun over his shoulder on the makeshift sling. Alder was a favorite resting place of both brown and black bears, and he did not want to stumble on a sleeping grizzly underprepared.

The terrain was uneven and ridged underfoot, and Stone supposed that much of the ground had been mined over the years and had now been reclaimed by nature. Behind him, the Pacific coastline; ahead of him, the ridge of snow-capped mountains rose high and acted as a barrier to the interior of Alaska. *It would be a different place in the winter,* thought Stone. Every region had its own geological idiosyncrasies that produced gold. Here, it would be the seams in the mountains ahead of him. Fissures of gold exposed by erosion and washed downstream. On the coast, they mined the stuff using barges and giant vacuum pipes right off the seabed. The end of the line, a journey taking a million years or more from the snow-capped peaks reflecting in the moonlight.

Stone eventually found himself on a ridge overlooking McBride's Folly. There were no lights. He had imagined them mining right on into the night, but he knew that later in the season the daylight would last until almost midnight and further north, there were eighty or more days where the sun did not set at all. Even so, there were arc lights and the vehicles had powerful headlights and spotlights that could have been used. Why had everyone gone home? Mining was a seasonal endeavor and depended upon people buying into the dream and going for broke.

The sheer scale of the mine lit only by the moonlight was considerable and he realized he had underestimated the task ahead of him. Getting across McBride's Folly and onto Tanner's claim would take more than thirty minutes, and the whole time he crossed the open ground, he realized he would be exposed. Silhouette was one of the key factors in camouflage and concealment – along with shine, sound, smell, and shape - and with the moon bright in the sky, anyone observing the mine would not fail to see him. There may well have been no lights, but that was not to say nobody was down there. Stone used the elevation of the ridge to traverse a shallow line of descent, much like a skier, and found the going easier as he maintained a slight angle to cover more ground. By the time he had dropped five-hundred feet, he was half a mile from the cabins and close to the far belt of trees marking out the northernmost end of the claim. Nobody would see him here, so he remained on the excavated ground and marched at a good pace until he reached the belt of trees on the west side of the claim. The forest was thick, but then Stone remembered Katy saying how it had not yet been excavated and tested, and that their focus had been on the other side of the claim. Which was what had drawn his attention to the west side. The land backed right onto Tanner's claim, and if Tanner was so keen to buy a mined-out claim, then Stone was sure the samples that Katy McBride's father had taken would be in this stretch of untouched forest.

The forest was thick and entirely overgrown with spruce. The trees were not huge, but this was gold mining country, and the land could well have been cleared years ago for access and reclaimed by nature. Stone estimated no more than twenty years of growth, judging by the ten-inch diameter trunks and twenty-feet of height. He trudged through, ever mindful of bears, but he was sure they would be far away from the machinery and noise of the mines, probably scared off by guns if they wandered too close.

After a few hundred yards, Stone came to the edge to what was clearly Duke Tanner's claim. Again, nobody was going for broke with night shifts, and the men clearly observed long daytime shifts. But there were lights on inside the cabins and trailers, so Stone stepped confidently out onto the heavily graded ground knowing that anybody up there would have had their night vision ruined by the ambient glow of lights, or if they were inside, would be completely night blind. As he drew closer, he could smell smoke and when he neared the camp, he saw the dying embers of fire and beer cans scattered where the men had gathered around the flames for a drink and to chew the fat after a hard day's work. They appeared to have retired to their trailers and Stone could smell chili and cooked meat on the cold night air. There were other smells, too. Perhaps coffee and tobacco. Music played, interspersed with the sounds of various movies or distant laughter, and Stone imagined tired men kicking back, soon to be working another shift.

Stone worked his way past the vehicles. The workers had all parked in a line away from the mining equipment. Everyone owned a pickup truck, and he could see there were both old and new alike. But no Chevy Tahoe that matched the truck the two men had driven at the hospital shooting. Stone moved on, using the shadows and vehicles for cover. He crossed a hundred feet of open ground walking tall and steadily. There was no sense in crouching and running. Walking normally would not catch in somebody's peripheral vision and if he acted casually and not suspiciously, then he could be mistaken for a fellow worker in the darkness. When he got into the shadows again, he edged along the machinery and headed for the cabins that acted as the mine's offices, which were the first buildings people would meet on the drive in. As Stone neared the offices, he could see a large mound of tarpaulin. He crouched down beside the mound and lifted the corner of the tarp. It was secured by guy ropes which were weighted down by rocks. Stone lifted a couple of the rocks nearer to the mound and easily lifted the slackened tarp. As he suspected. He moved more of the rocks and dragged the tarp clear. The first truck was an old Ford, and it was beaten up badly. Stone worked his way around the front of it and saw the scuffs of yellow paint. The bumper was missing, but Stone would not have bet against it matching the paint and damage to Katy McBride's Ford Bronco, and the debris at the scene of the crash being a match. Stone pulled away more of the tarp and instantly recognized the Chevrolet Tahoe that had tried to run him down at the hospital in Carlsson Sound. A neat bullet hole was in the center of the windshield and again, if the bullet was still inside the vehicle, Stone would not have bet against it matching the cop's weapon, fired in retaliation before he was gunned down. Two for two. The opportunity was too good to miss, so Stone took out his phone and checked around him before taking a photograph of each truck, and in particular, the bullet hole and the scuffed yellow paint left by Katy's Ford Bronco. The flash lit underneath the tarp like lightning, but he was confident the flash would not be seen further away. Nevertheless, he watched the trailers and cabins for a while before replacing the tarpaulin and kicking the rocks away to tighten the guy ropes.

Stone started back the way he had come but froze when the beam of a flashlight cut across his path. He dodged to his right and took cover behind an excavator, his hand gripping more tightly around the grip of the shotgun. The beam of light swept over the bulldozers and excavators in the row. Stone dared not move. The sounds of movement at night were greatly amplified, the stillness in the wilderness almost absolute.

The light skittered over the machinery, then played for a while on the tarpaulin. Stone froze, realizing that an edge of the tarp was still ridden up over the front bull bars of the Chevy. The flashlight turned to the offices and Stone used the change in direction to calmly cross the ground and step into the lee of one of the trailers. He glanced back and watched the light scrutinize the excavator where he had taken refuge, and then the man bent down and swept the beam underneath.

Stone had seen enough. He was not going to hang around long enough to see if he had been made. He turned around and headed back onto the plateau of lunarscape that made up the worked claim. When the darkness around him took on an ambient glow, he turned and looked back at the camp. Several trailers and RVs had their lights on, and more were flicking on by the moment as their occupants were being woken. Stone turned and ran for the edge of the claim, the belt of trees between Duke Tanner's claim and McBride's Folly would offer the cover he needed, but the ground he was now sprinting across was vast and exposed. The terrain was hard and uneven underfoot and he tripped and sprawled heavily. Winded and shaken, he rolled onto his side and saw the arc lights switch on, the camp illuminated like an evening game of baseball. Slowly, the arc lights started to move, and Stone watched as a quarter of the plateau behind him was turned into day, the light withering two-thirds of the length of the cut, casting shadows all the way to the trees. Stone struggled to his feet, picking up the shotgun and hobbling towards the boundary. His ankle and knee joints had stiffened and slowly loosened as he picked up speed. Behind him, the arc lights swept through the cut and fifty yards from the boundary, he was illuminated like the principal character on a stage. The first rifle shot kicked up dirt three feet ahead and to the right. That was an easy counter, so Stone darted right, slowed, then quickened his pace and dodged back left. Only more than one rifle fired this time and several bullets hit the ground around him simultaneously. He threw himself onto the ground and rolled, bullets passing overhead and pinging off into the trees. When he got back to his feet, he was nearing the edge of the light's reach, but the bullets were still hitting the ground around him. Another push, near exhausted by the pace, and Stone reached the trees and kept pushing until he was fifty paces deep into the trees, before diving onto his stomach, and then rolling onto his back to inspect the muzzle of the shotgun. Blocking a shotgun's barrel with mud or debris could prove catastrophic when the weapon was fired. The back charge as the burned powder, pressure wave and shot reached the obstruction and ruptured the breech or barrel could turn the weapon into a bomb and maim or kill the user as well as anyone standing beside them. Stone unloaded the weapon, upended it, then held his eye to the breech as he pointed the barrel towards the glow of the arc lights. The barrel was clear, so he quickly reloaded with the shells and got back to his feet. Behind him, he could hear baying dogs and urgent voices.

"You'd better run, gold thief!" a deep, Midwestern accent resonated through the night air. "That's my damned share!"

Another voice screamed, "Trespassers don't need no warning shots!"

Stone pressed on. Neither voice sounded like the two men he'd had the run-ins with, nor did they sound like Duke Tanner, for that matter. Stone imagined tough, innocent gold miners protecting their end of season bonus. If Duke Tanner suspected Stone had being snooping around, he could well have whipped his men into a frenzy. Perhaps even told them he had made off with a quantity of gold from the clean-up room. Stone did not want to harm innocent, though somewhat hot-blooded rednecks, but he wasn't going to go down without a fight. He pressed on through the thicket and when he reached the cut on the side of McBride's Folly, he turned back into the trees and headed north to circumnavigate the cut. Behind him, the dogs bayed more vocally, and Stone tore off his jacket, took out his knife and started to cut strips of fabric. He bent down and scooped up some dirt laden with stones and wrapped the debris in the jagged sheets and balled them up, tossing them further into the trees. He dropped a few pieces of fabric, too. Each time the dogs discovered the trail, it would take precious seconds for the handler to assess the find and command them to keep searching. Stone's pace was slowed by the process of laying the false trails, but he had managed to get a few bundles deep into the woods and he balled and tossed his jacket out into the cut, then pressed onwards. After fifty or so paces, he turned back towards the edge of the cut and took cover crouched beside a large spruce. In the ambient light from the distant glow of the arc lights on Tanner's claim, Stone could see the bulk of his jacket twenty feet out in the open ground of the cut. The dogs were baying loudly, and the voices were excitable as the dogs leapt out into the cut and savaged the jacket, tearing and pulling it between them, to the shouts of commands to stop by the dog handler. The two men stepped out into the cut and were silhouetted by the glow of the arc lights. Stone estimated them to be sixty paces from him as they approached the dogs, then picked up the jacket and looked out across the lunarscape. One of the men pulled out a flashlight and swept it across the open ground. And that was when Stone fired.

The man with the flashlight went down, and Stone had the next shell chambered, the pump action sounding crisp and threatening in the silence that always follows a gunshot. The second man aimed towards where the gunshot and flash had come from, but Stone had already rolled to the side and the shot went wide as Stone aimed and fired again. The man went down, grabbing his shins and howling in unison with the first. Stone backed away and made his way through the trees. Sixty paces and the shot would have punctured the skin, but he doubted whether the lead would have shattered bone. Much of the shot would have been dispersed and he was confident no more than twenty pieces of lead shot would have hit the men's legs. But it obviously hurt like hell, and they would both need medical attention in the form of tweezers, antiseptic, and gauze dressings, but not a whole lot more. A few days off work and they would both have a beer story forever more.

Thankfully, the dogs were scent hounds and not attack dogs, and the two men had wisely kept them back with them as they had struggled to their feet and limped their retreat into the tree line. Stone had traversed the steep incline and turned to watch the McBride's Folly claim, and the arc lights of Tanner's claim beyond. There were vehicles moving about and he could see men helping the two unfortunate trackers back across Duke Tanner's cut. By now they would have an idea what direction he was headed in, and what the lay of the land was. The road from Tanner's claim to McBride's Folly looped around the fast-flowing river to a bridge five miles to the west. But Stone was parked on the next track over, and that track was only reachable by a fork road that led back to Lame Horse or up to McBride's Falls. Stone knew that if he could get to his truck, he would travel parallel to the access road to the two mines and be in the clear.

But he had to reach his truck first.

Chapter Twenty-Three

Stone did not stray into McBride's Folly, but he saw trucks pull in, headlights blazing. It was evident somebody on site had woken, as he could see a figure with a flashlight greet the trucks. Stone was three-hundred yards away, with another three-hundred feet of elevation. He could not make out the figure, but assumed that it was Marvin, the mine foreman. Trusted employee, by all accounts, but that cut no sway with Stone. The man's friendships and loyalties were clouded. You either came down on one side of the fence or the other.

Stone saw the bright lights and heard the gunshots a second later. Muzzle flashes lighting up the dark sky like fireworks. He could not see where they were shooting, but it looked like two or more guns were firing indiscriminately around the cut and into the line of trees. He ducked his head instinctively, but they had not reckoned on him being high and east of the mine already, and the gunfire was of no concern to him. The gunfire eventually died down and the trucks headed back out. Stone pressed on.

He did not have much time.

Chapter Twenty-Four

"Goodness! You look like you've been to war!" Maude rushed over and guided Stone into the back office. "What in heaven's name have you been doing? You can't go hunting at night out here. There are special permits to get first."

Stone caught sight of his reflection in a wall mirror. He had not realized that he had been whipped and scratched by withies and branches, reddening his face with welts and tiny cuts, and that he had sustained a substantial graze to his cheek when he had fallen. "I wasn't hunting," he said. "But it's likely Duke Tanner and his boys will be here soon, and I need you to do something for me before they get here."

She frowned, cocking her head curiously. "What have you done?"

"Nothing," he replied tersely. "But they will certainly make some stuff up about me. I need you to send some pictures and a short report to the police. I'm guessing the nearest police are in Emmerson?"

"They are."

"OK," he nodded. "But I'd like you to send them to the police in Carlsson Sound as well." He paused. "An officer was shot there today, and I know who did it. The police in Carlsson Sound will most likely take the tip-off more seriously." He took out his phone and switched it on. He frowned as he saw an empty text message, discarded it then connected to the motel's Wi-Fi. "What's your email address?" Maude took the phone from him and entered it before handing it back to him. She watched as Stone uploaded the photographs he had taken at the mine and typed out a short email. "I want you to tell them that an anonymous traveler found the link between the shooting of a law enforcement officer in Carlsson Sound, and of a hit and run between here and McBride's Folly. Hell, this is Alaska, so they'll be glad someone cared enough to bring it to their attention. They will understand them not wanting to hang around. Oh yeah and delete my email afterwards."

"And these vehicles are being stored at Duke Tanner's mine?" she asked incredulously. "That's quite an accusation."

"It's a fact," said Stone. "That's where I've been, and that's what I found. I saw the same guys in the same vehicle when they tried to get to Katy McBride today…"

"Dear Lord!" Maude shook her head. "This has gotten out of hand!" She paused. "But Duke Tanner... are you sure?"

"You'd better believe it," he replied. He checked his phone. As well as the empty text message, he could see an email. It was not an email address he recognized, and he could see that there was no content.

She opened a drawer and took out an envelope. She handed it to him and said, "This came for you late this afternoon. By courier..." She looked at the letter quizzically, then looked him up and down as well. She guessed correctly that he was not going to enlighten her about the envelope. "Where are you going now?" she asked.

Stone shrugged. "Getting cleaned up, then expecting a visitor. Or visitors, I guess..." He kept scrolling on his phone, then closed the email app and switched the phone off, slipping it into his pocket.

"You should leave."

"No, I think I should stay."

"For Katy?"

"Yes."

"And the fact you don't like being pushed, huh?"

"That too."

"Games are only games until a line gets crossed," she said. "Then they become action and consequence."

"I hear that," said Stone. "But are you talking about Duke Tanner, or myself?"

Maude shrugged and looked at him plaintively. "I suppose, young man, that remains to be seen…"

Chapter Twenty-Five

Virginia

"Tell me you sent it."

"I sent it," Power replied quietly, looking at Liz Roper. "His phone was receiving, and therefore emitting a signal. But he's just switched it back off."

"Is he not just out of signal?" Liz Roper asked.

"No. There's no cell pulse, so he's switched it off for sure. Unless it's a battery issue."

"When will the patch activate?" she asked impatiently.

"The next time he switches on his cell phone and connects to a network." He paused. "The patch sends Stone a blank text. He won't have to open it, delete it, or save it. But from the moment it is received, and his signal reactivates, the patch will send back an open link on the line. From then on, we're tracking him until he turns the phone off again."

"And we'll know exactly where he is?"

"Yes."

She smiled, shaking her head. "Then, we've got him…"

"You can track him, yes. And you'll have a ballpark area if he switches off his phone again," Power replied. "But the next time he switches it back on, he could be two states away."

"But it's more than we've had before. More than the FBI and the Secret Service have had all this time they've been hunting him."

Power turned back to the screen. Part of him wanted Stone to ditch the phone, disappear for good. But he was being held against his will and he feared for the outcome, so there was a bigger part of him that wanted the man safe and well and completely discoverable. To put an end to all of this. An end to Power's incarceration at the hands of this deniable CIA operation and the beautiful and alluring, yet savagely ruthless woman keeping him from his freedom. Liz Roper was everything he would have ever looked for in a woman, but she was also dangerous. Like a black widow spider who would eat its mate after copulation. Power, who usually recognized his far higher-than-average intelligence as one of his principal attributes, was also aware how easily he had been sucked in by her. It not only irked him but made him wary of her, although he would never dream of showing it.

"This patch..." Liz Roper said. "You invented it?"

"It's not an invention," he replied. "It's not a tangible product. I wrote it. It is a sequence of coding, that's all."

"What the fuck's the difference?" Ted asked tersely from behind him.

"The difference, my intellectually moribund friend, is that coding exists, so cannot therefore be invented. I write codes in the same way a writer pens a story. The pen and paper already exist, the concept of fiction is not new, so the writer merely *writes* their story, while I merely *write* a sequence of coding."

"Sounds like you're splitting hairs to me," the man said.

"I imagine a lot of things sound that way to you, Ted."

"Keep up the lip, buddy, but we're not going to need you forever..."

He was cut short by a flash of anger from Liz Roper and the exchange was not lost on Power, but he did everything he could to avoid showing that he had seen. He merely flicked his fingers across the keyboard and watched the screen. Rob Stone had not yet switched on his phone, and for the first time since he had written the piece of tracking code, Power did not like his options either way.

Chapter Twenty-Six

Stone had returned to the room but had then moved two doors down as a precaution, paying for both rooms to show good willing and give both Howard and Maude some recompense. He inspected the letter which had arrived for him, but it was clear that it had already been opened. He shrugged it off. It was what it was, and the content was what he had expected, but he suspected he had now lost the element of surprise. He showered and changed and headed back into the motel bar where Maude had fixed him a burger and he had sunk half of a much-needed beer while he waited. There were no other patrons, and just a quiet soundtrack of country music and soft rock in the background.

Stone checked around him, then slipped out of his booth and bent down to examine the neighboring table. The legs were attached to the tabletop by two bolts and a pair of wing nuts. Stone set about undoing the nuts and tested the integrity of the table. It was still steady. On top were menus and a condiment holder with tabasco, ketchup, salt, and mustard. Napkins were tucked into the back of the holder. Stone pocketed the wing nuts and returned to his booth. He took out his own bottle of tabasco and used his knife to jimmy off the plastic neck. He left the cap off and sipped some more of his beer. He had only been seated a minute when Maude bustled out of the kitchen carrying a burger the size of a softball.

"I gotta say, hon, if there's anything else you need, tell me now because the kitchen is closed!" she said with a chuckle, but the undertone was not lost on Stone. He had put her to an inconvenience after she had now called it a night.

"I appreciate you staying open late for me," he said. "But I'm done. I'll tackle what I can of this monster and then I'm off to bed." He paused, then added, "Did you send the email?"

"I did." She smiled. "I gather they're going to head on over tomorrow morning. Now, if there's nothing else, I'll leave you to it."

Stone nodded his appreciation and watched her leave. He placed the tabasco bottle towards the edge of the table and started to eat. He had only managed about half of the burger and a dozen fries when two men walked in, checked out the otherwise empty bar, then made their way over to his table.

"Duke Tanner wants a word," one of them said. He was a tough looking guy around six-two and two-ten. Hands like shovels. And his face looked like it had been hit with one at one time, too. "Now…"

"If Tanner wants to speak to me, then he knows where he can find me," Stone replied.

"Don't make this difficult on yourself, Mister…" the second man drawled in a southern twang, but the tone had little in the way of intimidation to it, being a full octave higher than his companion's voice, and not in any way menacing. He was also six inches shorter than his buddy, and about thirty pounds lighter.

"Really?" Stone looked up and smiled. "That's your tough guy voice? I wonder if this place does karaoke. I guess you could always do a couple of Bee Gees numbers…"

"You'll think twice about using that smart mouth of yours when I've knocked some teeth out of it," the smaller man replied.

Stone shrugged. "We'll see," he said, taking another bite of his burger. He chewed unhurriedly, then swallowed and took another sip of beer. "Where is he?"

"At the mine," the larger man grunted.

"And he thought I'd just come willingly?"

"He knew you'd see sense."

"Interesting…" Stone said, as the larger of the two men lifted his shirt and exposed the butt of a pistol resting against his belly. Stone noted that he was soft around the middle. Probably drove a load truck or operated an excavator all day long. Sat on his ass for fourteen hours a day. Stone shrugged. "OK, then."

Stone edged out of his seat and slowly got to his feet. The two men stepped back to make room for him as he grabbed the bottle of tabasco and flicked it into their bewildered faces. Both men held their hands to the eyes, clawing at the liquid fire that had incapacitated them, giving Stone the opportunity that he needed to grab the leg of the neighboring table and yank it free. The table fell with a clatter on the hard wooden floor and both men were dancing about screaming as they rubbed their eyes. Stone felt the weight of the wooden table leg like a player going into bat. He brought the table leg down across the bigger man's shin and he screamed and fell, clutching his broken leg and forgetting all about the chili sauce in his eyes. Stone brought the table leg back down across the smaller man's knee and the effect was the same. Both men clutching their shattered limbs and rolling about on their backs.

"What was that you said about knocking out my teeth?" Stone gripped the table leg and held it high above his head. The man looked up at him, his left hand held in front of him in a feeble bid to deflect the impending blow, his other hand cradling his shattered kneecap. Stone grinned and dropped the makeshift club onto the floor. "I guess it's your lucky day cupcake…" He lifted the larger man's jacket and took the pistol, then crouched down and removed a small revolver from his companion. "You guys aren't cut out for this," he said. "You're gold miners. Stick to mining in the future…" He moved so that he was between both men and looked at them in turn. "The two gang bangers Tanner has working for him. Where are they?"

The larger man spoke through gritted teeth, he was not holding out. "They showed up right around the time you did…"

"Shut up, Chris!"

"Hey! Fuck you man! Our season is over! Whatever the hell Duke Tanner is doing, he can fucking well do it without me. I'm only here because he promised overtime rate and an easy job." He panted and puffed through the pain like a woman in the throes of childbirth. "Jesus…" He steadied himself then said, "I don't

know where those guys are. But they're bad news. Both of 'em…"

"I said, shut up!"

Stone bent down and picked up the table leg and watched the smaller man flinch. "I say, it's you who'd better shut up…" He turned to the larger man and said, "Where are they?"

The man shook his head. "Look, they haven't been at the mine, I don't know where they are."

Stone dropped the table leg on the floor and walked out of the restaurant, pausing at the front desk where Maude was hovering, her expression one of anguish.

"You're OK?" she asked.

"Sure, why wouldn't I be?"

"Those guys…" she trailed off. "I'm sorry, but Howard told me to stay out of it. He said you probably had it coming for what happened in the parking lot and that we shouldn't get involved."

Stone nodded. "Well, you are involved. Whether you like it or not. You claim to care for Katy McBride, but you should know that Duke Tanner is terrorizing her and has brought in people to do his dirty work for him. I get that you are all part of a community up here, but one of your number has crossed the line." He paused. "And as for having it coming, well, not this time. You might want to call nine one one and get those guys some medical attention, but I'm sure if Howard calls Duke Tanner first, he'll want the emergency services kept out of it."

"You figure?"

"Damned right. Go on, call Tanner, and see what he says. He's playing a dirty game and he'll want some sawbones in the boonies to patch them up. Got any good veterinarians in the community who want some extra cash? Tanner will try those first. Mark my words."

Stone stormed out through the door, aware that Maude was already making a call. He was not staying here tonight. Or any other night. Not with Howard blowing with the wind. He knew that somebody had opened the letter, and that meant his element of surprise was likely gone. He unlocked the door and tossed his things into his bag. He checked the shotguns and adjusted the .45 pistol in his waistband.

Outside, a large truck pulled into the parking lot and skidded to a halt, throwing up loose gravel. Stone had seen the truck before. A new model with an engine large enough to jump start a power station. Duke Tanner got out and strode inside the motel. Stone could see that there were two men still seated inside the truck, but neither man got out and there was not enough moonlight to see if they were the two gang bangers. Tanner returned a few minutes later, opened the door of the truck and the two men got out and went inside the motel. Tanner made a call on his cell phone, and moments later the two men came back outside helping one of the men between them. There were grunts and shouts and they carefully loaded the man into the rear door and positioned him carefully on the seat. They set back out for the motel when Stone stepped out of the darkness and into the ambient glow from the parking lot light. Duke Tanner looked up, the phone hanging loosely near his ear. He stared, but he did not move quickly enough to break his hesitancy and Stone made the first move, walking over the loose gravel and standing twenty paces from him.

"Your veterinarian is going to be busy tonight," Stone stated flatly. "You could always call nine-nine-one and get your guys some proper medical attention…"

"Still a smart-ass…"

"Well, it's better than being a dumb-ass." Stone paused. "How's that working out for you?" Tanner took a few paces forwards and Stone drew the .45 and held it loosely by his side, the muzzle pointing to the ground. The big man stopped suddenly, his eyes on the pistol. "That's close enough," Stone said coldly. He watched as the two men came out from the motel, the larger man cradled between them, hopping towards the truck. "The next time you feel you have a point to make, you might want to grow some balls and try and do the job yourself."

"You talk big with a gun in your hand…"

"Well, I'm not putting it down. I've got you all figured out."

"Really? And that's what, exactly?"

"A back-shooting coward." Stone paused. "The kind of man who has a woman beaten up just so you can get her to pack up and quit, then move in on her claim."

"And where's your proof?"

"Let me worry about that," Stone replied.

"Boss?" One of the men approached tentatively and said, "They're in a pretty bad way. We'd better get moving…"

"We move when I say we move," Tanner replied sharply, his eyes still on Stone. "You know, Jake? This is the guy who did that number on them. How about you and Dave do a little number on him?"

Stone stared at the man and said, "I've got no beef with you. Go and take good care of your buddies…"

The man looked at the gun in Stone's hand and shook his head. "It will keep, Duke. They need pain relief and Chris has a bone poking through…"

"Get out of here, Tanner," said Stone. "Like your boy said, it will keep…"

"This won't be the last of it," Tanner replied, his tone more of a growl than before.

Stone nodded. "You can bet on that…"

Chapter Twenty-Seven

"It's bullshit!"

"It is what it is."

"We'll see…"

Stone shrugged. "Get your kit, your truck, and hit the road."

"You'll be sorry…" Marvin took off his orange hardhat and flung it at Stone's feet. It bounced and Stone knocked it aside before it reached his own face, but he let it go as he watched the site foreman stride to his truck, kicking a clod of earth in rage on his way.

Stone had slept in Katy's cabin at the claim. It was a basic one room affair, but he had got a few hours' sleep and she had good instant coffee and some store cupboard ingredients enabling him to scramble some eggs which he had eaten with toast and his third cup of coffee. He had intercepted Marvin when he had driven in at seven-thirty AM.

"Anybody else got a problem with this letter?" Stone addressed the other seven men gathered around him. "I'm hiring and firing until the mix is right…"

There were grunts and shrugs, the men looking at each other. It was not the start to the day they'd had in mind. One of the men stepped forwards. He was about thirty and as rugged looking as the rest of them. "When is Katy getting back?"

Stone knew this man to be named Don. He was the site maintenance guy, and he was also Katy McBride's cousin. Stone was not sure if the man was a full cousin, or once removed, but the man was family, and he was keen to keep him on side. Katy had given Stone control of the running of the mine until she was well enough to take over. It had been a shock to most of the men, but Marvin had known already, and Stone had cursed Howard at the motel. He'd thought Katy would have had an ally there, but the man was sat on the fence with the best of them. Stone couldn't exactly blame him, he was only supposed to be passing through, after all. "A couple of days," Stone replied. "But she won't be ready to work for a while longer."

"She's OK, though?" Don ventured, watching Marvin drive across the rough ground at high speed, his tires throwing up gravel and mud in its wake. The other men all watched, too. Don looked back at Stone and said, "She'll be alright, won't she?"

Stone nodded. "She will be soon. She's bruised and grazed and has some broken ribs." He paused. "In the meantime, I'm in charge."

"With respect, mister…" a bearded giant asked. Katy had described him in her letter. A man called Jed from Oregon. A good worker, but a closed book. Again, everybody in Alaska seemed to be running from something. "But who the hell are you?"

"A friend," Stone said. "Someone who can see what is happening here and will see a stop to it."

"Yeah, I heard you started a fight with Duke Tanner's men. Some of us aren't so easily beaten."

Stone held the man's stare and said, "Jed, if you're not happy with the situation, then feel free to walk…" Stone eyed the other men in turn, then said, "I don't start trouble, but I'll end it. I'll kill it dead. I don't do anything in the daytime that keeps me awake at night, so if you fuck with me, I'll take you down and it won't worry me if you're fired, if you crawl away from here or if you have to be carried. Or buried. I'm looking after Katy McBride's interests until she is fit and well enough to return."

Jed spat a tobacco-stained glob on the floor and said, "Is it true she was beaten up?"

Don said, "No, I heard she fell…"

The other men all frowned and murmured. Stone recognized the need to get these men, these essential workers, on side. "She was attacked, yes. I've seen evidence at Duke Tanner's claim that two men firstly ran her off the road a few weeks back. I saw the truck at the mine, under a tarp. There was paint visually matching Katy's truck all over the fenders." He paused, allowing the men to take it in. "When I was visiting her in the hospital down at Carlsson Sound, one of the guys I suspected of performing that hit and run saw me and ran. A cop was shot in his escape. The police department at Carlsson Sound have been notified and I'm expecting action to be taken today."

"And this guy you saw, you think he put Katy in hospital?" Don asked subduedly.

"I do."

"Jesus…"

Stone nodded. "But right now, we have a problem. I'll lay it out plainly. The funds are about to run out. There's enough for a few more days of fuel to run the vehicles and the conveyer belt thing…"

"Trommel," said Jed.

"Yes."

"Jesus, and you're in charge?" Jed said, but through the beard there was the hint of a smile.

"Don has been made site foreman," Stone replied. "I'm just here to get it squared up."

"Really? I'm in charge?" Don replied, trying to hide his glee.

Stone nodded. "You are. And you've got your work cut out. Because the fuel is running low, and we have just a few days to find what Katy's father found in those test drills."

"Marvin said we're on it this time," Don replied. "The east cut will be the one."

Stone shook his head. "Duke Tanner is making it difficult for Katy because he knows she is running out of time. She says that before you concentrated on the east cut, you were going to start on the land bordering the two claims. I want you to divert your attention to that area of trees. Get the ground cleared, the overburden taken away and expose the ground underneath. Then we'll run some ground through the *trommel*…" He looked at Jed as he emphasized the piece of equipment and acknowledged his earlier mistake. "Don, get everybody where they need to be and make a start."

The men all gathered around Don as he gave them their instructions and Stone made his way back to his truck. Marvin had left in a hurry and Stone wanted to see where he had gone, and he would not have bet against it being straight to Duke Tanner's claim.

Chapter Twenty-Eight

Stone watched from the ridge. He could see Tanner and Marvin talking beside Marvin's truck. He checked his watch. The police from Carlsson Sound should have been here long before now. If they had already been, then Stone couldn't see how Duke Tanner would not have been hauled in for questioning. Especially as the driver of one of the hidden trucks had shot one of their own. Police tended to band together, and he was sure that if the connection had been made, then the mine would have been as good as shut down while a team of CSI were put onto it. Of course, Stone knew that the likelihood of the trucks still being there was slim, it could only have meant one thing. Maude had not sent the email to the police. Could Howard have warned her against it? He could have sworn the two were on the level, but ever since Stone had injured the man in the parking lot, the balance had changed. He was sure that Howard had pinned his colors to Duke Tanner, but what about Maude? Surely the way Katy McBride had been treated would have united a sense of female solidarity? Stone needed to know for sure, but right now he had a long drive ahead of him, because Katy had just called the site phone and asked if he would come fetch her from the hospital. She was checking herself out and couldn't think about staying with so much riding on the mine. Of course, Stone wanted to stay and see what transpired with Duke Tanner, but even if there was the vague chance of the police getting here later than anticipated, Stone wanted to keep a low profile. A few hours on the road would also give him the chance to reset and re-evaluate. In Stone's experience, every conflict needed a pause and a chance to strategize.

Chapter Twenty-Nine

Washington DC

He was tall and heavy, but it was muscle and bone and a corn-fed upbringing in the Midwest. Barely a shred of fat. He could remember playing high school football, but the memory is like that of a dream and the longer he tries to recall it, the more it fades until eventually he is staring at the bare wall and can recount nothing at all. He likes football, though. But he supports no particular team. He has no affinity with anywhere, no draw to people or accents or a pin on the map.

He is lifting weights and he is naked. His body is scarred and each of those scars tells a story, but again, he can barely recount them and when he tries, they fade like every dream he has ever had. The apartment is bare. Just a double bed to accommodate his massive frame, a chair, and a bookcase, although he can't ever remember having bought a book. The kitchen is both well-stocked and well-equipped. He takes nutrition seriously and there are plans and menus and recipes on the wall in laminated sheets, but he did not put them there. He is deadlifting three-hundred pounds in reps of ten and sets of fifteen. It is a colossal workout, and the final part of his routine. He has already bench-pressed two-fifty in reps of ten and sets of twenty and spent an hour on working his core with weighted sit-ups and squats. He has planned a spinach and carrot smoothie, a five-egg omelet, and a pound of shredded roast turkey breast when he finishes, and he can feel the fat burning and muscle building and it spurs him on to finish the set. He is hungry, but first he must warm down with some stretching and take an icy shower to repair the muscles. He does this every day for ninety minutes and each day works a different part of his body. His routines change every two weeks, and they arrive by email from a no reply address. He has no contact with anyone, except for one man, and the physical meets have been less and less over the years. But he once again has his orders and all he is now waiting for is for the woman he has been told about to make contact and confirm a location. And then he will go to work.

Chapter Thirty

"So, what is this place?"

"My friend's cabin," Katy replied. "She was left it a few years back, it belonged to her aunt."

Stone could see that the cabin was old, or at least weathered, but it had been well looked after and judging from the newer looking boards and wooden roof tiles, maintenance had not been skimped on. There was a covered porch going all the way around, or at least the two sides he could see, and the side wall was stacked with logs from the deck to the eaves. Beyond the cabin a small lake glistened in the sun, and the far side looked to be thick forest all the way to around halfway up a jutting mountain that was still capped with snow. It was idyllic and looked like the sort of image *Microsoft* used as a screen saver.

"Will you be alright out here?"

"I figured you'd be here with me," she said a little meekly. "Or at least I was hoping."

"I need to be at the mine," he replied. "Sure, I don't know a thing about it, but I think

I've shaken them up and set them on the right course."

"Don can handle it. They'll be taking off the overburden for the next two days." She opened the door and eased herself out carefully. "How about we get settled in, I'll get us something to eat."

"I can get that sorted; you can rest up."

Katy smiled and closed the door after her. Stone noticed how stiffly she walked, how every movement caused her pain. He had expressed his concern at her not heeding medical advice and checking out of hospital, but she had been adamant that it would be for the best. Knowing that the men who had put her in there had come back only terrified her more, and Stone understood that she felt protected when she was with him, and that being at home was sometimes the best road to recovery. He picked up the two grocery bags and followed her across the dirt drive. Fallen pine needles had created a carpet over the dirt, and they crunched noisily under their feet. "I really appreciate this," she said. "Over and above. Most people have a few dates before they get into this kind of shit. Movies, meals, skating, art galleries… We're just here saving businesses, sorting out this gal's problems," she laughed. "You're one in a million, and I don't even know your last name."

Stone smiled. "Well, if you ever get back into law, I'll spot you that dollar and client confidentiality will be firmly established…"

"Oh, God. Is it really that bad?"

"It's complicated."

"I'm not so sure that I even want to know now."

"Best way." He paused as she unlocked the cabin door. "I'll fix us something to eat…" He was cut short as she pulled him towards her and brushed her soft lips against his own. Stone struggled with the bags, then dropped them on the porch and kissed her back. He wrapped his arms around her, and she gasped, a wince of pain upon her face. Her lips were thick and swollen and he knew how tender her ribs must have felt. "I'm sorry, perhaps we should just…"

"No. I want you," she said, but her eyes were teary, and she looked fearful.

"What's wrong?"

"Nothing," she replied. She caught hold of his hand and led him slowly off towards the bedroom. The cabin was a single level affair, with just two rooms leading off the open-plan kitchen and living area. She stroked his chest, then shuddered. Again, Stone frowned, but she simply said, "Please be gentle with me…"

Stone got it. He knew there had never been a fall. The gang banger turning up to the hospital had confirmed that for him. Whether he was just finishing the job, or whether he was there to intimidate her further and silence her, he did not yet know. She had been beaten, and she was willing to push through the pain for some tenderness and care. Although Stone was more than willing to offer the tenderness she craved in the shape of a movie and a snuggle up on the couch in front of a log fire. But now, as she led him towards the bedroom door, her hand in his and the promise and expectation of sex growing ever closer, he found himself highly aroused and drunk on anticipation.

Katy set the pace, slow and sensuous. Stone was ready for more passion, but he knew that she was in pain and allowed her to take charge. In his experience, good love making required one person to take control and the other to follow. It did not matter who took the role, but when two people operated on a different agenda it made for awkwardness and frustration.

Stone kissed her body gently all over. The

bruising was off-putting because he did not want to hurt her and wasn't even sure they should be doing it. But Katy drove them forward and when he finally entered her, he was swallowed up in a wave of pleasure, but strangely, never truly felt she was involved. He wasn't entirely sure if she had orgasmed, and knew it was a ridiculous thing to ask, and when he finished, she rolled off him and went to the bathroom, Stone catching a glint of tears in her eyes. He waited for her to return but gave up after fifteen minutes and decided to get them something to eat rather than wait for her to return and dissect what they had done, and what the problem had been between them, or more accurately, on her part. He pulled on his clothes and went out to the kitchen, where he saw her standing in the window, wrapped in a fleece blanket, and staring out at the lake.

"OK?" he asked.

She turned around, her eyes still moist and glossy. "Fine," she said quietly. She walked up to him, reached up and kissed his cheek softly. "That was lovely," she said and walked back into the bedroom.

Stone stared out at the lake, feeling dejected. They hadn't clicked, and that was fine because you could not hope to have that special connection with everyone you slept with, but he liked her, and they had connected so well on their first night together at the motel. But she had been run off the road and attacked in the dark. Perhaps she had felt obligated, needed to feel secure and protected. Had he over thought their connection? He didn't think so, but they had merely gone through the motions in the bedroom, or at least she had. Had they moved too soon? They were into the realms of relationship and the hours they had spent together since he had met her three weeks ago could be rounded up to a day at the most. He sensed she regretted moving so fast, and now he had gotten to know her and her family's history at the mine, he felt that if he bailed out on her now, then he would do so knowing that she would lose everything. But what could he hope to bring to the party? He had quit an engineering degree to sign up and go to war. A rash act of vengeance after his fiancée died in the nine-eleven Twin Towers attack. He couldn't even bring a wealth of skills with him that would get gold out of the ground, but he could bring muscle, and perhaps that was all she needed.

Chapter Thirty-One

"Why the hell are you not digging where I said you should?"

"We're committed to the east cut. It makes no sense to strip new ground at this stage in the season." Don protested. "Marvin had a lot of experience…"

Stone stared at him and said, "Until Katy gets well enough to return, I have the final say. As far as I can see, you've wasted a whole damned day." He paused. "I'm heading into town now, when I get back, I expect to see work started, or you're gone as well. Family or no family, I'm working in Katy's best interest. Got it?"

The man nodded reluctantly. Stone had reached the rank of master sergeant in the Airborne Rangers, and he knew how to use his voice to make a grown man tremble, and it wasn't all about shouting. Just the level of voice and conviction of statement. "I guess," he replied.

"Then why the fuck are you still standing here?"

Stone watched Don walk back to the ATV

that he would use to ride back to the cut. Excavators and trucks were expensive to run, and Stone had noticed the men ferrying themselves back to the recreation room for toilet breaks, lunch and at the end of the shift like they were Uber drivers for each other. Stone had noticed two quad bikes were parked up under a tarpaulin and now the men would use these and potentially save a fortune on profitless fuel. He had felt psyched relaying this to the crew, feeling he at least had addressed an issue to the financial security and smooth running of the mine, even if he did not have a clue how to effectively get the gold out of the ground.

Stone headed for the edge of the claim and started to climb the wooded slope to the top of the ridge. When he reached the summit, he was afforded a view of trees and grassy clearings, of lakes and mountains, and as he turned to his left, he could see distant glimpses of the Pacific. It was quite something, but he had not climbed the slope simply for a panorama of middle Alaska. He turned his eyes back to the western end of the claim. Duke Tanner's mine was running and there was a hubbub of men and equipment and vehicles. The police were still not there, and Stone was confident they had not been there earlier and would not be turning up anytime soon. The email had not been sent and he needed to find out why.

The road back to the highway had been constructed decades before from tailings – the waste stones and rocks left over from running the pay dirt through the conveyors and bars and grates that separate the gold and fine sand from the waste – and had been compacted over the years. It was as good as tarmac, but the top inch or so was mud that washed down from the slopes and whether it was wet mud, or bone-dry dust, the surface always felt loose, and the truck drifted through the turns like riding on ice. The grip of the vehicle never actually gave completely, but it always felt like it would. It was enough to contend with. Which was why he did not notice the pickup truck in his rear-view mirror until it was too late.

Chapter Thirty-Two

Stone could feel the truck pulling towards the ditch lining the road and he knew that the offside tires had been shredded. The truck was both difficult to control and acceleration had been affected. He glanced into the rear-view mirror and saw the truck gaining on him. Forest lined the road and ahead of him the mountain range loomed. Lame Horse was behind him, too far to get to with the shredded tires and besides, he had to get the truck turned around and avoid the two men in their own vehicle. Not an option. He turned his eyes back to the mirror and could see one of them leaning out of the window and aiming the automatic weapon. He had managed to successfully hit Stone's rear tires, had reloaded, and was getting ready to fire again. Stone knew the man's chances were good. There was only seventy yards separating them, and they were gaining on him quickly. He pulled the truck over to the left, forcing the man to lean further out and aim across the hood. Stone swung the truck back, then snaked back over to the left. The man was way out of the window and attempting to get a decent aim with the rifle. Stone veered right, slammed on his brakes, and waited for the driver to take evasive action. He stood on the brakes, swung to the left to avoid a collision, and the man with the rifle was cast sideways out of the window. Stone saw flailing limbs and the weapon fly through the air, and then the man landed in a heap and skidded on the dirt road. Stone already had the shift in reverse and the last thing he saw was the man scrambling in the dirt to get clear. There was a noticeable bump as he hit the man with the tailgate and towing hitch and even above the rumble of the V8 engine as Stone selected drive and floored the gas pedal, the man could be heard screaming.

Stone only drove another twenty yards before slamming the gear shift into park and stepping out with the shotgun. He raised it to aim but was met with a barrage of bullets from the driver, who had simply fired his weapon through the windshield of their truck and was getting more accurate by the second. Stone flung himself clear of the truck and returned fire, peppering the windshield, and forcing the driver to duck down into the passenger seat. Stone pumped another round into the chamber and fired again, this time catching the other man in the road as he scrambled for cover. The shot hit his right butt cheek, and he arched his back and screamed as he disappeared behind the rear of the truck. The driver had got back into the fight and was firing again, but a shotgun was no match for an AR-15 assault rifle and Stone made the split-second choice to get into the cover on the fringe of the road, as most of the rounds were directed towards the truck. As he landed in the brush and crawled forwards on his belly, he could smell fuel and suspected the fuel tank had been ruptured. There was a pause in the shooting and Stone knew the man would be switching to another magazine. He knew what was coming next, and he was up and running for the thicker trees, reaching them as an entire magazine was unleashed in his direction, thirty 5.56mm high-velocity bullets cutting through the undergrowth, some pinging off into woods as they ricocheted, having a second chance to find their intended target.

More rounds came after a short pause in the volley of fire, but Stone was already working his way down a steep hill with plenty of trees behind him to stop a bullet's path. As he reached the bottom of the slope, he heard the 'woof' of ignited fuel and a secondary explosion. He risked a glance over his shoulder and saw a large mushroom of acrid, black smoke rising high in the air. They had set fire to his truck, or the vapors from spilt fuel had ignited on something hot – perhaps the rims of the wheels had become hot enough with the tires shredded – but either way, his transport was gone and everything he carried onboard. After another hundred yards, a large fallen tree provided Stone with a lying up place where he could evaluate his situation and provide himself with cover and observe whether he was being followed. There was moss on one side, and he knew from being in the northern hemisphere that side would most likely be pointing north. Moss thrived under damp conditions with the least amount of sunlight. He had fallen for this before though, as it can sometimes be other factors that prevented the light breaking through, such as overhangs, fallen trees or even the forest canopy itself, so he looked around him and saw other tree trunks with a semi-circular wrap of moss – enough for him to make an informed decision which way was north, and in doing so, a ballpark direction back to Lame Horse, which was the nearest town.

Stone checked his pockets. He had three shotgun shells in his jacket, and he took two and loaded them into the underside of the shotgun, where they nestled up against the other shells in the tube and were held in place by a smooth flap of metal on a spring-loaded hinge. The shotgun now had a round in the breech above and four in the tube. He rested the shotgun against the trunk of the fallen tree and continued to check. Apart from his folding lock-knife he had a hundred dollars in tens, his cellphone, and some pocket change. He checked his cell phone signal, and he had a single bar and over half the battery. But who was he going to call? He was a wanted man. He was on his own. He only ever used the phone when he could use the Wi-Fi in a motel or public area and wondered why he even bothered carrying it with him, but he already knew the answer to that, and that one person was laying broken and bruised and mending in a remote cabin on her own and waiting for him to return. For a moment he wondered whether that would be their next move – to backtrack and go after Katy while he was alone and on foot with no transport. That was what the smart money would say. But in answer to his fears, he heard the unmistakable sounds of someone pushing through the brush in the direction he had come. Stone picked up the shotgun and crouched slowly, not making any unnecessary or sudden movements. His phone vibrated, a text delivery showing with only a partial number. He frowned, assumed it was junk mail and switched off the phone before pocketing it and tightening his grip on the shotgun. Stone then turned his eyes to the undergrowth and waited for the fight to come to him.

Chapter Thirty-Three

As the distance between them closed, Stone's advantage with the shotgun increased. Only ever effective up to fifty yards, a shotgun was better up close. The closer the better. Loaded with any kind of birdshot it was the most devastating weapon imaginable at twenty feet, and utterly redundant at a hundred yards. But his enemy knew this, too. And at fifty yards, Stone caught a movement behind fronds of bracken and thin saplings, all enough of a barrier to slow or deflect the shot at this distance. He did not want to waste a shell unless he could guarantee a 'stop shot'.

There was movement to his right, also. Which meant although he had hit the man in the butt, he had not been put out of action. Maybe the guy's wallet had taken some of the sting out of it. Whatever had happened, Stone could not afford to be flanked. He did not imagine that they had seen him, but the two men knew enough about terrain and the wilderness to know a killing ground when they saw one and they had held back. Which told Stone two things. The men knew how to hunt. And now they were hunting him.

Chapter Thirty-Four

Stone was bugging out. A tactical withdrawal. He was lying prone on his stomach, the shotgun cradled in the crooks of his elbows, and he eased himself from side to side, his elbows and knees doing the work as he almost slithered out from behind the fallen tree and into the brush behind. Sound was the most important thing now, hearing the most valuable sense. With his back to his pursuers, he needed to hear them approach. But he had been given no choice but to give up his hide. With assault rifles and the two men unwilling to cross the open ground, Stone knew that their next move would have been to start putting some rounds into the undergrowth. Stone's shotgun would not penetrate much in the way of the foliage – even the saplings, let alone larger branches - but the 5.56mm bullets from their AR-15's would devastate such cover and reach out far beyond. Stone needed them closer, damn near close enough to see the whites of their eyes.

Stone had barely made it twenty yards when the first gunshot rang out, closely followed by two more. He quickened his pace, then when he came to a short slope, he held the shotgun close to him and rolled down the slope, splashing down into a shallow creek. The water made him gasp. Icy glacier water, not much above freezing temperature. He had enough gradient of the slope above him to get to his feet and take off up the creek, the water hiding his footprints and eliminating the chance of stepping on dry twigs or branches that could give him away. Behind him, the gunfire erupted into a melee, and Stone could tell from his combat experience that both weapons had unleashed on the clearing. He used this to his advantage, racing hard up stream, confident he would not be heard and still unseen from the ridge above. By the time the gunfire subsided, he had enough distance between himself and his pursuers to step out of the creek and run flat-out up the incline, where he threw himself onto his stomach with the shotgun ready at his shoulder. He was now looking down on the clearing and the fallen tree that he had used as cover. He had line of sight to the edge of the clearing. Forty yards with thirty feet of elevation. At the fringe of the clearing, he could see broken branches and cuttings of bracken from where they had unloaded on and around the fallen tree.

But no gunmen.

Again, Stone wondered whether the two men had returned to their vehicle, but got his answer when a shot rang out, followed by three more in quick succession. Clods of earth and leaf debris flung up into his face and he rolled away from it, hoping he had moved further away from the gunman. He registered the noise to his right and fired a return shot, more of show of force and to make the gunman duck for cover than to expect a successful result, and he rolled further away and started to scramble back down the slope. Another volley of gunfire came from his left, and Stone realized that despite his best efforts, he had been pincered. He knew the ramifications of this, had trapped Taliban fighters himself when he had operated as a small recon team in Afghanistan. It never panned out well for the man with his enemy on either side of him. Stone fired at the movement and pumped another round into the shotgun as he slid back down the slope and made for the fallen tree. He loaded his last round into the weapon, fired a shot in both directions, then jacked the final round into the chamber. A lot of effort. All of it wasted. He was back where he had started, and his enemy now knew exactly where he was.

"Come out and we'll talk!" shouted one of the men.

"Yeah, real friendly, like!" the other shouted.

Stone said nothing, but he now had a good idea of where the two men were. He looked around him, but he could hear them making their way hesitantly through the brush.

Perhaps it was time to talk…

Stone hastily unthreaded his boot laces and tied the two ends together. He applied the shotgun's safety, attached one end around the trigger and nestled the shotgun into the crook of a branch on the fallen tree, the barrel poking out a few inches and two feet off the ground. He made sure the butt was firmly wedged, then threaded the laces back around a sapling and then off to one side at approximately forty-five degrees. He looked up and listened. One of the men had started tentatively down the slope. Stone looped the end of the lace around the toe of his left boot, then bent down, flicked off the safety and grabbed a handful of leaves and shook them out over the lace. He then opened his folding lock knife, placed it on the ground and stepped on it with his right foot. He could tell one of the men was near and sure enough, the older and larger of the two men edged out from behind the tree and Stone raised his hands, keeping eye contact with the man.

"I lost my shotgun when I fell down the embankment," Stone said. "I'm unarmed…"

The man looked past Stone at his brother who had just made it down the slope. The younger man limped, grimacing in pain and his brother said, "Frank will want to have words with you," he growled at him. "Seems you put a dozen or more BBs in his ass…"

"Fuck yeah!" Frank replied, stepping around Stone and giving him a wide berth. "Where's his gun?" he asked his brother without taking his eyes off Stone.

"The pussy lost it when he fell…"

"Is that a fact?" the younger brother said. "I didn't see it, Kurt…"

"Well, it ain't in the son-of-a-bitch's pocket!" Kurt snapped. "But you can check him, anyhow…"

"Put your hands on your head, you fucking pussy…" Frank put down his rifle and looked at his brother. "Just make sure you cover me, Kurt."

"It's done. Now check the son-of-a-bitch so we's can have us some fun…"

"Couple of good'ol boys like you want to make me squeal like a pig…?" Stone sneered. "The film *Deliverance* is just a family documentary for you guys. I bet prison sex is all you pair of idiots are used to…"

Frank frisked him firmly and quickly, then stepped back and picked up his rifle before saying, "I made that bitch of yours squeal, though…" He paused, then grinned when he saw Stone's expression. "Right… she didn't tell you!" he laughed. "How about that, Kurt? The dumb bastard doesn't know she's spoiled goods!"

"Women sure do keep their secrets…" Kurt said dryly. "Normally I don't go along with Frank's ways, but…" He shrugged haplessly. "That Katy McBride sure is a sweet piece of ass… I just couldn't say no."

"But *she* sure did!" Frank wailed.

Stone watched Kurt take a step closer. He was aching inside, his heart thudding at the revelation. Was it true, or were they just trying to irk him? It would certainly go with her lack of involvement last night. But surely if what the two men said had happened really did, she would not have wanted to sleep with him last night. Stone tried to put the thought aside. "You're a couple of big men, aren't you? So, you raped a woman. Taught her a lesson. What, was that on Duke Tanner's orders?"

"What the hell does it matter to you?" the older man asked. "You ain't getting out of here, boy."

"I guess that's the case." Stone shrugged. "So, indulge me…"

Kurt shrugged. "Tanner wanted her softened up."

"But did he order you to rape her?"

"He wanted her beaten to a pulp. He was pretty darn specific about that, and that's what he got."

"So, you raped her as part of that arrangement?"

Kurt shrugged. "He knows us. Knows what we've done in the past, seen our rap sheets. He didn't hire a pair of fucking monks." He paused. "Frank has a liking for pretty women like Katy McBride, even if women like her don't tend to share the same attraction. Duke Tanner knew what Frank went to jail for, what he did to that young girl…"

Stone felt his neck and cheeks flush, his heart hammering against his chest. He could feel his legs stiffening, the stress threatening to incapacitate him. He had seen it before, felt it before, even. Kneeling before a Taliban commander, watching the ground where the shadow wielded the sword above his head. A split second before SEAL Team Six had rescued him. But there would be no rescue today. He was on his own.

"You'll pay for that," Stone said coldly. He stared at the older man in front of him. "You and your pervert brother..." He was cut short by a jab to his kidney with the barrel of the assault rifle which nearly felled him. But he could not afford to go down. That would be the end of it for him if he did. He steadied himself and said, "I get that this piece of shit does what he does. But surely as his older brother, you should steer him clear..." He paused. "Mothers expect that of sons."

"What the hell are you bringing up my mother for?" Kurt took a step forwards, the rifle raised at Stone's head.

Stone shrugged. "I had an older brother," he replied. "Our mom always told him to look out for me. I guess she didn't do that with you, huh?" He paused. "I guess she was too busy sucking dicks for cash in the front seat of some punter's vehicle…"

"What the…?" Kurt took another step forwards, as his brother brought the frame of the rifle down on Stone's shoulder. "Get outta the way, Frank!" He shouted, struggling to aim at Stone's head while his brother was directly behind.

Stone bent double, the impact almost dropping him. He glanced at the protruding barrel of the shotgun, the angle, and of Kurt's legs. It was as good as he would get. The shot would spread. He snapped his left foot backwards and the shotgun blast took the man's left leg off at the shin. Stone was already moving and had the knife in his right hand as he smashed the rifle out of Frank's clasp with his left. The knife drove deeply into the man's groin and Stone swiped the blade upwards, the *Spyderco* serrated blade slicing clean through the man's testicles and penis and up to his navel. Stone whipped the blade out and jabbed it into the screaming man's chest. It was a precision strike, driving a full four inches up to the hilt and deep into the man's aorta. He snapped his arm back, withdrawing the blade and pushed him to the ground. Blood was already soaking the man's sweatshirt and jacket. He had seconds to live rather than minutes. Stone turned to the other man, only now registering the screaming as he clawed through the leaf mulch of the previous fall. He had dropped his rifle, fight or flight kicking in and his lizard brain telling him to reach safety. Stone bent down and picked up the rifle, calmly pulling back the charging handle and checking the chamber. He glanced at the safety. It was good to go.

"Shit, that's got to smart a bit," he said, looking at the severed lower part of his leg. It was still attached by some skin and sinew and following him as he continued to drag himself away. "Don't worry about me, I'll just be here watching until you give it up..."

The man stopped and rolled onto his side, looking up at Stone, who saw the fight leave his eyes as he knew what would be coming next. A man who knew there were no chances left. "Get on with it," he growled.

"You beat and raped a young woman..."

"Fuck you! Just do it!" He swallowed hard and rasped. "Get it over with..."

"It's far too quick for the likes of you."

The man grimaced, but through the agony he forced a smile. "I think she enjoyed it," he said coldly. "Even through the screaming and fight she put up. Part of her enjoyed being taken by a couple of real men. Not just another pussy like you…" He trailed off, his face a ghostly white and his chest heaving as he struggled to breathe through the pain.

Stone tossed the rifle aside, bent down and grabbed the man and dragged him up to his one good foot. The man screamed in protest, but Stone dragged him to the fallen tree and pushed him down onto his backside. The man's foot was still attached, but only by the thinnest thread of sinew now. Stone pulled out the shotgun and unfastened the shoelaces. He then went to Frank's body and unfastened his belt. The man had carried a folding lock knife in a leather pouch attached to his belt and Stone took it out and thumbed open the blade as he walked over and looped the belt around Frank's neck, then stabbed through the belt, pinning the man to the fallen tree. The belt was tight, but not so tight that the man could not breathe, although he certainly wasn't going anywhere.

Stone gathered up the two rifles and a couple of spare magazines, then sat down on the forest floor and refastened his boot laces. As he tied them, he stared at the man and said, "You're going nowhere. You're not getting out of here. And nobody is going to come and save you."

"Fuck you…" Stone got up and walked over. The man was trying to move away as he knelt in front of him, but the belt pulled as tight as a cinched noose, and he could not manage to move more than a few inches. Stone slapped him across the face, and he jolted to attention. He was perspiring despite the chill air, and he had turned a whiter shade of pale, not only with the pain and magnitude of what trauma he was going through, but with the loss of blood as well. Stone doubted he had more than a few minutes before he bled out. "I'm not going to beg, you son-of-a-bitch…"

Stone almost recoiled at the man's breath. Stale and heavy with cigarette smoke and poor food choices. It had an odor of dog shit about it, too. The worst breath he had ever had the poor fortune to smell. He stood up, then bent down and picked up the lower part of the man's leg. He gave it a tug and the sinew held. The man winced and looked like he was about to vomit. Stone shrugged and snatched the limb away, the sinew snagged then tore free. He tossed the limb into the man's lap, then turned and picked up the two rifles and the shotgun and walked out of the clearing. He slung the rifles over his shoulder on their slings and did not look back as he left the man to die.

Chapter Thirty-Five

As he drove back to Lame Horse on the dirt track, Stone could feel the anger welling within him. His stomach felt hollow, and his neck felt flushed and hot. Knowing what the two men had done to Katy galled him to the core. The physical attack would have been brutal, both men using her for gratification and showing no remorse. Stone imagined the man's effluvium being the final insult she would have to endure. But it was so much more than that and he knew she had been in emotional toil when they had been together last night. Try as he might, he could not work out her reasoning for sleeping with him at the cabin. She had clearly been in pain, and she had been under no pressure from him whatsoever. He could not hope to understand what was going on inside the mind of a woman who had endured such a horrific experience, but he was left wondering whether making love with him had been cathartic for her in some way. He could not imagine putting a time frame on when normal sexual relations would continue after such an experience. If at all. But what did he know? He wasn't a psychologist. And no gender fully understood the other, add to which, different peoples' personalities, resilience and coping skills and he pictured concentric circles in his mind, with no chance of seeing an image that would fit a given scenario. But as Stone drove on, the truck no longer handling skittishly as he joined the asphalt of the highway and left the loose surface behind, he remembered his first *real* love affair which had been with a married woman, just before he had started college. She had been in a mentally abusive relationship with the same man since high school and had started her affair with Stone when she had discovered her husband had cheated on her all over town. The man in question was a slob, who expected to be greeted from work with a beer and a smile and would strip down to a 'wife-beater' singlet vest and sit on the couch sipping beer and scratching his balls in front of the TV until she got dinner ready. A taste for steak but with a hamburger budget, the man never once complimented her on the wizardry she had performed out of the dregs of housekeeping money and offers at *Target*. Stone remembered the woman fondly and the sex had been amazing between them. He had learned much from her, and it afforded him locker room bragging rights and a sense of manhood he had not felt to that point in his life. Bragging and exaggerating blow-by-blow details of the sex he had just had, and what a loser her slob of a husband was, one of his more perceptive friends – soon to take a psychology degree at Harvard – had commented, "It doesn't sound as much as though she's fucking you, but more like she's *unfucking* her husband…" Stone had been somewhat irked by the comment, but it had stuck with him over the long, hot summer and he had managed to make a clean break of it, gone on to study engineering at MIT and had met Sarah. They had become engaged in their third year. Stone had barely thought about the married woman since, but for some reason, his friend's comment had emerged from the recesses of his mind, and it started to make a great deal of sense to him. On reflection, his torrid affair had been one of release for the woman and a journey of discovery for Stone. She had not loved him, probably spun him a line that he was the first man she had cheated on her husband with, and most likely had not thought about their affair since. But Stone knew that his friend's words had been true, and in all likelihood, Katy

McBride had put herself through the motions with him to try and undo what had been done to her, in her mind at least, if not her body.

Stone sighed, the feeling of rage subsiding and a sense of despair rising from within. He felt ill-equipped to support Katy. The manly stuff was done. Both men had paid the price for their actions, but it could never undo what had been done. Revenge never did. Stone was on the run. He could not afford to stay in this part of Alaska for long. Already there was a trail and likely a shitstorm on the horizon.

Actions and consequence.

He needed to bug out. Live to fight another day. But he also knew that running was the hardest thing to live with and the expression could easily be reversed to *fight to live another day…* For Stone, he knew that he needed to cut loose. He was not looking to stay, and as much as he liked Katy – even fallen for her - after what she had been through, it would not be fair for her to pin false hopes on him. Tear the band aid off quickly. Keep on driving. Which was exactly what he did. Right past the motel. Until he saw Duke Tanner's truck parked outside.

And that's when he hit the brakes.

Chapter Thirty-Six

Stone watched Duke Tanner step down the three wooden steps of the motel office and restaurant block and look up as he swung the pickup truck into the parking lot. Tanner walked over, a gloating, self-satisfied expression on his face. A man on a winning streak. He frowned and stopped suddenly as he realized it was Stone behind the wheel and not the two men that he had sent to kill him.

Stone wound the window down. He had one of the AR-15 rifles resting across his lap, the muzzle touching the door and his right-hand hovering near the trigger. "What's up? Cat got your tongue?" Duke Tanner's hand hovered near the pistol on his belt and Stone shook his head. He had noted it was a Glock, and by the thickness of the frame it was a .45 or a 10mm. The guy had gunned up. Done away with the wheel guns and joined the twenty-first century. "I've got a nice Smith and Wesson AR-15 on you and a full clip just waiting for an excuse to empty itself. It will cut through both this door and you like a hot knife through butter…"

"Your prints are all over the inside of that truck, and I believe it will be found on CCTV at Carlsson Sound hospital. Right around the time you were there, and a cop was killed."

"Is that the best you've got?" Stone paused. "I've got pictures of this vehicle at your mine two nights ago, along with the other truck used to run Katy McBride off the road a few weeks back."

Tanner shrugged. "That could have been anywhere. There's nothing on my claim tying me to anything." Stone felt his finger edging towards the trigger, but he glanced past Tanner and saw both Maude and Howard hovering in the entrance to the motel. Maude appeared worried, but Howard looked resolute. Tanner glanced behind him, then looked back at Stone with a wry grin. "Old friends, known each other for decades…"

"I would have sent that email!" Maude shouted. "But Howard stopped me…!" Howard stopped her again, bustling her back into the motel, glaring at Stone as he shoved Maude inside and slammed the door behind them.

"Funded them when the bank wouldn't sign off on the loan they applied for. I guess they know which end of the knife to hold. Well, one of them does, at least." He paused. "I used to shack up with Maude, I guess she still holds a grudge about me cheating on her. But, not enough to refuse my money…" Stone said nothing. It made sense. Coming to Katy's aid that night was one thing but turning against Duke Tanner when he probably still owned the deeds to the motel until the loan was paid was quite another. "Money talks, I guess. So, there will be no police presence at my claim, nor down here at Lame Horse." He stepped aside and allowed two SUVs to drive past him and park directly in front of the motel. They were both new models - a BMW X5 and a Range Rover Velar - covered in dust and grime from some hard driving, but in these parts, they would be called 'soccer mom' SUVs and the four men who got out of them stretched and acknowledged each other, then opened the rear doors and started to take out their cases were clearly not from these parts. Stone could see gun slips and fishing gear and figured they were office types up from Seattle on a few days' 'mancation'. Tanner smiled and said quietly, "Not quite the right time or place to use that AR-15 you say you have in there…"

Stone lifted the muzzle to show Tanner,

then dropped it back down out of view. "Perhaps not," he replied. "But there soon may be…"

Bolstered by the witnesses and his correct assumption that Stone would not simply gun him down in cold blood, Duke Tanner smiled and said, "Be on your way, boy. You're not ready for big boy games…"

Stone nodded sagely as he put the truck in gear and drove back out onto the highway. Words did not hurt him, but they could certainly help him. Giving Tanner a win would fuel the man's ego and likely lull him into a false sense of security. The man was a bully and a tyrant and was clearly a big fish in a small pond. He would have funded Maude and Howard not for reasons of altruism, but for the power it handed him and the credit it would give him for their loyalty. People like that had power and the thing they feared most in this life was losing that power. Stone had met people like Duke Tanner before. And it had not ended well for them.

Chapter Thirty-Seven

Stone had driven into town and stopped beside the estuarine river, the tide clearly out. The mud smelled of rotten fish and seabirds and waders were picking through the mud for softshell crabs, oysters, and carpet clams. On the far bank, Stone could see a brown bear rooting through a bank of oysters. He checked his phone, frowned once more at the blank email. He needed to get to a computer as the phone was a cheaper model and had a limited capability. He looked about him, but Lame Horse was a basic settlement. He couldn't very well use the computer at the motel, but he supposed the auto parts store with its reliance upon ordering specialist parts would be his best bet. He drove on and parked up on the forecourt, and the guy who had repaired his tires came out to meet him.

"No can do, my friend."

"I haven't asked anything yet."

"No need. Duke Tanner has a stake in this place, and I can't very well go against what he says. Not when he is here all damned year, and you're just a guy passing through. My advice is to keep on driving while you can. I haven't seen the fella's heckles so ruffled in years!" He paused, wiping his oiled hands on an even more oily cloth. "No offense, mister. It is what it is…"

Stone nodded. He looked at the man's arms, and like many in his job they were sinewed and muscled and scarred. Sleeves rolled up, getting down and dirty. Stone could see the USMC tattoo and smiled. "Is Duke Tanner a vet?"

The man smirked, then said dismissively. "No."

"But you are."

"Seventeen years. Marine Corps. Got out in ninety-eight and headed up here."

"Semper Fi."

The man scoffed. "You ain't no jarhead!"

"No, sir. Army artillery…"

"Say what?"

"Good one," Stone smiled at the man's humor. Artillery specialists tended to get tinnitus and lose the best of their hearing a few years into their service. "I went into Airborne Rangers, and then recon. I worked with a few jarheads, though. And SEAL teams."

"From your age, I'd figure Afghanistan?"

"Yep."

"I was in the Gulf War, myself."

"You boys had a good Burger King, I hear…"

The man laughed. "Yeah, it was over pretty darn quick. Still shit scary, though."

"I hear that." Stone paused. "First deployment is the worst. You never know how you'll cope when the bullets start to fly."

"It was my second deployment. I was in Grenada in eighty-three…"

"Damn, what is it with you? You can't fight for a full week?" Stone laughed and the man joined in, too. "You make it the full three days for that one, too?"

"Well, I think we ended up with more days spent surfing than fighting." He shrugged. "And the Gulf was a six-month deployment…"

"With a full three days on the trigger."

"I never fired my weapon after Desert Shield. Every Iraqi I saw had his hands on his head or was waving a white flag!"

Stone chuckled. "Well, jarhead. You going to help out a fellow vet?"

"That depends on what you're going to ask."

"You have a computer and internet?"

"Yep."

"Say if I walked in there, used it for ten minutes and left a hundred bucks on your desk. No comebacks, no way Duke Tanner will ever know."

"Then, I guess I could do with a donut to go with my coffee. I'll be back in about fifteen minutes, and no offense, I don't want to see you again..."

The office was a clutter of invoices, delivery notes and used coffee cups. Nude glamor model calendars from vehicle parts and tire companies were displayed on the walls, some dated from ten years previous. There were also posters of cars and posters of girls. And some posters of girls sprawling across cars. The chair behind the desk had torn and lost the majority of its sponge stuffing years ago.

Stone had logged into his account and opened the email, then checked his text messages alongside the time and date of the email. The text and the email were sent within a minute of each other, and neither sender was known to him. He frowned and logged into his mail account on the desktop computer. The email came up with no subject. He scrolled over the page where a body of text should have been, clicking the left button, where lines of invisible text highlighted. There was still nothing to read, but *something* was there. He highlighted the entire page and searched the toolbar for fonts and colors, but there was no option for this, so he right clicked the highlighted lines, and copied it. He then opened a new Word document and right clicked the paste icon. Stone stared at the text, his heart racing, and a hollow feeling in his stomach.

Rob – I'm in trouble. I have been abducted and am being forced to help my captors. I think they are CIA, or perhaps something even darker, but they are hunting you. There is an encryption in this email, and it activates when your phone is switched off and then reactivated. They are a team of three. A red headed woman and two jocks, both blond with military cuts. I heard them talking about a 'specialist' they are bringing in – can only be a bad thing. Good luck, my friend, I am so sorry – Max.

Stone looked at the phone and shook his head. He had been so careful, so sure he could evade the 'deep state', but he should have known better. He switched off the phone, unclipped the back case and removed the battery and SIM card. He pocketed all three, when his instinct was to tread them all into the ground. He checked his watch and the date. He figured if the signal activated when he first noticed the incoming email, then he had until tomorrow morning before they reached him. It was possible they could have taken flights and arrived a mere five hours later, but this was Alaska and even a flight into Anchorage was going to be met with car hire, or if they were FEDs, then they would have to liaise with the local contingent. However, Stone doubted this would be above board and constrained by protocols. He imagined they would have to source vehicles or perhaps close the ground by chartering light aircraft or helicopter flights, but they would still need vehicles when they got here and to arrive in the dead of night was tactically foolish. They would need to regroup, plan, and do a reconnaissance of the area, gather what intelligence they could before making their move. And by ceasing the signal, Stone had given them a ballpark location. He just needed to keep moving and avoid leaving a trail.

Chapter Thirty-Eight

Stone found what he was looking for when he was around three miles from McBride's Folly. Katy had told him where her father had died, and he could not help thinking that the two gang bangers had missed a trick when they had first attacked her. The road to the mine was relatively straight, but for a series of three switchbacks that remained with the river's course. One of the switchbacks had been washed deep into and even someone's attempts at constructing a barrier had clearly not been enough to stop her father's truck crashing through and into the fast-flowing river. Ironic in that it had been Katy's grandfather who had brought down half the mountain with dynamite to expose a seam of gold, and in doing so, had steepened the river's gradient so much and created the rapids which now made this corner so precarious. Stone shuddered to think what it would be like to go over into those rapids in a vehicle. The three switchbacks looked identical, and he imagined that in the darkness, they had misjudged the location and sent Katy's truck into the ditch a full corner short of the perilous corner where her father had died. Either that, or the other explanation could be that what they had eventually done to Katy had been in their plan all along. Stone thought of the way one of the men had been bent over her, for a moment thinking he had been giving her CPR, only to be draining her consciousness so that he could have his way with her. He shuddered again, this time imagining what both men had put her through. They were no longer a threat to her, and hopefully that would give her some comfort, but he also knew that he could never tell her. It would be up to her to say what had happened, and from the way she had acted since he had brought her home from hospital, he doubted she ever would. Some secrets were taken to the grave, and he imagined this would be something Katy McBride would never speak of again, and Stone realized it was not for him to deny her that.

Stone stopped the truck facing the apex of the corner. He put the gear shift in park and left the engine running while he salvaged what equipment he could take with him, then he crossed the track and cut an alder with his knife and sliced off the tiny branches. He was left with something the size of a walking cane and he reached back into the truck and pressed one end onto the gas pedal and bent and pressed the other end into the underside of the seat. The gas pedal was mashed to the floor and the engine was howling. Stone closed the door, reached back inside, and pulled the shift back into drive and pulled back out of the way as the truck lurched forward, crashed through the remains of barrier, and surged out into the void before the hood tipped down under the weight of the small block V8 and the entire vehicle somersaulted in the air before crashing down into the water and rolling onto the roof. Stone edged nearer the precipice and stared at the boiling water thirty feet below. The truck was already fifty yards downstream, just the two rear wheels, axle and the last four feet of flatbed visible as it pirouetted lazily in the flow. After another fifty yards it sunk completely. Stone imagined it washing up on a shallow bend further downstream, his prints and DNA either wiped clean or unusable in the event of an investigation. He had realized that any investigation from now on would be in finding him, and not looking for evidence in the attack and sexual assault of Katy McBride.

Stone picked up the best-looking AR-15 and fired three shots at a large rock on the side of the road, approximately fifty paces away. He saw the three strikes, chipping off fragments where he had aimed. Good enough. He took the spare magazines and stashed them in his jacket pockets, then picked up the other AR-15 and pressed the button on the left-hand side of the frame that popped out the pin on the right. When he drew the pin all the way out of the frame, the weapon scissored in half, and Stone removed the firing pin assembly before tossing it upstream. He threw the AR-15 downstream, then shouldered the other rifle on its sling and headed down the road.

Chapter Thirty-Nine

CIA Headquarters,
Langley, Virginia

Mike Rogers sat back in his chair and re-read the email. As deputy director he had run his section with a free rein and that had been his biggest failure. He had amassed a financial deficit which had been allowed, unchecked, to spiral out of control. And now an audit under the Democrat administration would surely discover it and the paper trail would end at his door. With just three more years until his retirement, he was not going to outlive this administration, even if he could outlast the elderly president. Sooner or later the bean counters would come knocking and with them they would bring the strongarm officers of internal review and affairs.

Rogers wanted Stone. The man was at the top of both the CIA and FBI's most wanted list, and he knew that Stone had walked away from whatever the hell he had been involved in with millions. Tens of millions. And right now, Rogers could think of no better way of killing two birds with one stone. He smiled at the play on words. Did he believe that Stone had been set up? Yes. Undoubtedly. Would proving the fact help Rogers in any way? No. But if he could have Stone forced into a corner where his arrest was not possible, have the man killed, then it would be a glorious win in the eyes of the Democrat administration – naturally and historically wary of the Central Intelligence Agency – and if he could find the whereabouts of those funds, then he could bring his account back into the black and put some aside for his retirement before handing the rest to the treasury.

Liz Roper had her team on it. The Secret Service techie with the ridiculous name was helping them to close in and Rogers had ensured that by using his asset, they would succeed in taking down a man with Stone's abilities. The asset was the last of his kind. Part of a long-canceled black-ops project using drugs and hypnosis and gene therapy to create a team of perfect assassins. The project had been a failure, and the subjects – the best men and women that the military had to offer, but all suffering from schizophrenia due to the drugs that had been administered during the experiment – had been terminated. Stone had been up against one of these 'freaks' before. Rogers had discovered that Tom Hardy, the CIA officer in charge of the program had retained one for his own agenda. The asset had been used long after the program had been thought to be extinct. That same asset had been responsible for the scheme Stone had found himself unwittingly part of. An earlier confrontation between the two had left the man with a head injury that should have killed him but had in fact shaken something loose. Allowing him to regain his memory. Knowing who he was and what he had been 'altered' and trained to do, he had capitalized on it and Stone had found their paths crossing once more, with Stone taking the fall. Mike Rogers cursed Tom Hardy, but the irony was not lost on him. Rogers had also kept one of the assets in operation, away from the CIA's knowledge and records, and now that man would close the circle and finish Rob Stone once and for all.

Chapter Forty

Despite the chill in the air, the early spring sun still overpowered by the bitter cold of the wind, Stone arrived at McBride's Folly hot, perspiring, and desperate for a drink. He could have slaked his thirst in the river, but knowing it ran through various gold claims, and the excavation in place, and the run-off of mud and top-soil and whatever heavy mineral deposits made its way into the river, he decided to wait the hour or so of hard marching he had adopted to reach the mine as quickly as possible.

Ignoring Don, he made his way into the recreation room and picked up a bottle of water, drained it as he poured himself a coffee from the jug on the pot warmer, then picked up a couple of stale Danish pastries and sat down heavily at a table, only then unslinging the rifle and backpack.

Don walked in wearing a concerned expression. "Are you OK?"

"Busy day."

"We're on the cut now," he said. "We should know if there's gold in the first test."

"How much are you running?"

"Three tons."

"Run ten."

"Ten?" Don looked perplexed.

"That's right. You got a problem with that?" Stone asked sharply, tearing off some of the pastry and drinking some coffee to help him chew.

"No…"

"And use a good selection of the paydirt. Don't run it all from one place."

"Right…" Don stared at him and said, "It's not as simple as that…"

"What's the problem?"

Don shrugged. "We're getting low on fuel."

Stone nodded, drank down some more coffee and said, "Get me something with your fuel supplier's name and number on it. An invoice or something like that." He got stuck into the second Danish and most of his coffee when Don returned with a crumpled sheet of paper. He looked at the last fuel delivery receipt and bill from a company called Galveston Fuels. It was five thousand dollars for their minimum tanker for something called red diesel. Stone had heard the term before, a dyed fuel with a higher sulfur content that while it would not harm road vehicles, was illegal to use in anything but agricultural or construction equipment. The lower taxation meant lower costs passed on to food and houses. He guessed gold mines came under the same bracket and dodged the full fuel tax. Stone reassembled his phone and as he switched it on, he told Don to get back to work before dialing the number. He may have been Katy's cousin, but he thought the man should have had her back more. Marvin had been influenced by Duke Tanner and as a miner with experience, Don should have seen the writing on the wall. Costs were spiraling, gold wasn't in the pan and Katy was out of her depth. As family, Don should have been more proactive. As far as Stone was concerned, the man had better come around quickly, or he would be walking down the road.

Stone told the woman on the end of the phone where he was from but was curtly told that they would no longer deliver fuel to McBride's Folly or its directors.

"I understand that a community this size hears rumors," said Stone matter-of-factly. "But I have card details I can give you, so the fuel will be paid for before your truck leaves."

"I'm sorry, but we are no longer dealing

with McBride's Folly Mining..." the woman replied, though somewhat awkwardly if her tone belied her true feeling.

"I have the money. It will be paid in full before your tanker pulls out of the yard."

"I'm sorry..."

"Could I speak to somebody senior?" Stone paused, knowing how that always sounded. I want to speak to the manager. What was the male version of a Karen? "You see, I'm helping Katy out while she's convalescing..."

"Oh dear, what happened to her?"

Stone could not give her the whole truth, as much as he wanted to shout about what had happened thanks to Duke Tanner's heavy handedness, so he said, "She was beaten up by people paid by one of her closest competitors."

"Really?"

"Yeah." Stone paused. "So, I'm guessing your company is being paid off, or pressured for loyalty by someone. And that would be the same person who beat up a young woman who just didn't want to sell. I'll offer ten grand for the same delivery if you can leave the depot now," he said firmly. "That's five grand in your boss's hand for nothing more than being a dick, but finally seeing some sense..."

There was a pause, then the woman said, "Sorry, but it's been made clear to me."

"Damn. I was hoping to appeal to your better nature, your womanly solidarity. A thirty-year-old woman shouldn't be beaten up by two guys and hospitalized, just because she won't sell her family's legacy. What the hell kind of place is this?"

There was a muffled sound on the phone, and then after a few seconds the woman said, "Kolinski and Sons... just outside Whittier. It's a fair drive, but if you can offer a load minimum of ten thousand dollars, they'll start the drive immediately. I'm sure about that. You'll also get ten grand of fuel that way, too."

"Thanks."

"I don't like these games," she whispered. "I'm sorry about Katy. I never met her, but we used to have a good gossip on the phone when she put her orders in. Wish her well for me..."

The connection was cut, and Stone sat staring at the phone. He wondered whether his pursuers had gotten enough. He stripped the phone down again and removed the SIM and battery. Would Max Power report the contact, or would he try to hide it? He knew the man was in a tight spot but forewarned was fore armed. He had to forget about Max Power. He could not fight a war on so many fronts.

And right now, Stone was getting ready to fight.

Chapter Forty-One

"Take three rooms," said Liz Roper. "The place looks deserted. Get them in a row with one of them on the end. Then we can take two adjoining and use the third room as a buffer to stop anyone listening through paper-thin walls."

"I'll try," Ted replied.

"Try harder. Use one of your fake IDs if you have to. The FBI one generally gets the job done." She looked at the man next to Max Power in the rear seat. "Bob, you and Ted will share a room together. I'll take a room with Power..." She looked at him and said, "Don't get any ideas, Max..."

"Oh, you can bet your life that emotion has long since passed," Power replied tersely. "The thought makes me want to vomit, let alone take a shower..."

Liz Roper caught Bob smirking and she glared at him. "Something you want to say?"

Bob shrugged. "No, all good here..."

Roper turned back in her seat and stared at Ted. "Why are you still here? Three rooms, get..." She watched as the agent got out, closed the door, and headed for the reception. "Jeez, it's a good job he's pretty…"

"Are you sure you want to share a room with the asset?"

"For God's sake, Bob, must you call me that?" Power said indignantly. "I thought we were best buds…"

"I can't seriously call you *Max Power*." He shrugged. "What the hell were you thinking when you came up with that?"

Power turned and stared out of the window. "Maxwell was my middle name. The world didn't need another John. Besides, I was young and hopeful," he replied quietly. He knew enough about emotional distancing to know that Bob's hesitance to use his name meant that he had not got through to the man, and in all likelihood, it would be Bob who took Power for a one-way walk in the woods when they completed their mission. He felt he had bantered and formed a close enough bond with Ted. He would have to try harder, seal the deal emotionally. The man was younger and far more impressionable. Liz Roper was a closed book. She was all about the mission and the step up it would give her in her career. But Power had still to strike a close bond with Bob. He knew that if he was ever going to project Stockholm Syndrome on them effectively, then Bob was the essential link. He could not imagine Liz Roper doing the dirty work herself. That was what the two hulking men, high in testosterone and low in IQ were for. Besides, she would not want a person's death on her record – either officially or unofficially - she was all about deniability.

"Power won't give me any trouble," Roper said eventually, looking at him in the vanity mirror in her sun visor. "Besides, if we're running the tracking system, then I want it close to me."

"Still don't trust me?" he replied tersely.

She smiled. "I've studied Stockholm Syndrome enough to know that you neither have a convincing case of it, and nor do any members of my team lean towards your vulnerability with any true empathy." She paused. "So, understand this; know your place, do what you do, what you say that you are more capable than anyone else of doing, and you *may* get out of this alive. Play games with us, try to fool us and warn Stone that we are coming for him, and you won't hear the gunshot that kills you…"

Chapter Forty-Two

Stone had managed to secure a fuel delivery and was told it would arrive tomorrow morning. The two drivers would travel the five-hundred miles through the night, taking turns to keep the wheels rolling. Stone had paid for the load by the Visa debit card linked to the Spanish bank account Max Power had set up for him, one of several in a variety of names all over the world. One day, Stone hoped to hand the money in – it was blood money after all - but only as soon as his name had been cleared of the heinous crimes he had been accused of. He still saw the images as he drifted off to sleep, or occasionally, he would be plucked from his sleep and fail to get back off again as his demons teased him into the early hours. The stage at the memorial, the somber crowd, the President, the first lady and their two boys…

Two hours after he had secured the deal on the fuel, then checked that the men at the mine were in fact working on the eastern cut, Stone arrived back at the cabin. He switched off the engine and stared at the cabin as he gathered his thoughts. Katy had been through so much. He knew that he needed to be strong for her, but he was also aware that if people working for the state had got a fix on him - and it was more than likely now with Power's mention of the trace – then he knew he would have to leave sooner rather than later. He could not allow Katy to know that he was aware of what had happened to her. To leave after such a revelation would affect her for years, possibly for the rest of her days, making her feel that she was sullied and tarnished and not good enough for him. She would have her own battle to put the attack behind her – if indeed she ever could - and she could not be burdened with anything else. He would have to play ignorant, and in doing so, he could not mention what had happened between himself and the two men, nor what had become of them.

Stone breathed a deep sigh and got out of the Bronco. The truck was old and made from the type of steel that rarely dented, and the door closed with a heavy 'thunk'.

The door to the cabin opened and Katy walked out unsteadily. She smiled and waved as he caught her eye. She frowned at the rifle in his hand. "Going hunting?"

"Maybe."

"Well, we don't need anything. I've got a couple of steaks out of the freezer for later, and there are some potatoes in the store as big as footballs," she smiled. "I make a good garlic and herb butter to go with baked potatoes. I will let you grill the steaks. I believe that's classed as man territory," she smiled again. "There's a grill out back, and some charcoal."

"Sounds perfect," he replied. "I'm no chef, but I do like to poke at a fire with a stick..."

"How's it going at the mine?"

"Fine," he said, not mentioning the fuel crisis.

"Fancy a swim in the lake?"

Stone frowned, then pointed to the mountain ridge behind them. "There's snow on those mountains," he commented flatly. "That water will be barely above freezing."

"You say freezing, I say invigorating!"

"You're still not selling it to me."

"They do this sort of thing in Sweden all the time."

"Yeah, but I heard they jump right back into a sauna straight afterwards..."

"Come on," she said, touching his shoulder tenderly. "Where's your sense of adventure? Let's go right now, you can leave the rifle here."

Stone smiled and followed but the AR-15 came along all the same. "I'll keep it for the bears," he explained.

She shrugged. "I've never had a problem with bears," she said.

"But the day you do, you'll wish you had a rifle with you." He scanned the tree line, but he was not looking for bears. He knew it was only a matter of time before the team found him. "Anyway, we don't seem to have swimming costumes."

Katy turned around when they reached the shoreline. The beach was all gravel and she started to undress as she looked at him. Stone shrugged, put down the rifle and started to undress. "That's the spirit," she said. "Live a little…" She touched him, smoothing her hands over his muscular chest and firm stomach. "I've missed you…"

"It's only been a few hours."

"You have that effect on me…"

Stone found it difficult to get the images of the two men, and what they had done to her, out of his mind, but Katy was sensual and warm and smelled good. She smelled of summer meadows and blossom and it took him back to his youth and his affair with the married woman and their intimate, sometimes reckless lovemaking in fields and beside lakes very much like this one, only that had been in the Midwest and during a hot and heady summer he would always remember.

They made love on the beach, slowly and sensuously, and gently throughout because of her bruises. Afterwards, Katy got up and waded into the lake and started to swim. Stone followed but was startled at just how cold the water was. He panted and gritted his teeth and eventually dipped under the surface.

"You're such a wuss!" she exclaimed, wading with no discernible effect from the cold water.

"It's freezing!" he said defensively. "I'm just glad we did that first," he smiled and winked. "I'm almost transgender now…"

"Lucky me!" she laughed, then almost instantly, she stopped. She looked as if she was about to cry and dived under. When she surfaced, she was twenty feet from him with her back to him. She waded back to shore, picked up her clothes and walked quickly back to the cabin.

Stone followed, but he had already decided she needed space. He had buried the symptoms of his own PTSD from what he had seen and experienced on his tours of Afghanistan, and he already knew that Katy was having recall flashbacks of the attack. There was nothing he could do and speaking to her about it was no longer an option because she did not know that he knew. And now, having kept quiet, and suddenly announcing that he knew would likely make things worse. Put a barrier of distrust between them. He used his sweatshirt to towel himself off, then hurriedly dressed against the cold and picked up the rifle. His muscles felt tight and stung as he warmed quickly. He made his way back, stopping behind the cabin and dragging the grill and a bucket of charcoal around to the front to catch the setting sun.

"I'm sorry," she said. She was dressed in baggy sweatpants and a thick sweater, sitting in the swing seat and Stone had missed her in the shadow of the porch. "I don't know what came over me."

Stone said nothing.

"I feel a bit out of sorts. Maybe it's the new relationship thing, perhaps I'm not ready…" She paused. "Sorry, you look kind of sad…"

"If you're calling it a day, can you at least wait until we've had those steaks?"

"Jerk," she grinned.

"And I wasn't aware this was a relationship…"

"You've been there for me, you're running my damned mine for Christ's sake, I'm pretty sure this has entered the realms of relationship…" She paused. "Or are you just a sucker for a damsel in distress?"

Stone said nothing. He could not remember a time in recent years when he hadn't been helping a woman in trouble. He shrugged and said, "I should have been born in a different century, I guess."

"Like a knight. I suppose you were born on the wrong continent as well. You should have been Sir Rob, The Protector," she giggled. "OK, Sir Rob, I command you to do battle with fire and slay two enormous ribeye steaks before hunger lays siege and all hope is lost…"

Stone performed a mock bow, rested the rifle against the handrail of the porch and set about lighting the grill. He enjoyed Katy's company and admired her resolve and tenacity.

She would have been a good match for him, but if he was to remain a free man, he knew he could not stay. The thought saddened him, and his mood was suddenly melancholic as he scooped up handfuls of pine needles for tinder and wondered if the two of them could have had a future together had they not been such damaged and complex souls.

Chapter Forty-Three

The laptop was all set up and working off the Wi-Fi and there was no sign of a signal from Stone's phone. While 'testing the system' Max Power had typed out another quick email, using white font on a white background and sent it to Stone while the others were checking their equipment, loading up on coffee and day-old donuts and waiting for something to happen.

"You've sent another email?" Liz Roper asked.

Power nodded like it was nothing. "A blank one, of course. If he opens it, we'll have a brand-new bearing." He paused. "Instead of going off the last one, which is thirty-miles due east of here. A stretch of dirt road and forest near a series of claims.

"Claims?"

"Gold mines," he replied. He could see the notion was lost on the woman from DC. Even though his experience of the wilderness extended only to a few camping trips as a child, he could tell that Roper was a city girl all day long. "They take areas the size of a dozen football fields and scrape off the topsoil, then run the ground underneath through conveyer belts and grating, washing the dirt away with water and catching the gold. The gold is heavier, so sinks to the bottom."

"And that's it?"

"Well, they need to know if the ground has gold deposits, so I guess that's the skill right there. They can't just dig anywhere."

Ted and Bob had finished cleaning their pistols. Power glanced at them as they reloaded and holstered their weapons. He knew nothing about guns, but he doubted they had done anything to get their pistols dirty, so he wondered whether it was an exercise in focus. Like when athletes wear a lucky sock, or a tennis player bounces the ball before service a certain number of times. Getting into the headspace. Which told Power they were close to a conclusion. Confident they would catch Stone soon. The notion of his friend being cornered, drawn into a fight was overwhelming. But it was the notion that he would have outlived his usefulness that scared him the most. He could feel a case of IBS coming along and excused himself.

"Not again," said Bob.

"The guy's nervous, what do you expect?" Ted replied. "Hey, tech boy, open the fucking window this time!" he laughed and responded to a high-five from Bob.

Power flushed red and headed into the bathroom. He could hear a sharp knock at the front door. He frowned, but time was not his friend and the nerves had gotten to him.

Liz Roper frowned also. She drew her Glock 19 pistol and held it by her side as she stepped towards the door but seemed to have a change of heart and nodded for Ted to get the door instead.

Bob was up on his feet and peering through the blind. "One guy, white, six-four, two-fifty. Built like a line-backer. Black suit. Looks like a Fed."

Roper frowned. "What the hell would the FBI be doing here?" She paused. "OK, Ted. Open the door. Slowly…" All three had their weapons drawn. She looked towards the bathroom door, but Power seemed to be in there for the long haul. "Easy guys…"

Ted opened the door and stood back while the man filled the doorway in its place. There was no light allowed in, such was his height and breadth.

"Liz Roper?" the man said, looking past Ted having apparently taken no notice of him. "I'm Mr Black…" She looked him up and down and nodded. "You people want to holster your weapons?"

Roper nodded. "Search him, Ted."

"I really wouldn't, Ted," the man glared at him. "We don't want to go down that road…"

Ted took a step backwards and raised his weapon. "Get your hands up and face the wall…!"

Mr Black smiled, looked past Ted, and stared at Roper. "Our mutual acquaintance said you requested a person with my particular skillset." He paused. "You either need me or you don't. I will be in the third room you've taken, and you can pick up my tab. I will be dressing for the great outdoors, and I have my own equipment for the task. All I need is a when and where from you." He backed out of the doorway and headed down the porch, where they could hear him opening the door to the neighboring room and closing it behind him.

"Who the hell was that?" Ted asked, looking between both Bob and Roper. "I thought Bob and I were the muscle on this job?"

Roper shrugged. "Stone goes down. We're not making an arrest here," she said, then whispered, "And that goes for him in there, too." She nodded towards the bathroom. "Muscle is one thing. But cold-blooded killing is quite another. Unless either of you want to walk him into the woods and put a bullet in his head…?" Both men glanced at each other and remained silent. "Didn't think so. You can still go up against Stone, but let's send in *Lurch* first and see how he does, and we can hang around on the side lines before making our play."

The atmosphere had changed and there was a distinct chill to the air. Maybe it was the open doorway, or maybe it was the ramifications of what had just been said hanging in the air like a bad smell. Either way, it had just got real. They were close now.

And people were going to die.

Chapter Forty-Four

Stone stared at the cell phone on the table in front of him. Three parts. Body, battery, and SIM card. Next to it was his bottle of Coors beer and it was bitingly cold, the glass and label wet with condensation. He took a sip and reached out to turn both the steaks. The charcoal was hot and glowing red and white and the steaks sizzled on the grill, but he had made sure to mound the charcoal in the middle and was cooking on the edge of the grill with no coals underneath the meat. He wasn't a great cook, but he enjoyed grilling with fire. Primeval and instinctive. He remembered his father holding a beer as he tended the grill with both he and his brother vying for attention and the chance to turn a burger while his mother – who cooked every meal apart from barbeque – bustled in and out of the house with salads and bread and left the men to burn and char and play with flames. He smiled at the thought. He missed them all. His father had died right after his retirement, and his brother had been killed in the line of duty with the FBI. His mother had remarried, and Stone had not been her new husband's biggest fan. She had a whole new life, but Stone never felt a part of it and even his memories seemed tarnished now, knowing how she moved on. It may have been five years later, but for Stone it had felt rushed and insensitive. He knew he was being unreasonable and now that visiting her was not an option, he missed her more and more and figured he could finally get past his misgivings, but like everything in life, you did not know what you had until it was gone, and you always missed what you could not have.

"Jesus, I don't want mine well done!" Katy chided.

Stone realized he had been daydreaming too long and pulled the steaks off the grill and put them on a couple of plates. Katy had brought out the enormous baked potatoes wrapped in foil and a dish of the garlic and herb butter that she had made. It was a simple, yet excellent meal and the two ate hungrily and finished off a Napa Valley Merlot and watched the flames, Stone having added some logs to the charcoal to turn the kettle grill into a firepit.

"I was saving this for something special," she said.

"This isn't special enough," he smiled.

She shrugged and smiled, but it was a little mirthless and Stone imagined she was thinking back over what had happened. A man on the run and wrongly accused of the most heinous crimes, and a woman who had been brutally attacked and sexually assaulted while desperately fighting for her livelihood and fending off imminent bankruptcy. It was not a foundation for a successful relationship. Stone knew they were doomed, but he took solace in moments like this. Fleeting moments of the ordinary that reminded him there was the possibility of a normal future, and one day he may well inhabit such a place again.

But now he would break the ordinary and let reality catch up with them both.

"I need you to stay someplace else," Stone said.

"What?"

"There are people after me. I told you this when we first met."

"I didn't know what to believe."

"It's bad. But now they have caught up with me. So, it's worse than it's ever been."

"What did you do?"

"I can't say."

"Give me a dollar," she said. "I'm still a

licensed lawyer. I will be your counsel and that will grant me lawyer-client confidentiality. We joked about it before, but now I'm deadly serious."

Stone said nothing. He finished his wine and placed the glass measuredly on the table.

"I'm falling for you," she said, but she looked sadly at the deck between them. "The timing is terrible, though…"

"Tell me about it."

"Give me a dollar."

Stone reached into his pocket and came out with a five-dollar bill. "Here. Consider this a retainer." He paused and smiled. "But I think you had better get another bottle of wine."

"We're down to beer," she replied.

"That'll do." He waited for her to get out of her chair and head back inside the cabin. She returned with a bottle of Coors and a bottle of Budweiser and held them up for him to choose as she curled up into her chair. "Thanks," he said, taking the Coors from her and sipping a mouthful of foam. It tasted bitter and sweet all at once after the expensive Merlot and he took another sip to get used to it. "I'll start at the beginning," he told her. "Do I need a receipt to keep it legal?" he asked but was not serious. He doubted the contract between them would hold up, but he needed her to know. Especially as what he secretly knew about her left him feeling burdened with guilt.

"No, you have my word."

"Secrets have a habit of changing things."

"They do…" she replied quietly. She wiped her eyes and Stone noticed they were moist and glistening in the firelight. "The really big secrets can change things for the worse."

Stone shrugged. "Perhaps we should leave the secrets where they are?"

"I have a secret, too," she replied.

"You don't have to tell me."

"I think I need to…"

Stone sipped some more beer for a distraction. He could only assume that she was going to tell him about the attack, but now he felt he would be doing her an injustice because he already knew, and she would be sharing her innermost emotions with him. Simply already knowing her secret felt akin to cheating within a relationship. And his reaction would likely inform her that he already knew. He was no actor and did not want to start now.

"I know all about it," he said sharply,

then his tone softened as he looked at her. "Those two gang bangers were hired by Duke Tanner to drive you out of McBride's Folly and sell to him. He paid them, and they did that terrible thing to you." He paused, taking in the horror on her face. "I'm not saying Tanner knew they were going to go as far as they did, but the guy knew their rap sheet and he wanted a message sent to you."

"Oh, my God… You know?" She shook her head, tears welling up and trickling down her cheeks. The tears that followed ran more quickly over the wet skin. "How…?"

"I killed them both," he said.

"What?" She stood up and paced across the porch deck, spoke with her back to him. "How…? When…?" She paused. "I'm so confused right now…"

"They came after me. Tanner wants me out of the way, too. Without me, he can get to you more easily." He paused. "They shot at me, I shot at them. They thought they had me and confessed to what they had done, or rather taunted me with it. The tables turned and they're both dead…" Stone told her everything. He left nothing out. Maybe it could give her the 'closure' everyone was always so eager to talk about. Knowing that she would never see them again, never feel threatened and fearful they could do it again.

"Just like that?" she said flatly and turned around to face him. Her eyes glistening in the light of the fire. "We need to report this. What they did, they did. And they should have paid. But murder?"

And there it was. She was still a lawyer. A lawyer playing at being a gold miner to honor her family. What was it? Not enough attention from daddy? Proving she could finish what his own father had started? As far as Stone could tell, she had her own demons to slay, and it was not so much about her desire to make McBride's Folly work but proving she could do it when everyone else had failed.

"I didn't kill them for you," he said. "They were trying to kill me, and it was self-defense."

"A man tied to a tree with his own foot in his lap?" She scoffed. "I wouldn't want to be defending a client with that…"

"So much for my five bucks…"

Katy tore the bill out of her pocket and screwed it up before throwing it at him. Stone instinctively blocked it from his face and batted it into the kettle grill where it glowed before combusting and lighting their faces for an instant.

"Well, if that was ever a fucking metaphor for us," he said solemnly. "Burning fiercely, then out. Just like that…"

"The police will find your burned-out truck," she said matter-of-factly. "They'll search the area and find the bodies. They'll ask around, Maude and Howard will ID your truck, tell them all they know about you, they'll swab your room, eliminate fingerprints and DNA and they will find you on the system. Secret Service agents, like the FBI, are routinely DNA tested and logged."

Stone nodded. "It was good while it lasted but doomed from the beginning." He paused. "Are you going to report me?"

"Of course not," she replied quietly. "I've fallen in love with you…"

"But we're done…"

"It can't work, Rob. You're a wanted man." She paused, wiped her eyes with the back of her hand. "But if you stay, you'll be caught." She shrugged. "And I still don't know what you've done…"

"What I've been accused of," he corrected

her. "I was set up to get to the President. It worked. I sent evidence of my innocence, but still they haven't dropped the charges, and until they do, I am not going in. There's another agenda here, something that means that it's better for someone for me to take the rap, and this means sending a team after me and taking precautions that I don't ever get to see the inside of a courtroom." He paused, shaking his head. "I have someone on the inside and have been informed that the team have located where I am but are yet to pinpoint my exact location."

"And that's why your cell phone is in bits?"

"When I connect to the network, they'll have me."

"So, don't connect."

"These people won't give up."

"And nor will you," she commented flatly. She walked towards him and held out her hand. Her movements were slow, and he could tell she was still in pain, the bruises working outwards. But there was a brightness, an alertness in her eyes that told him she would be OK. She had character and spirit and resolve, and the two hired thugs had not, and would not decay that. She had won and they had lost. Stone took her hand and stood up. "Let's go inside," she whispered. "You have no choice but to leave tomorrow, but I want to spend a night with you that we'll always remember…"

Chapter Forty-Five

They had eaten in the room the previous evening to keep a low profile and there were cartons and food wrappings, and empty drinks bottles everywhere, the room smelling of grilled cheese, potato chips, smoked meats, and stale air. Max Power was seated at a chair in front of the laptop and both Ted and Bob were sprawled on the beds watching the sports highlights on the small television screen. Liz Roper was seated at the tiny table scrolling through her emails.

"I could sure do with some eggs and coffee," Bob announced. "Ted, you want some breakfast?"

"Sure."

"Forget it," Liz Roper said tersely. "Take Power with you. Ted stays here." She looked at him and said, "You go for some breakfast when Bob gets back. I don't like this guy Mr Black next door."

Bob nodded and looked at Max Power. "OK, nerd. Let's go."

Power shook his head. "My IBS is flaring up. All that grilled cheese and nacho chips. When we stop somewhere a little more civilized,

I'll need to eat somewhere that has some wholegrains and vegetables on the menu…"

"Wuss." Bob shook his head despairingly and said, "Just put hot sauce on everything and your gut will be just fine…" He looked at Roper and said, "Liz, breakfast?"

"No, you go ahead. Power is right, too much crappy food on the road. I could do with fasting and a calorie deficit this morning. Get out of here…"

Chapter Forty-Six

Katy had been right. Stone probably would never forget the night they had just shared together. He had never known a sense of intimacy like it, and now in the cold light of day, he realized that it was over. All of it. Everything. They would both go their separate ways and have only memories. To stay was to be captured – if not today or tomorrow, then eventually – but to leave would mean he would live to fight another day.

They had eaten a breakfast of fried eggs and toast and drank strong, black coffee and when they had finished, Stone had driven Katy to McBride's Folly, where she said she would stay and go through the invoices and check the progress of the western cut. He had taken the Bronco back to the cabin with him. He looked at the cell phone in its three component parts. He wondered how close the team would be. He estimated that he needed an hour or so to make some preparations, so he did not want to connect the cell phone too soon, but part of him was tired of waiting. Tackling this team would not solve his problems, but it would give him a sense of turning the tables on them. Even if he emerged victorious, there would not be a happily ever after in Alaska, no beginning of something wonderful with Katy McBride. There would only be more teams, more people hunting him. All he could do was keep moving, but not before he found out what this team knew about him and whether more were on the way.

Stone checked over the AR-15 and the spare magazines. Katy had told him that there was a .44 magnum in the cabin, top drawer in the dresser. The revolver was in case of bears and her friend always kept it loaded. Stone found it and checked it over. It was a Smith & Wesson model 29, made famous by Clint Eastwood in the Dirty Harry movies. When Dirty Harry would say to the bad guys, *"This is a forty-four magnum, the most powerful handgun in the world, and it could blow your head clean off..."*

Stone wielded the weapon. He had fired one before, but its size and weight meant that it was extremely controllable with no more felt recoil than a heavily loaded .38 snub-nose detective special. It measured a foot from the tip of the muzzle to the end of the butt and was a cumbersome handgun for combat, but it was a one-shot-stops-all weapon, and he was glad of the addition. There were more powerful handguns available today, of course. And Stone had used some of them, too. But the .44 magnum offered the best all-round package when it came down to powerful pistol ammunition, and in his opinion, it worked best of all in the gun he was holding in his right hand. After he had stashed it safely from view in the dresser near the door – to use as a stashed weapon if things became desperate - he assembled the cell phone and waited for the signal to show. Just to make sure he was discoverable, he used the cabin's basic Wi-Fi and connected to his email account and checked his in box. There was another email there, and like the previous one it was blank. But simply having his phone and with no access to a computer, he could not copy it into word and change the color of the font. He would have to take it on face value and hope that whoever was after him had not called in the entire United States Marine Corps.

Chapter Forty-Seven

"Is that what I think it is?" Liz Roper asked.

Max Power's heart skipped a beat as he saw the marker on the screen.

It was on.

"Jesus, Power, whose side are you on?"

Power did not answer the obvious as he reluctantly leaned forward and brought an overlay map on the screen, the red dot giving a four-meter-square pinpoint. "I wasn't withholding anything," he protested. "It's only just activated."

Bob had breakfasted and Ted should have been on his way back from the restaurant any moment. Liz Roper checked her watch, then jotted down the coordinates and took a screenshot of the map on the screen using her phone. She looked up as Ted knocked twice and entered using his key card. "Here's how it's going to play out..." she said.

"He's active?" Ted asked excitedly, looking around the room at the expression on their faces. "How far?"

"Less than thirty miles," Power replied with a grimace.

"What the hell's up with you?" Roper asked tiresomely.

"It's my IBS again," he said. "I think it's the stress…"

"Right," she replied, shaking her head. "OK. Bob, I want you to stay here and mind Power…"

"What…?"

"That's an order!" she snapped. Bob shrugged, but his face said it all. He was a player and he had just been benched. "Ted and I will go with… Mr Black…" She shook her head feeling ridiculous saying the man's name. "I don't trust him, but we have to use him," she said. "Ted, keep an eye on him at all times. Power, you keep monitoring the screen and the signal, because we will not have Wi-Fi on the road, and Lord knows what the cell phone reception would be like for roaming. Here you have a great signal and if he moves, you can call or text in the route and coordinates to us as we're on the move."

Everyone nodded. Ted was beaming at the chance for some action and Bob was dejectedly pulling out a chair so he could sit beside Power in front of the screen.

"Ted, get Mr Black and bring him in for a

briefing," Roper looked up as Power stood up. "Where are you going?"

"The bathroom," he replied. "I'm sorry, first it's the food, now it's the stress and nerves…"

A minute later, Ted returned with Mr Black, who was dressed like a hunter in camouflaged cargo pants and a green sweater under his green jacket. He carried a large pack on one shoulder, the strap pulled taut under the weight.

"What have we got?" he asked, his voice coarse and deep and quiet. "He dropped the pack on the floor and leaned in towards the laptop screen.

"Rob Stone is less than thirty miles from here," Liz Roper replied. "His coordinates are there on the screen and the map shows he's a few miles off the road. Looks like a remote property, most likely a cabin in the woods…"

The silenced gunshot cut her off as the left side of Bob's head blew out and splattered her with blood and brain and bone fragments. Ted went for his weapon, but Mr Black moved the pistol fluidly and shot Ted in the knee, the end of the suppressor just inches away from the man's kneecap. Ted dropped to the floor and as his head moved past the suppressor another shot fired and Roper was covered in the man's blood and brains. The weapon moved again, this time stopping right in front of Liz Roper's face. She opened her mouth to say something, but the bullet cut her short and went through her right eye. She fell forward onto her knees, blood gushing out of her eye socket like a tap. Mr Black reached out and pushed her backwards and she fell onto the floor. Her feet were twitching and more out of annoyance than to speed up the process of her dying, he shot her twice through the heart, then pulled some of the complimentary tissues out of the dispensing box and wiped the laptop screen. He reached for his phone and took a picture of the screen and the static red dot marked with the coordinates. He tucked the silenced Walther back into his pocket as he picked up the pack and opened the door, using a tissue to wipe the doorhandle clean, he stole a glance at the scene, then closed the door and crossed the parking lot to his vehicle.

Chapter Forty-Eight

He was sat frozen to the spot, still holding his breath. Pants and trousers still loose around his ankles and the roll of toilet paper in his hands, a length trailing to the floor. All he could think was that if he was to die, he would do so humiliated on the toilet. Such an undignified way to go. He had always said his IBS would be the death of him…

He had heard the silenced gunshots. They sounded nothing like they did in the movies, and yet, he knew instinctively what they were. He had heard the bodies fall, too. More than a heavy weight, something discernibly different. Hollow, wet, and final. As if he had heard their organs or bowels slopping around inside when they had landed on the hard floor. And then silence. Ominous. Final. Power had to fight emptying his bowels, his entire insides feeling as if they had turned to liquid. Desperate to remain silent. Praying the killer did not open the door.

He had no idea how long he had been sat there after he had heard the door open and close. His brother used to use the tactic when they played hide and seek as children. He would wait for him to step out of the closet, then surprise him. Power waited. And waited.

After thirty minutes, his legs went numb and as he tried to stand, he felt the blood releasing and flooding his veins, the sensation of pins and needles so severe, that he almost cried out in pain. He was in a fix now, because not only could he not pull up his own trousers, but he was involuntarily making noise as he battled through the pain. But he realized that he was in the clear because the man would surely have made his move by now. Power knew that the man was long gone, he had simply lacked the courage to move until now. And the courage to cope with what he would see inside the room.

He cleaned himself up, pulled on his trousers and fastened his belt. He looked at the sink but decided not to risk making noise running water to wash his hands just yet. Not until he knew for sure. He eased the door handle and opened the door a crack, peered through, then eased it open some more and tentatively edged out into the room.

What he was greeted by sickened him to the core. Living, breathing people reduced to corpses in just a few seconds. Liz Roper's remaining eye stared at the ceiling. Power could see grey matter through the damaged eye socket.

Her face was covered in congealing blood, some looking like crimson tears on her cheek. Both Bob and Ted had a small hole on one side of their heads, with exit wounds that a clenched fist could go through on the other. He looked at them all with mixed feelings of sorrow and relief. Sorrow, because he had spent weeks in their company and had often fallen into the beginnings of Stockholm Syndrome before catching himself in time. And relief because he was finally free. Whoever these people were, and however unique their remit was within the CIA, Power could return to the Secret Service and tell them what had happened. He would first take the laptop with him and find somewhere to dispose of it. Damaging it was no good. But there were bays and fjords and lakes on the drive back south and he would lose it forever in the depths. That way, he could give Stone a chance to stay ahead of the Secret Service when they learned of Power's story.

Power disconnected the laptop, picked up the keys to the SUV and headed for the door. He stopped himself short, turned around and surveyed the scene. Ted had gone for his weapon, and it was lying on the ground beside him. Power slowly made his way over and carefully picked it up. He did not like firearms, was an advocate for total gun control, but if he was to be asked right there and then, the gun in his hand made him feel a hell of a lot better than he had felt before he had picked it up. Suddenly, he felt protected, and the feeling of vulnerability was ebbing as he stood there with the 9mm Glock in his hand. He looked around again, then took Liz Roper's purse out of her handbag. He went through and took out a wad of notes totaling five-hundred dollars. Enough to fuel both himself and the SUV until he got to Seattle. He knew that the Secret Service were located on 4th Avenue, and they were a sizable entity. They would fly him back to Washington DC and take care of the situation here. He did not want to involve the police at this stage, and he wanted as much distance between himself and Mr Black as possible.

He opened the door, checked all around, then scurried across the parking lot and opened the door to the SUV. Within a minute he was on the highway and heading south.

Chapter Forty-Nine

Stone had made all the preparations he could. He did not have a crystal ball, but he knew how these things generally played out. The team would be small. Power had told him as much, but he suspected they would leave Power out of it. And that meant somebody would remain behind to babysit. Perhaps act as a support unit. Monitoring the tracker homing in on his phone signal, providing logistical support, even if it was just using *Google Maps* and predicting the route, should Stone attempt to flee. So, he figured that the woman would come along with one of the men acting as muscle. And that just left the specialist. A team of three.

Stone had thought long and hard about how he should play this. If it was a team of US Marshals or the FBI, then he would have turned heel and made a break for it. Canada, perhaps. Or just head south and keep going for the Mexican border. He was considering whether Central or South America may be the way to go anyway. But this team was operating under the radar. A team of CIA operatives who had called in the services of someone altogether darker.

They were not playing by a set of rules and Stone would meet them head on. No mercy.

It was him or them.

He watched the ground ahead of him, the cabin looking small from this distance. He had a good view of the lake, the Ford Bronco parked on the open ground and the sparse forest beyond. The buds were out, but the trees were still a few weeks from being full with leaves, and the only trees with any cover were the pines and furs. Stone kept the rifle firmly into his shoulder, the open sights still good for the two-hundred yards to the cabin. He had good cover, but he was far from camouflaged. He had to rely on keeping a low profile and using the saplings and fallen branches he had built into a hide for him to remain unseen.

A gunshot sounded and echoed through the valley. And then another. He could not hear the 'whizz' of bullets near him and did not hear them impacting on the ground around him. He figured it was a hunter, and if he was to estimate the distance by the report, then he would have said half a mile or so. Another gunshot echoed, this time sounding closer, and a full minute later, another shot rang out. Stone craned his neck to see. There was no movement in the trees, no signs of a vehicle on the track. Another gunshot, this time louder and he guessed it to be a heavy hunting caliber and estimated a distance of five-hundred meters. Nobody hunted like that. Not unless they had multiple sightings of prey and were a terrible shot. Another two shots rang out in as many minutes and Stone frowned. This time, they sounded close. He moved out from behind his hide and craned his neck for a better view. Again, another shot, but no sound of a bullet hitting the trees or ground. He had been under enough gunfire in Afghanistan to know the sound. And then, five successive shots, a few seconds apart and all the bullets hitting the ground around him.

"Don't move!"

Stone froze.

"If you move, you're dead!"

Stone had only felt like this once before. The moment he had been taken prisoner in Afghanistan. The man was close, and he was directly behind Stone. If he rolled with the rifle, then he would be cut to shreds.

"Don't even think about it..." the man said, much closer now. A few paces away, no further. "Drop the rifle..."

Stone complied and tossed it a few feet in front of him.

"Hands on your head. Ease up onto your knees and cross your ankles."

A pro... thought Stone. His heart started to race, and he had a well of dread in the pit of his stomach. He did as he was told, still no idea just how far away the man was, nor what he looked like. He assumed he was on his own. As Stone knelt back on his ankles, he was aware of a 'whirring' sound growing louder and a large black drone powered by multiple pods of helicopter rotors appeared before him in a hover. Stone could see a rig underneath and fixed firmly and facing downwards at forty-five degrees were two Glock pistols with extended magazines. Stone could see they were longer and chunkier than the more commonly used 9mm 17 and 19 models and assumed they were either 10mm or .45. The drone gained height to around twenty feet and leveled with one of the weapons pointed right down at Stone, the other pointing towards the cabin.

"The camera has now enabled the software to *paint* you with facial recognition." The man paused. "So, by just using voice command, I can order it to fire. And it will do so in triple taps. I wouldn't try anything if I were you, Agent Stone..." He laughed. "I found you with the drone using heat-seeking technology, and then I was able to sneak up on you while I fired a few rounds over the other side of the valley. Now the drone has me covered, while I do this..."

Stone felt something heavy and metallic smash into his skull. He fell and rolled near to his rifle, but the drone dropped in height, pitched slightly as it hovered, and the muzzle of one of the Glocks was frighteningly near his face. He stopped, raised his hands, and turned around slowly. The drone whizzed over his head, turned, and hovered in front of him.

"Know when you're beat, Stone..."

Stone looked at the man. He was four inches taller than Stone and thirty or forty pounds heavier. He held a Heckler & Koch UMP 9mm submachine gun in his left hand, and in his right, supported by a webbing neck strap, he held the control for the drone, complete with a built-in video monitor. The man had taken high-tech military technology to an ambush in the woods and Stone never stood a chance.

"Now, keep your hands on your head, turn around and make your way back down to the cabin." Stone followed the man's orders, the drone hovering above and in front of him. "And remember, it's now flying itself and only needs my command to fire three shots at a time into that pretty little face of yours…"

Stone trudged down the slope and onto the path. The path was naturally worn – nothing fancy with stone chippings or wood bark – just one of a series of paths around the cabin. The woodshed, an outhouse from days preceding the basic bathroom, a tool shed, and a massive woodpile were all interjected with pathways that Stone's father had always called fox runs. When Stone rounded a sharp bend in the track around an old rotten tree stump as he neared the cabin, he took an extra-long stride and continued.

"Wait…" the man said, and the drone stopped moving and hovered in front of Stone. "What have we got here?" Stone did not turn around, but he could hear the man scraping something on the ground. "It's OK, Agent Stone. Perhaps you will turn around slowly and show me what you have been making…" Stone could see the edge of carpet had been exposed. The man had dug away some of the mud. Stone squatted slowly, took his hands off his head, and caught hold of the edge of the square of carpet he had earlier removed from the cabin. "That's it… pull back the wrapper and let me see what you had in store for me…"

Stone pulled back the carpet and layer of mud to reveal a three-foot deep hole. At the bottom of the hole, ten sticks sharpened at both ends had been stuck in the ground. The tips looked like needles and would have easily speared through the square of carpet and the man's feet with the force of his two-hundred and fifty pounds falling directly on top of them.

"Sneaky," the man said. "But what else have you in store?"

"Nothing."

"You expect me to believe that?"

"I don't give a fuck what you believe." He paused. "You're one of them, aren't you?"

"One of whom?"

"One of Tom Hardy's freaks."

The man stared at him and frowned. "How do you know about Tom Hardy?"

Stone thought back to Vermont and his search for a missing virus. He had not killed Tom Hardy, but he had been there when the man had died. "You're one of his toys…"

The man glared and said, "I think I'll kill you now…"

Stone shook his head. "No, you won't."

"I won't?" the man scoffed.

"No."

"You're very confident…"

"You're a freak. One of many belonging to a project that was supposedly shut down. You have orders, and I'll bet they involve finding out where I stashed the money from a project that one of your number was involved in."

"One of my number…?" the man trailed off. "I don't know what you mean, but you're certainly right about telling me where the money is. And you *will* tell me. I can guarantee that. I can be *extremely* persuasive. Now, turn around," he ordered, then jabbed Stone with the muzzle of the submachine gun.

Stone climbed the wooden steps and pushed the door open. He stepped over the threshold and every muscle in his body tightened, the pain excruciating and he was aware only of falling forward, rigid, and helpless. He crashed face-first into the wooden floor, his back arching, and his entire body shuddering. The man kept his finger on the trigger for a few more seconds, then released and the Taser stopped sending 50,000 volts of electricity through Stone's body.

Stone felt his arms being pulled back and taped. His ankles also. The two darts that had delivered the shock were ripped out of his skin and he heard the Taser clatter across the floor. Then he was pulled up and dropped roughly in the chair. At the back of his mind, he realized just how strong the man was and that his chances of survival were slim. Unless he could divulge the information that the man required in such a way as to remain useful. The thought that he had been out maneuvered started to weigh heavily on him and it was all he could do to tell himself to remain calm and bide his time.

"Congratulations," the man said. "You didn't wet your pants. Most people do when they have been tased."

Stone said nothing. He couldn't care whether or not he'd wet himself. He had been under torture interrogation before and knew the degradation could get a whole lot worse.

"You have something I want."

Stone shook his head and said weakly, "Correction. I have something your master wants."

The man shrugged. "Same thing."

"How are the headaches?" Stone asked. The man frowned. Stone coughed, clearing his throat, his blurred vision from the jolt of electricity started to clear. "Or the dreams…?"

"What?"

"Can you picture mom and pop?" Stone sneered. "Your high school prom date, your college sweetheart, your military service. How's all that working out for you?"

"I…"

"You don't know, do you?" Stone stated flatly. "Just another genetically altered freak with a frontal lobotomy and so many pills to take daily that it's as if you're munching on M and M's…" He shook his head. "Jesus. Do you even know your own name?"

"Of course, I do!" the man snapped. "It's Mr Black!"

"Mr Black?" Stone laughed. "Whatever Hardy's Dr Frankenstein did, he certainly created his monster. Even if they didn't give you all the most original names…" He smiled when he saw the confusion on the man's face, the look of doubt in his eyes. "You're the product of a CIA program. An experiment. Certain people in congress found out about it and shut it down. I was sent to hunt down the last of your kind and discover the identity of the last man involved in the project. That man was Tom Hardy, a veteran of the CIA with almost thirty years' service. He had been involved in just about every controversial operation the agency every mounted. Only, the subject I killed clearly wasn't the last of the freakshow exhibits. Just like Hardy wasn't the last person in the chain. You have a master I didn't know about, and you clearly slipped through as well." Stone paused. "It could all come back to you. I could give you your memory back." He thought of how he had knocked something loose inside the man's skull before he had escaped. Two years later Stone was pulled into the man's plot for revenge, and ultimately, the reason Stone was now on the run. Given the opportunity he would like to smash something heavy against this guy's skull, and not stop until there was nothing left.

The man stared at Stone for a while. And then he took off his jacket, reached around behind his back and drew a wickedly sharp looking knife. It was a small Bowie style with a dull-colored blade, but for the glinting sharpened edge which ran to a needle-sharp tip. The top third of the blade's spine was also sharpened from the tip backwards. "Enough talk," the man said quietly. "Until, that is, you feel like telling me where you have hidden the money..."

Chapter Fifty

Katy McBride put down the empty coffee cup and looked out of the window of the cabin onto the claim and the machinery excavating the cut in the distance. The fuel had been delivered and the invoice had showed it had been paid. She had called the fuel company and been told the name on the card, but she had no knowledge of the name. All she knew was that it had been Rob's doing. Hell, she did not even know the man's surname. And yet…

She could not let him leave without telling him exactly what he meant to her. The mystery man whom she had fallen in love with. The stranger who had blown in with the wind of change and helped her when she had needed it most. And now he would deal with his problems, and then he would leave. He had not said as much, but deep down she knew. She had called her cousin, Don. Ordered him off the western cut and back to the office, where he would drive her back to the cabin. She could assist the man she loved, or at least tell him how she felt and work on a plan together. She just hoped he felt the same way about her.

Don had parked the ATV near the fuel

dump and was ambling over, talking on his cell phone as he walked. She cursed his lack of urgency, rapped her knuckles on the window to gain his attention. He looked up, nodded at her, and casually finished his conversation. As he slipped his phone back in his pocket, she met him on the wooden porch.

"As I said, I need you to drive me somewhere," she informed him. "Twenty miles, drop me off and then head back here and continue with the cut."

"Where are we going?"

"I'll let you know when we're on the road." She paused. "Have you run any test soil from the cut?"

"We're doing it this afternoon," he replied.

"Is it looking good?"

"There's some color in the grates," he said with a nonchalant shrug. "Maybe we'll get enough back to pay *lover boy* for all the fuel…"

Katy stared at him and said, "What gets paid is my business. The bills are for me to worry about." She walked stiffly to Don's Dodge Ram pickup truck and got in the passenger side. "And don't worry, I'll slip some extra fuel money into your pay-packet when we do the clean-up. Wouldn't want you out of pocket for this trip…" She stared straight ahead as Don got inside. She knew she was losing her employees' faith. She needed a good clean-up, or she knew the men would be making other plans for the season. Jumping ship before it sank completely. At the moment, it was listing badly and being constantly bailed out. The fuel comment had irked her, and she still had no way to repay Rob's kindness unless she saw some gold.

"What pay-packet?" Don replied curtly as he swung the big truck around and powered out of the site onto the dirt access road. "We haven't been paid for close to three weeks…"

"It's coming," Katy replied solemnly. Her father had once told her that when staff lose faith in their boss, there was no turning them around. She should have known then that her father had experienced the same problems, his father most likely before him, and that McBride's Folly would always live up to its name. Pride and stubbornness had made her stay and finish what her grandfather had started, but perhaps the old man should have quit decades ago. "We just need to run all the ground in the western cut…"

Katy winced as Don swerved wildly to avoid a pickup on the apex of a tight corner near the river and swung across the road onto the beginning of the mountain track away from town. It was the same stretch of river that her father had drowned in when he had left the road in a tipper truck. She grabbed the door handle to stop herself rolling into Don, then straightened up as the two vehicles passed. She looked right into Marvin's eyes, and then looked in the wing mirror and watched his truck disappear down the road. She had not spoken to the man since he had left, and now she felt she was surrounded by failures. Failure to see that Marvin had been sidling up to Duke Tanner, failure to see that she had lost the trust of men she trusted. Men like Don, her own cousin. Who else at the mine was close to walking, close to crossing the boundary and working for Duke Tanner?

"You should have sold out to Duke Tanner," Don replied cuttingly. "I'm twenty-seven and have wasted ten years on chasing a McBride's dreams…"

"Then go your own way," she snapped. "Don't let me stop you…" She regretted it instantly and was about to apologize when Don cut into her.

"Maybe I will," he said coldly. "Maybe I already have…"

"You're leaving?"

"In a manner of speaking."

"Look, it's been rough. Daddy left me with debts. We hit poor ground with the eastern cut. We kept digging when we should have moved elsewhere. I thought Marvin was to be trusted…"

"You don't know shit from Shinola…"

"Don…" She trailed off as she saw the road they were taking. "Where are we going?"

"To the future," he said quietly.

"The future?"

"Where the money will be made."

"How will I make money going this way?"

Don laughed as he swerved the truck around a tight bend on an incline and the wheels tore into the track. They were heading to McBride's Falls. The place where her grandfather had dynamited the mountain to divert the river, so he had all the water he needed to sluice his paydirt and expose more of his cut. The place where he returned to, in order to redivert the river when his mine turned out to be a bust. The place where he went but was never seen again. "There's no *I* in this," he said. "Well, not for you, anyway…"

Katy watched the track narrow ahead. She looked at the parked truck and at the man leaning against it. He was smoking a cigar and in his left hand he held a Winchester lever-action rifle. A short carbine. The gun looked tiny in the big man's hand. Like a child's toy.

"Tanner…" she said quietly, then turned to Don. "What are you doing?"

"Oh, come on!" he snapped. "You're the hot-shot lawyer. You understand a hostile takeover when you see one…" He shook his head. "The fucking mine should belong to me, anyway. What made it *your* birth right? Alan McBride was my grandpa, too! It's all in a fucking name, isn't it? Handed down from father to son, but daughters? My mother should have been a part of it all! Well, you're the daughter now, so why the hell don't I deserve more than minimum wage and a share of fuck all? At least with someone who knows what they're doing in charge, the boys will get a chance of a share in the gold. Right now, we've all got squat…"

Katy grabbed the wheel and pulled as hard as she could. Don tried to correct in time, but she had caught him by surprise and the wheel snatched onto full lock all too quickly. The truck veered to the left, and she opened the door and rolled out, the rear wheels almost rolling over her as she sprawled. The nearside wheels of the big Dodge rode up on some raised ground and the weight of the mighty V8 engine helped over balance it and it started to roll in slow motion. Don scrabbled to get out, but he had forgotten his seatbelt and as he struggled to free himself the truck rolled over and crashed down heavily on the roof. Don's seatbelt finally unbuckled as he was inverted, and he landed heavily in the footwell. The passenger door had torn free, and the Dodge started to roll slowly, Don still unable to get clear. The truck gained momentum, then as if speeded up remotely, it rolled roof over axle and continued to increase in speed until Don was thrown out of the open doorway ahead of the vehicle like a ragdoll, only to be crushed a split second later by the roof as the Dodge continued to roll. The sound of crushing metal on rocks, breaking glass and shattering plastic sounded like gunfire and when the vehicle smashed against a rocky outcrop and finally came to a rest, the sound echoed across the valley in what seemed like perpetuity.

As silence returned to the wilderness, Duke Tanner stared dumbly, his mouth agape. The cigar had dropped to the ground. He looked to where Katy had leapt out, but she was nowhere to be seen. He turned to Don's body, flattened by the enormous force and weight of the leviathan of the road. The man looked like day-old roadkill on a busy highway. Tanner cocked the rifle and headed to where Katy had tumbled. He looked at the ground, the faint footprints leading off the muddy hillside to the forest beyond.

There was no more intimidation to be done. Now, only action mattered.

Now, it was time to hunt.

Chapter Fifty-One

He had beaten Stone for more than ten minutes. Never too much to the mouth – he needed his questions answering after all – but he had worked punches into his eyes, temple, and cheekbones, and a few to the mouth for good measure, but mainly to the chest, ribs, and stomach. Stone knew the drill. Softening him up. No questions, just pain and no idea when it would end.

And then came the cutting.

The man used the compact little Bowie knife. He pulled the backside tip down the length of Stone's right cheek. Not a deep wound, but it bled from the first to last moment, and he did it real slow. To the man's annoyance, Stone did not flinch, and nor did he scream. But he got satisfaction when he jabbed the tip of the blade into the meat of Stone's shoulder. He drove the blade deeper, smiled as Stone struggled against it and gasped when the tip of the blade met bone. The man wiggled the blade, then pulled it out slowly as Stone grunted. When the blade was clear of his flesh, the blood flowed down his arm and pooled on the floor.

"You will now tell me where the money is hidden," the man said. He took his phone out from his pocket and opened the record app. "Nice and clear, for the microphone..."

"Fuck you..."

"The money."

"For your handler?"

"For my country."

Stone shook his head. "Someone in an anonymous office wants it for themselves. They are senior enough to have control and access to you, and considering your project was shut down and the other freaks eliminated, then I'd say we're talking deputy director level." Stone paused, wincing at the stinging in his shoulder and the dull ache at the root of the wound, where the metal had scraped the bone. His lips were thick and painful, and his eyes were swelling and bruising, and his left eye had started to close. "That should narrow it down for me."

"For you!"

"Yeah."

"And what are you going to do?"

"Find out who wants me dead. Find out who is pressing ahead with hunting me, keeping me a fugitive. Despite me providing evidence that it wasn't me. That I was set up."

The man glared. "You're not leaving this cabin alive!"

Stone shrugged. "Then why would I tell you anything? What's in it for me?"

The man looked at him, clearly needled at throwing in his hand so early. He tore off his sweater, untucked his shirt and rolled his sleeves up. "Then, I had better do such a good job on you, that your deal will be getting the swift end that you will no doubt beg for..." He stepped forward and caught hold of Stone's shirt and sliced it open. Then, he sliced across Stone's right pectoral muscle. "Just a little bloodletting... before we get to the more sensitive regions..."

Stone gasped, clenching his teeth together, panting through the pain. "It will be easy for me to work this out..." He said through gritted teeth. "Now that I know the freak that I killed wasn't the last of your kind... Now that I know that you knew who Tom Hardy was... It will be easy for me to draw Venn diagrams and leave a name in the center."

"But you're not getting out of here..." The man tore wildly at Stone's trousers and grabbed at his appendages. Stone cried out involuntarily as the man caught hold of his penis and genitals and yanked them out. He bent down with the blade, smiling as he slipped the cold steel underneath his scrotum. "Where is the fucking money…"

The gunshot was deafening in the confines of the cabin. The man released his grip on Stone's balls and dropped the knife, where it clattered underneath the chair. A rose of blood collected at the front of the man's shirt. Just right of center beside the huge mound that was the man's right pec. He turned around slowly and stared at Max Power, who stood in the doorway, the gun clenched between his shaking hands. He started towards Power, then ignored him and continued past through the doorway as Power stepped aside, his hands still shaking and the pistol moving wildly. The man made his way outside, his legs unsteadily taking him to safety.

"Max, get me free!" Stone shouted. Power walked towards him, averting his eyes from Stone's crotch. He reached for the knife, then worked at the duct tape securing his wrists. He slipped and sliced into the skin. "Fuck! Don't *you* start cutting me…" When his hands were free, Stone snatched the knife from Power's hands and sliced cleanly through the tape securing his ankles.

Stone got unsteadily to his feet and fastened his trousers and belt. He headed for the dresser drawer where he had stashed the Smith & Wesson .44 magnum and headed outside. Ahead of him, the man was trying to take one of the Glocks out of the drone's rig. He looked back at the cabin steps, where Stone was dropping down the last of them to the pathway. The man gave up on the gun and dropped the drone beside the control unit and started to run. Stone raised the heavy revolver and watched, working out the man's stride, the speed. He estimated he was six-five, so his normal stride would be half of that, then close to fifty percent more when he ran. He was right on target. Stone lowered the pistol and waited.

The man dropped three feet lower to the ground and there was a pause before he screamed and shattered the silence.

But scream, he did.

Stone approached cautiously. But he figured if the man had been intent on the Glock attached to the drone, then he would not have a weapon on him. Stone cocked the revolver, and now the trigger only required four pounds of pull instead of ten. He edged around the hole he had previously dug and filled with sharpened sticks. The man was whimpering and tugging at his ankle, but he had three, foot-long stakes in his foot and another through his calf muscle.

"That's gotta hurt…"

"Fuck you…"

Stone could see there was a lot of blood. Some scraps of flesh hanging from the sharpened tips that had gone through and through. The last time he had seen a man in this state, he had cracked a rifle over his head and left him, assuming he was dead. That lack of thoroughness had led Stone to being on the run. Being here.

Stone saw the amount of blood collecting on the man's chest. A 9mm bullet through the back and out of the chest. He would not be leaving here. But Stone had been wrong before. Another time, another place. He leveled the revolver between the man's eyes. "Are you going to tell me who's working you?"

"No."

"Are you going to give me a name?"

"Never…"

Stone fired, and the top of the man's head

disappeared.

"Dirty Harry was right," Stone said quietly. "Clean off…"

Chapter Fifty-Two

"I was heading south," Power said, watching as Stone sliced off strips of duct tape and secured them across his recently cleaned wounds to act as sutures. "I only wish I'd made it here sooner…"

"Don't. He'd have undoubtedly killed you." Stone paused. "That drone of his had heatseeking technology and a facial recognition program. Once it's locked onto a target, it hunts it until the target is dead. There wouldn't have been any escaping it." He shrugged. "I guess I was in an old school mindset. The game is changing…"

Power shuddered. He had fled the scene at the motel but had a crisis of conscience about ten miles down the road. He had turned around, returned to the motel room, and used Ted's phone to take a picture of the laptop screen. The phone had been locked and he had struggled to use Ted's thumb print to open it. Hands shaking, stomach convulsing, it had finally opened. He had then reset the phone password and headed to the final coordinates, unsure what he could do, and terrified of what he would find. He had held the gun on the center of the man's back, willing himself to speak up and command him to stop. But he couldn't. He had closed his eyes, heard Stone's desperation, and fired.

Stone packed the wound to his shoulder with some clean dish cloth strips. He would have to soak them with saline before removing them later, but he secured them with more tape and buttoned up his shirt. Rudimentary first aid. The cut to his face had stopped bleeding, but he was left in no doubt it would leave a faint scar. Power had offered to help, but Stone had refused. Part of him was ashamed by what had happened, of the fact that he would still be secured to the chair, appendages removed and likely begging for the swift release the man would have dangled in return for the information, had Power not found him in time. The man had gotten the better of him. and Stone knew from his experience on his first tour of Afghanistan, that the sense of vulnerability and failure would live with him for some time to come. But live he would. Fate and happanstance had aligned once again in his favor.

"What now?" asked Power.

"He killed your entire team?" Stone asked, swallowing down a handful of painkillers he had found in one of the kitchen cupboards. They were sugar coated and went down like candy.

Power nodded. "But they weren't *my* team," he replied. He wasn't about to show Stone the scarring to his genitalia caused by Liz Roper dowsing him with hot coffee and bound to a chair as Stone had been. "They abducted me, and tortured me, also…"

Stone nodded. He had already thanked him. "You're in the clear, Max," he said. "Call the Secret Service and report everything that happened. Leave out the fact you warned me, and say that I tricked you into freeing me, then gave you the slip."

"You're not coming in?"

"No."

"I can vouch for you."

"I know. But somebody in the CIA with enough authority and reach is determined that I take the fall. The money we hid is their motivation."

"Then we should hand it in."

"I still need a bargaining chip for the charges to go away." Stone paused. "I have the accounts, but I have also moved and stashed physical money around the country."

"And as long as you have the money, then there will always be somebody who wants it."

"But I suspect just one person knows the extent," he said. "The man behind the scheme at the island had to have had help." Stone paused. "A dark web killing game with online betting was one thing. But to switch to international terrorist organizations bidding to wipe out the President's family is quite another. He could not have become so connected in such a short period of time. I smashed his head in during my investigation into the missing virus…"

"This is the *Ares* virus?"

"Correct. I was investigating the CIA's black-ops assassination program. The assassination program had been shut down, but Tom Hardy had kept one of the subjects off the books and this assassin was being used to hunt Isobel Bartlett, the bio-technician who snatched it when she overheard a plan to profit from the vaccine. From then on, the two matters were linked. Two worlds colliding…" Stone shook his head. "When I battered the man on the head, I shook something loose, the man regained his memory. But I should have known that he had inside help from somewhere. And that person is the same person who had you abducted to find me. They obviously kept another one of these assassin experiments," he said, nodding to the open doorway and the body of the man outside. "Find this person, and the whole thing will be put to bed." He paused. "But the worst of it is that someone inside the CIA knew what would happen to the President's family. They were going to collect the money all along."

"So, that's it?" Power asked. "I just tell them everything, and I'll be, OK?"

"You've done nothing wrong." Stone shrugged. "Press upon your abduction. Insist that you talk only to the Secret Service, and if the FBI get involved… which they undoubtedly will… then only talk to them if you have Secret Service representation. The important thing is to make sure you see everyone's credentials. But more importantly, see that those credentials are verified."

"The CIA?"

Stone nodded. "The CIA are fine." He paused. "It's the scope for people operating on tangents that go way beyond their remit that's the problem."

"But I shot a man."

"To save me," Stone replied. "Like I said,

tell them everything. You didn't see what happened out there. That's on me." Stone gathered up his rifle and made his way outside. "Get back to the motel and secure the scene. Wait for the Secret Service to arrive…"

"Secure the scene? But I'm a computer technician!"

"You're a member of the Secret Service. Put your big boy pants on and take charge before Alaskan State Police walk muddy footprints all over the crime scene. Securing the scene safeguards both you *and* your story."

Stone walked over to the drone and unfastened one of the .45 Glocks. He used some of the spare, clean dishcloth that he had rammed into his pocket to change his dressings later to wipe the weapon over and removed his own fingerprints. He carefully placed the weapon in the dead man's hand and stepped backwards. It would have to do. He was never going to let the man get away, but he was not going to give his detractors anything else to use against him. He had been tortured by the man, saved by Power, and forced to shoot the man when he drew a pistol and had given Stone no choice. That was the story the investigators would be presented with, and it was up to them to prove otherwise.

Stone got into the Ford Bronco and fired up the engine. Power had parked the SUV near to the man's vehicle a few hundred yards further up the track. He did not offer Power a lift. It was crucial that his DNA was nowhere near the vehicle to risk countering his account in the subsequent investigation.

Stone drove out past the two SUVs and onto the backroad south. He needed to find some wheels before he left. There were some cars and trucks for sale outside the auto parts store in Lame Horse. He had not taken any notice earlier, but there would be something for a few thousand bucks and he could trade it in further south. A few different vehicles between Lame Horse and Seattle would not hurt his escape strategy, either.

He thought about Katy McBride as he drove. He couldn't hope to stick around after what had happened. The feds would be crawling all over Lame Horse and his own Secret Service would struggle to maintain control of the investigation. He just hoped Max Power could hold up under interview and that the involvement of a black-ops CIA asset would bolster the Secret Service's resolve to reach out to Stone and see sense. Now that it was clear that the deep state had an agenda, then it could only go towards clearing Stone's name further.

Stone slowed the truck at the turning. Left for McBride's Folly, straight-on for the highway and Lame Horse. And south. South made the most sense. He could buy a set of wheels and leave Katy's Bronco at the garage. He could pay the guy to drive it to McBride's Folly, as he had done before when he had paid for it to be made road-worthy after being forced off the road.

And then south to the lower forty-eight.

No awkward good-byes, no questions, no looking back. Stone shook his head. Katy had been through too much, and even with time such a precious factor, Stone made the left and headed down the trail. He had barely made it a hundred yards when a truck rounded the bend, wide on his own side, forcing Stone to slow. Stone could see that it was Marvin at the wheel. The man slowed, eased his hand out of the window and flagged Stone down. Stone reached across the seat and eased the AR-15 a little closer, flicking off the safety on the left-hand side of the frame.

"Thought that could only be you in that old Bronco," Marvin said as he pulled alongside. He had a rifle on the seat beside him and a whitetail deer sprawled in the flatbed, a bullet hole behind its left shoulder and blood on its lips. Alaska's equivalent of going to a farm shop to buy a roast. "Just seen Katy and Don heading up to McBride's Falls."

Stone shrugged. "It's a free country."

"Don't make no sense," Marvin replied. "It's the only place the road goes and there's nothing up there but unstable ravines and raging rapids. Don's her full cousin, and that ain't the kissing kind. Not this far north, at least..." He paused. "Ain't no other reason to go up there."

"*You've* been up there."

"To bag a deer for the larder." Marvin shook his head. "Don was driving pretty erratically. You should perhaps check it out."

Stone frowned at him. "Why?"

Marvin shrugged. "Because you've clearly got her back." He paused. "I worked with her grandfather when I was a boy, then for her old man. Not all the time, just between salmon fishing and working on other mining concerns. But I was around enough to think of Katy as a proxy niece. She's fallen for you. And you know Jack shit about mining, but you know when something's off. You've got good instincts, except about me, that is. You see, Duke Tanner is my friend, I've known him a long time. But he's obsessed with having McBride's Folly. And that don't make sense, because the one thing that ground hasn't given up over the years is gold. Sure, some good clean-ups here and there, but largely it lives up to its name. I guess I didn't want to work the western cut until we had absolutely everything out of the eastern cut. And then there's the fact that once the western cut is down to bedrock, then that's it. The place is done. And Katy will be done, too. And that will be the whole McBride family saga over. She'll go south to the money, back to practicing law, and the girl I've seen growing up from a baby will be gone, and I guess with her, her pop and grandfather, too." He paused, his emotions starting to get the better of him. He wiped his face with the back of his sleeve and said, "If there's even the hint that Duke Tanner had her hurt to run her off the claim, then I want nothing more to do with him. I drove on out there a few days ago to tell him the same thing. But I've heard that young Don has been friendly with Duke Tanner lately. And now that I'm not at the mine, and I've had time to hunt and fish and sit on my porch, well the more I think about it, the more it just doesn't make sense. Of course, that is, until it does…"

Chapter Fifty-Three

She was running scared. Her limbs and ribs ached from not just the injuries she had sustained in the beating, but from throwing herself out of the truck as well, and now every footstep hurt, every breath spread like wildfire within her ribcage. The crash had bought her some time. The noise of the rolling vehicle had sounded like gunfire and echoed across the valley, canceling out any noise she had made as she had scurried across the rock scree of the slope and into the trees. Tanner could have seen her, of course. But the truck had been between them and would have been an incredible sight. She had not seen her cousin thrown from the cab, did not know his fate. And nor did she care. Don had betrayed her for a shot at the gold. Lord knew what Duke Tanner would have promised him, but he would have been unlikely to deliver. A man whom the town all owed something to, and by no means a sense of gratitude. Tanner had made investments, and from what she had heard, he collected often, and his benevolence came at a high price.

It had been many years since Katy had been hunting. She had never enjoyed it but being raised in Alaska had come with learning how to use the wilderness, and the great outdoors was more than recreation up here. It was a larder. She knew all about tracking and sign, of sound and movement and color. She was wearing a beige sweater underneath her blue jacket, and right now, getting clear of Tanner was more important than thinking how much she would need the jacket when the sun went down. The here and now. And right now, a man was out here, and he had a trail gun and was going to use it. Katy had long given up on the thought that Tanner was out here to talk. The two despicable thugs he had brought in to change her mind about staying told her all she needed to know. She ditched the coat by balling it up and throwing it as far to the right of her as she could. Closer to the mountain slope. It only traveled twenty feet or so before opening and parachuting to the ground, but it was twenty feet off her trail. Next, she picked up a fallen branch with a few twigs on it and started to brush behind her as she walked, enough to disrupt her shoe treads and scatter debris over crushed ferns and grass and fallen twigs and branches. She interspersed this with running fifty paces or so before clearing after herself again. Enough to break her tracks and slow down her pursuer. But she knew that Duke Tanner was a bigtime hunter, who often illegally bought other peoples' hunting quotas and often exceeded his own, too. The trade in meat in Alaska meant that people bartered a side of mule deer for a quart of logs or mended your fence and gates for a hindquarter of moose. Tanner killed and butchered deer, caribou, moose and bear for both favor and labor. He was an excellent tracker, woodsman, and marksman. Katy had not hunted in twelve years. Her skills were rusty and as she pounded through the forest, she knew she was running out of time.

The gunshot confirmed it. A branch splintered near her head, the gunshot reverberating through the trees. She screamed and sprinted, dropping the branch and heading into a thicker belt of trees, the thunderous sound of McBride's Falls suddenly audible as she sprinted down the other side of the ridge and lost height.

Chapter Fifty-Four

Stone heard the gunshot as he approached the hairpin corner and steep incline. He selected low gear and the Bronco struggled to gain traction as it turned. He planted his foot on the gas and the truck jiggered and shuddered. The impact knocked him into the steering wheel and the sound of metal on rubber thudded loudly, but the old Ford Bronco propelled forwards rapidly. Stone got himself back into his seat to see the large hood of Marvin's Chevrolet in his rear-view mirror. The truck was massive with practically enough torque drive up a vertical slope. Stone had to press the gas pedal flat to the floor and shift into drive to get away from Marvin's fender. Stone braked and stopped beside the wreckage of Don's Dodge Ram. He got out, the assault rifle in his hands and stared back at Marvin.

"Figured she may be in trouble and that you could do with a hand…" the old timer reached into the cab and retrieved a bolt-action Remington rifle with a scope.

Stone nodded and headed up the slope. He paused briefly beside Don's body but moved on quickly. Crushed organs, stomach contents, bowels, and human excrement smelled as bad as it sounded and both men fought the urge to vomit as they made for the top of the slope. Duke Tanner's vehicle was parked at the top of the slope, its driver's door open.

"Duke never leaves home without a gun," Marvin said. "Usually, a trail or truck gun. His is a forty-four magnum. A Winchester lever-action. There wasn't anything in the rack in his truck, so I'm guessing he'll have it with him…"

Stone did not comment, but he pointed at the ground and said, "Katy's footprints…" He bent down and pressed his fingers into the dirt. "Matches her weight, and the distance between tracks matches her height and stride…"

"You know your shit, mister…" Marvin paused breathlessly as they walked on. "Hunter?"

"Soldier."

"Right…" He paused. "Well, thank you for your service…"

"It's thanks enough that you're out here helping me," he replied. "I'm sorry I misjudged you."

Marvin shrugged. "I'm too old for mining," he said. "Prefer fishing and hunting, anyway."

"Is McBride's Falls over the ridge?"

"Yes."

"Kind of high for a waterfall."

"Wait until you get to the top," he said. "This is a false summit, there are three mountain summits beyond and just about every drop of water flows down and is now funneled into the ravine caused when Alan McBride, Katy's grandfather, dynamited the mountain and changed its course."

"Proactive guy…"

"This is Alaska. You don't like something, you change it."

Stone stopped walking and frowned. "The trail has gone." He scoured the ground intently. There were traces of tread, but debris had blown over it and rendered the trail both confusing to read and time consuming to make out. "I think she's brushed the forest floor," said Stone. "Clever girl…" He looked at Marvin, who was a few feet away and studying the ground. "Does she have hunting experience?"

"Yep. Hank, her father, was a great hunter and teacher of fieldcraft. Hell, most people are up here." He held up a hand and said, "I've got Tanner's prints right here."

"We'll go with those. He's the threat, let's stick with him and just hope Katy will be OK…"

Chapter Fifty-Five

She stopped at the edge of the ravine. The water raged and frothed fifty feet below her and the spray up the sides of the ravine as it was funneled into a narrow flume that dropped two-hundred feet onto bare rocks below. This was a new waterfall and had yet to erode the rocks, but the water soon formed a torrent and fast-moving river, bypassing McBride's Folly and cutting through the softer ground. A whole new river created by a stubborn man and a whole lot of TNT.

"End of the line, Katy…"

Katy turned around, surprised that Tanner had caught up so quickly. "Duke…"

"I'm sorry… there's no other way." He paused, the short rifle held in just his right hand, the muzzle pointing at her stomach. "You should have accepted my offer…"

"Duke, please…" Katy McBride stared at him. The river spray had formed a fine mist and her face was wet, but Tanner still saw the tears in her eyes.

"Turn around…"

"No."

"Don't make this any harder than it has to be…"

"What the hell did you do?" she asked. "You had those men try to kill me…"

"They were never meant to kill you. Just scare you away, make you want to sign over the mine to me."

"They fucking raped me!" she screamed at him.

"I'm sorry…" He shrugged. "I didn't know they would do that…"

"Fuck you!" She took a step forward and he raised the rifle to her face, forcing her to stand still. "It was my grandpa's mine, my father's mine. I was just trying to finish what they started…"

"Your daddy couldn't find a quarter in a bucket of fucking sand!" Tanner snapped. "Alan couldn't find a quarter in an *empty* bucket! He honestly didn't know shit about it. He dynamited these damned falls and caused no end of trouble with the river. Roads and tracks washed away; farmland turned into wetland as thoroughly as if a thousand beavers had made dams!" He shook his head. "He was all but going to sell the claim to me, then changed his mind because your useless father wanted to play at being a gold miner, too. The stubborn god-damned bastard wouldn't change his mind. The old coot had to pay…"

Katy stared at him, mouth agape. "You killed him?"

Duke Tanner laughed. "Right where you're standing now, missy. Mighty fitting when you think about it. What with you going the same way and all…"

"You pushed him into the falls…" she said quietly, her voice barely audible over the tempestuous water below.

"He wanted my help dynamiting the damned river course again. He wouldn't sell to me, so I figured I'd have more luck with your father. It must have been quick because I never heard him scream…" He shrugged. "And then your father wouldn't sell either!" Tanner shook his head. "Only he wasn't as dumb as your grandpa. At least he actually had the sense to drill some test holes. The dumb bastard never said where they were, though. It doesn't take a fucking genius to guess they would be in the bends and oxbows of the old river's route. It's just that what they didn't know was that the old river was diverted by the old timers during the goldrush. Your father stumbled across the fact, drilled his holes in the original riverbed and found the gold. That's why I had to stop him…"

"No!" Katy sobbed. "Not my daddy…"

"That's it, Tanner. I've got a gun on you…" Marvin stepped out from the tree line, the rifle shouldered and aiming at him.

Stone stepped out thirty feet further down. Flanking Tanner but without Katy being in the line of fire. He had the short AR-15 shouldered and his finger hovering over the trigger. "Put the gun down, Tanner. It's over."

Tanner glanced at Stone, but he still could not see Marvin, who was directly behind him. There was no way of shooting either of them. They would cut him down at once. But his weapon was still aimed at Katy, and he knew it. "Drop yours or she gets gut shot. They're hollow points, so that'll be it…"

"The moment you fire, you're dead," Stone replied. "But I won't kill you with a gunshot. I'll put my knife in your ass and see where it leads me…"

Tanner clearly gave this some thought. "It's my word against hers," he said.

"I fucking heard you," Marvin replied. "You confessed!"

"A good lawyer will get the charges

dropped," Tanner sneered. "You fitted me up. I was going after her because she killed Don when she snatched control of the steering wheel..." He paused. "I built this town. Nobody would be anything around here without me..."

In Stone's sights, Tanner's hand moved three inches and the muzzle of the carbine, nineteen inches away from his trigger finger cleared Katy by six inches and an angle approximately fifteen degrees. Stone fired a single round through Tanner's hand and the butt stock of the rifle. It went clean through and grazed his gut on the other side. As he dropped the rifle, Katy leapt out of the way and ran behind Stone, and Marvin stumbled forwards almost tripping as he lunged and kicked the rifle over the edge of the ravine and into the water below.

Duke Tanner screamed and clasped his hand, blood pouring down his forearm. He looked at the three of them and spoke through gritted teeth. "You'll damned well pay for that," he sneered. "I'll get the best lawyer in the state. In the fucking country, even. And I'll see that she gets charged with Don's death and the two of you are charged with coercion and kidnap and assault. Whatever it takes... I'll walk free and the three of you will…"

Katy dashed forwards and shoulder barged the man. Despite his size and weight, and perhaps because of the fact the bullet had blown a hole through most of his hand, Tanner offered little resistance until it was too late. Teetering on the edge of the ravine, he mouthed something, but the noise of the waterfall drowned him out. Katy barged him again, driving all her weight and momentum into him, and he went over the edge. There was no scream. No sound of him hitting the raging and frothing water below. Stone darted forwards and saw a brief flash of color in the froth and then Duke Tanner went over the falls.

Two hundred feet to the rocks below.

His body was broken and twisted as the torrent of water washed him off the slabs of rock and into the raging river below that everyone in the area agreed flowed too fast all the way to the Pacific Ocean.

Stone thought briefly about what Katy McBride had said to him.

Don't ever cross the river east of McBride's Falls. You'll end up washed away and lost forever…

Chapter Fifty-Six

Montana
Two weeks later

Idaho was just behind him and at this point the landscape was still the same as his past three hours' driving. But borders were always so. Nothing ever changed once you crossed an imaginary line. The changes were always gradual and largely unnoticeable until you looked around and realized things no longer looked the same.

Pines and mountains with grassy slopes stretched out as far as he could see and a crystal-clear lake off to his right reflected the landscape so perfectly that the water was difficult to see. Like an illusion. Gradually the pines and slopes would give way to vast grassy plains as he headed towards North Dakota. The season was five weeks ahead of Alaska and it truly was early summer with rising temperatures to reflect as much. Stone had traveled through this part of the Midwest before, and he knew the region had baking hot summers and frozen winters with little in between. You either swam in the lakes or you skated on them a few weeks later.

He had not said a proper goodbye to Katy McBride. But he knew she would be OK. There had been no chance of a future and prolonging the inevitable goodbye and risking his own capture would not help anyone. Katy had driven back to McBride's Folly with Marvin, and Stone had taken Tanner's truck, but he had swung a left and headed south into Lame Horse. He had stopped at the auto parts store and three thousand bucks and twenty minutes later he was in an eighties Buick Le Sabre and heading south as far as it would optimistically take him. Which had not been that far. A Ford Taurus had gotten him out of Alaska and a Ford F150 pickup, consistently one of America's bestselling vehicles, had taken him into Idaho.

Before crossing into Montana, he had stocked up at a truck stop with travel snacks and drinks when he had filled with fuel. Too many potato chips and cans of cheese, and too much soda. He had bought the 1970 Pontiac GTO from a garage in Boise that had a line of American muscle cars for sale in various states of repair. The vehicle's body needed attention and a respray but was mechanically sound and its brawny V8 ran smooth and torquey and after driving trucks around Alaska's terrible road network and a problematic journey in a Le Sabre that should have been scrapped a decade ago, Stone had negotiated a good deal on the old F150 and a further $8,000 dollars. He had also bought a newspaper at the truck stop. Only because the headline had grabbed his attention. He didn't even need to read the frontpage story, but he would.

The lake was serene, and he stopped the GTO just off the road where people had stopped over the years to photograph the splendor of the lake and mountains beyond. He watched for a while. No traffic in either direction. He reached for the paper and read the headline and smiled. She had done it. Where her grandfather and father had failed. He hoped she knew they would have been proud of her.

Largest Haul of Gold in US history!

A female lawyer who gave up her practice in San Francisco to take over mining her family's claim struck on a seam of record gold reserves. Katy McBride (31) took over at McBride's Folly, near the small town of Lame Horse, Alaska, after her father who had been mining the ground was tragically killed in an automobile accident last year. Mining the last of her claim and close to bankruptcy, the seam of gold was discovered and mined in just ten days and has now been weighed and valued. After completing the excavation and running the gold deposits (called a clean-up), the final gold tally was twelve-thousand, two-hundred ounces estimated to be worth $23,059,494 on today's market. The largest single haul of gold in the history of the United States.

Katy McBride's grandfather, Alan McBride, controversially dynamited a section of mountain to divert a river which increased the size of his claim. He had always thought gold would be found in the bend of the river, but subsequently never found it. He was killed after he fell into the rapids attempting to dynamite the ravine to redivert the river when he failed to find the gold that he felt sure was there. The nearby waterfalls became known as McBride's Falls. Alan McBride's son, Henry (Hank) McBride later worked out that the river had taken another path before the end of the last ice age and ran record-breaking test samples but died before he could work the ground in question, or indeed let anyone know where he had taken the samples.

McBride Falls claimed two lives two weeks ago when neighboring gold mine owner Duke Tanner and an employee of the mine at McBride's Folly, Donald Boux were killed while prospecting for a *possible new claim. It is thought Duke Tanner slipped and fell into the ravine and Donald Boux rolled his truck as he went for help. When asked for comment, Alaskan State Governor Michael Blache said, "Alaska giveth, then she taketh away. She is a hardy state with opportunity galore, and a cruel mistress where even the most experienced of wilderness and mountain men can fall foul to its dangers. A place where true adventure can still be found..."*

Katy McBride intends to mine the rest of the claim, then fund the replanting of 50,000 trees and allow the mine to be reclaimed by nature. She will give profit shares of 5% to her existing seven workers and 10% to her family's foreman of thirty years, Marvin Jacobson. She has indicated that she will move back south and return to law, offering 50% of her work as 'pro bono' to victims of historical rape and sexual assault who are on low incomes.

Stone was still smiling at the article when he folded the paper and tossed it onto the rear seats. Katy McBride would be OK. Or at least as much as anyone could be after such an experience. But it looked like she had already found a way to channel the trauma of what had happened to her and turn it into a positive by helping others. Especially those who could not afford a talented lawyer and would therefore be unable to produce counterclaims and retrials of perpetrators who had escaped justice or were otherwise released without charge through a district attorney's heavy case load and only a fifty-fifty chance of prosecution. He checked his watch. The next town was eighty miles away and he hoped there would be a motel. It would not be the first time he had slept in the car if there wasn't. He could not search the internet for motels as he still had not picked up a phone, and he preferred it that way. He would let things settle before he bought one and sought out Max Power to find out what had transpired. But that could wait for now. Low tech was the key to keeping under the radar. He switched on the ignition and the engine warbled into life. Still no traffic had passed in either direction and as he pulled the old muscle car back out onto the highway, he enjoyed the feeling of isolation and the beckoning road ahead. Stone floored the throttle and the car fishtailed down the road, heading into the sun.

And nothing but uncertainty beyond.

Or opportunity.

Author's Note

Hi – thanks for reading and I hope you enjoyed reading my story as much as I enjoyed writing it! I plan to give Rob Stone another adventure soon and hope you will be coming along for the ride!

If you have time to rate this story, or even leave a short review on Amazon, then you will make this author extremely happy. If you would like to know more about my books and new releases, then you can sign up to my mailing list at **www.apbateman.com/sign-up-now**

Thank you for reading!

A P Bateman

Printed in Great Britain
by Amazon

66278967R00225